PRAISE FOR DONNA GRANT'S BEST-SELLING ROMANCE NOVELS

"Grant's ability to quickly convey complicated backstory makes this jam-packed love story accessible even to new or periodic readers." - *Publisher's Weekly*

"Donna Grant has given the paranormal genre a burst of fresh air…" – *San Francisco Book Review*

"The premise is dramatic and heartbreaking; the characters are colorful and engaging; the romance is spirited and seductive." – *The Reading Cafe*

"The central romance, fueled by a hostage drama, plays out in glorious detail against a backdrop of multiple ongoing issues in the "Dark Kings" books. This seemingly penultimate installment creates a nice segue to a climactic end." – *Library Journal*

"…intense romance amid the growing war between the Dragons and the Dark Fae is scorching hot." – *Booklist*

DARK KINGS SERIES

Dark Heat ~ Darkest Flame ~ Fire Rising ~ Burning Desire
Hot Blooded ~ Night's Blaze ~ Soul Scorched ~ Dragon King
Passion Ignites ~ Smoldering Hunger ~ Smoke and Fire
Dragon Fever ~ Firestorm ~ Blaze ~ Dragon Burn ~ Torched
Dragon Night ~ Dragonfire ~ Dragon Claimed ~ Ignite
Constantine: A History Bundle ~ Fever ~ Dragon Lost
Flame ~ Inferno ~ My Fiery Valentine ~ The Dragon King
Coloring Book ~ Dragon King Special Edition Character
Coloring Book: Rhi ~ Ignite the Magic (Prequel)

DARK WARRIORS SERIES

Midnight's Master ~ Midnight's Lover ~ Midnight's Seduction
Midnight's Warrior ~ Midnight's Kiss ~ Midnight's Captive
Midnight's Temptation ~ Midnight's Promise
Midnight's Surrender ~ A Warrior for Christmas

CHIASSON SERIES

Wild Fever ~ Wild Dream ~ Wild Need
Wild Flame ~ Wild Rapture ~ Chiasson Series Bundle

LARUE SERIES

Moon Kissed ~ Moon Thrall ~ Moon Struck ~ Moon Bound
LaRue Series Bundle

DARK BEGINNINGS: A FIRST IN SERIES BOXSET

Chiasson Series, Book 1: Wild Fever
LaRue Series, Book 1: Moon Kissed
The Royal Chronicles Series, Book 1: Prince of Desire

<u>**HISTORICAL PARANORMAL**</u>

THE KINDRED SERIES
Everkin ~ Eversong ~ Everwylde ~ Everbound
Evernight ~ Everspell

KINDRED: THE FATED SERIES
Rage ~ Ruin ~ Reign

DARK SWORD SERIES
Dangerous Highlander ~ Forbidden Highlander
Wicked Highlander ~ Untamed Highlander
Shadow Highlander ~ Darkest Highlander

ROGUES OF SCOTLAND SERIES
The Craving ~ The Hunger ~ The Tempted ~ The Seduced
Rogues of Scotland Box Set

THE SHIELDS SERIES
A Dark Guardian ~ A Kind of Magic ~ A Dark Seduction
A Forbidden Temptation ~ A Warrior's Heart
Mystic Trinity (a series connecting novel)

DRUIDS GLEN SERIES
Highland Mist ~ Highland Nights ~ Highland Dawn
Highland Fires ~ Highland Magic
Mystic Trinity (a series connecting novel)

IGNITE THE MAGIC

Sneak Peek at: **DARK HEAT**

www.DonnaGrant.com
www.MotherofDragonsBooks.com

THE ORIGINS OF THE DARK KINGS/DRAGON KINGS®

IGNITE THE MAGIC

NYT & USA TODAY BESTSELLING AUTHOR

DONNA GRANT

DEAREST READER

Writing a prequel story wasn't something I had thought about. Ever. Not until my agent brought it up during a conversation. As soon as I started thinking about it, I couldn't stop. The story unfolded so beautifully that I had no choice but to sit down and write it.

For those familiar with the *Dark Kings* and *Dragon Kings* series, you'll see a familiar name at the end of the book. Melisse. This is her origin story—or rather, her parents' beginning. I can't begin to tell you how I have fallen head over heels in love with Lennox and Ailis. Some books are difficult to write. Some are a tad easier. Then you have ones like IGNITE THE MAGIC that almost write themselves. The characters have been a part of me for a long time, but they sat back and patiently waited for their moment. And this is it.

From the sheer number of emails I receive about Melisse and Henry, I know many are anxiously awaiting their book. This prequel flows wonderfully into theirs. I haven't been able to state when Melisse's book will be out because I didn't know. But now, I do. Look for their book in the summer of 2024. She and Henry are demanding their time. And I'm excited to tell their story.

xoxox,
DG

CHAPTER ONE

Long, long ago

It was now or never. Ailis's heart thudded against her ribs in an erratic rhythm. She was out of time. She'd thought she would have at least half a day before they tracked her, but it appeared as though her luck had run out.

She gripped the small book firmly between her hands. Its weight was solid—dense, even. The leather had darkened in spots, while other sections possessed a sheen from countless hours of handling and sunlight, leaving marks to create a one-of-a-kind appearance. But she wasn't looking at the book. Instead, her attention was focused out the window of her hiding spot on the fifth floor of the building, where she'd caught sight of the king's guards approaching her. The jig was up. They knew.

Ailis immediately teleported to a different location. It would take the soldiers a little while to find her. Giving her just enough time to formulate a new plan. She had known the guards would come for her. After all, no one stole from the king's sister and got away with it. But Ailis had counted on being out of the city when that happened. Someone—or some*thing*—must have alerted the guards. Not that it mattered now. She had what she needed.

She glanced around the area to ensure she was alone, her heart tripping over itself. Her hands wouldn't stop shaking at what she had dared. She couldn't get caught. She had planned everything meticulously, down to the last millisecond.

But she hadn't factored in Fate. She should've known the tricky bitch would cause trouble. She always did.

One way or another, Ailis wouldn't be on the Fae Realm when night fell.

She didn't pause to take in the splendor of the lush hillside as she usually did. Though she probably should. It would be the last time she saw it. This plan had been set for months, but part of her would miss her realm. This was her home, despite the seemingly constant bickering between the Dark and Light Fae. Things had taken a drastic turn of late, however. There was talk of war. And not the small battles that had been happening—an all-out civil war. If that happened, there wouldn't be time to feed her adventurous soul, the wanderer spirit that begged her to discover what awaited.

Besides, she had seen all there was to see on her realm. It was time for something new, maybe even something dangerous. Ailis hurried toward the small cottage near the river. Aunt Beatrix had left it to Ailis when she passed on from this life. Bea was all she'd had, and with her gone now, nothing was holding Ailis here. She and Bea had been kindred spirits—adventurers eager and impatient to explore.

Ailis held up her hand, whispering the words to unlock the wards she had put in place. Her boots thumped on the wooden porch as she swung open the door and quickly stepped inside. Her gaze moved over the eclectic knickknacks Bea had collected throughout her long life. Fae could live for thousands of years, and Bea had filled each day with various escapades—and spent her final years looking back on all of them fondly without an ounce of regret. Ailis wanted that with every fiber of her being.

Each unique item in the cottage had come from their realm, but Bea had often spoken of yearning to go to other worlds. Bea had known it was possible, but despite her attempts to learn how, she never had. Ailis had taken it upon herself to do what her aunt hadn't been able to do.

The past handful of years had been devoted to discovering if travel to other realms was possible. That had taken much longer than anticipated. So many Fae said it was impossible. *A fine notion, indeed, but not something any Fae will be able to do for generations.* Yet she'd looked at the stars and knew it was possible.

A select few believed it could be done but were unwilling to talk. She'd settled on one and earned her trust over many months. Even then, the professor hadn't shared everything. Once Ailis had the basics, she focused on what she needed to accomplish her task. In her mind, magic was magic. All she had to do was discover how to work it. However, it hadn't taken Ailis long to realize it wasn't nearly as easy as she had believed. It wasn't just creating a

Fae doorway. She had to get the location correct so she didn't walk through and find herself in space—or a volcano. Creating that kind of doorway took an astonishing amount of power, knowledge, and expertise. Not to mention the restraint needed to control the magic used so she didn't rip a tear in time and space.

Of course, that was the theory. Or so she'd been told. But she had to start somewhere.

Ailis had meticulously studied everything about developing her magic. All Fae were inherently born with it. It was a part of them, like talking and breathing. For some, the ability to master complicated magic was easy. For others, they had to work at it. Always, though, Fae craved to be more powerful. Ailis was shocked at what she'd learned and how much her magic had flourished just from taking the time and absorbing the lessons in the numerous books she read.

She stood in the middle of the cottage and held the small book between her hands, wishing Bea was with her. But Ailis would take this adventure on her own. She cracked open the book, the pages yellowed from time cracking as they separated. It was this little tome that had put her into her current situation. She had stumbled upon a contact who'd spoken about the book in soft whispers, glancing around to make sure no one heard him. From then, she had made it her mission to locate it. Sadly, that had taken far longer than she had hoped. But if Bea had taught her anything, it was to never give up.

Once Ailis discovered who had the book, she'd sought out the owners and offered to purchase it. They'd instantly rejected her. She'd then offered payment if she could study it

—in their home if that's what they wished. They also refused that proposal.

So, she'd done what any adventurer being denied something would do—she'd borrowed it. Ailis had every intention of returning it when she finished, but she'd made the mistake of not waiting before she stole the book. The fact that the owner happened to be the king's sister made an already complicated situation volatile.

And when the king sent his guard, it told Ailis they wouldn't give her time to explain. They were after her head. At the end of the day, she had taken something that wasn't hers.

Ailis inhaled deeply to calm her racing heart. Sweat beaded on her forehead, and her hands shook. Was it excitement or fear? A little bit of both. She couldn't remember ever being so terrified and enthusiastic at the same time. She had dreamed of this moment for what felt like a lifetime. She'd thought she would have more time to study the book and ensure her magic was ready before creating the doorway and walking through. Fate had decided differently.

"Best laid plans and all." She whispered Bea's favorite saying.

She glanced at the door. They would come here for her. Family was always the next stop. She needed to go somewhere else, a place no one would think to look. Somewhere she'd have the opportunity to read at least the section she needed, if not the entire book. She mentally ticked off locations one by one but none of them seemed right. With her blood pumping in her ears, Ailis teleported a dozen times in rapid succession. It was rare among the Fae for someone to be able to follow another's magic when they jumped, but the King of the Dark recruited those who could do it to find any Fae on the run. The ability was time-consuming, and the more stops Ailis made, the more time it would take the Fae to locate her—and the more time she would have to read.

Time. She'd always had so much of it, but now it ran between her fingers like grains of sand. The tighter she held onto it, the faster it seemed to disappear.

She finally stopped teleporting. A quick look around confirmed the only thing Ailis would run into was one of the black deer that called the forest home. She sat beneath a colossal abifer tree covered with moss and opened the book, her eyes quickly scanning the words. The author described a realm just as verdant and abundant as theirs. A world with many treasures to be discovered. *That* was the place she wanted to visit.

Chapter after chapter, the descriptions entranced her. It had to be real. No one could describe such details without having been there. Yet this was the only copy of the work. Thousands had been burned three generations ago when both the Light and Dark Kings demanded to know if the author had actually gone to the new realm.

He'd vanished, never to be heard from again. And with his disappearance, his credibility crumbled. The entire realm was in an uproar about whether the story was fiction or truth. Light and Dark Fae alike began attempting to cross realms to prove the author right, and thousands upon thousands died in the process. The Light King demanded that all copies be gathered and had them burned. Even the Dark King agreed, ordering his subjects to destroy every copy. It seemed everyone listened but one.

Ailis read the last page and softly closed the book. She smoothed her hand over the cover before setting it on the grass. It had taken hundreds of books and dozens of meetings with some of the most dangerous Dark known to acquire the knowledge needed to build her magic enough to create a doorway to another realm. She'd never told anyone about her plan and carefully worded each query. The instant her questions caused alarm, she ended the conversation and severed all contact.

She had read and studied everything she could. She had practiced. All that was left was to actually try crossing the realms. She rubbed her hands together nervously. This was the first time she was undertaking this. She had thought to have as many attempts as necessary to create the doorways before ever stepping through.

"Seems Fate has other ideas," she murmured.

The Dark Fae were all about power. And if someone thought another attempted to gain more, it garnered everyone's attention. Quickly. The fact that every Fae was born a Light and *chose* to become Dark by action and deed said something about the Dark Fae—including her.

Ailis shoved that out of her mind. She needed to focus. There was no time to reminisce. She had devoured the words in the book and had an excellent memory. She didn't need the tome anymore, but it wasn't as if she could leave it. Nor could she return it. There would be too many questions, and if the king discovered what she was about, Ailis would never see the light of day again.

"It doesn't matter," she said to herself as she tucked the book into her bag before standing. "I won't be around for them to find. And when I come back, they'll applaud what I've done. Hopefully," she added with a grin.

She walked from under the shade of the tree. Once in the sunlight, she took a deep breath and mentally went through the checklist of what she needed to do. Then, she held her hands before her, palms out, hesitating for a moment. A surge of exhilaration shot through her as she focused on her magic, letting it build as she pictured the realm in her mind. She imagined it by the words in the book, letting images fill her mind's eye, all while imagining herself there.

When the magic thrummed through and around her with enough intensity that it vibrated, Ailis swept her hands up and outward as if outlining a door while her magic poured through her hands. At first, she felt nothing unusual. Then the pinpricks of discomfort began, quickly turning to sharp, stabbing pain. That led to unbearable agony. She tried to calm her breathing, refusing to look away from the doorway for fear her skin was ripping from her body. Ailis gulped, and her stomach roiled violently. Her fears of not correctly forming the door might be for naught. It was highly probable that the toll this took on her body would kill her before then.

She focused on the door and the realm she sought. Her knees quivered. Her lungs seized painfully. Then, blessedly, she spotted a shimmer of air like sunlight on water where her hands had been. Her legs gave out. She crumpled to the ground, catching herself with her arms that also threatened to give way. Despite the agony that lanced her, she didn't look away. She couldn't. Somehow, she was still alive, and she wanted to see if she had succeeded.

Gradually, a doorway appeared.

Tears pricked her eyes as she released a half sigh, half laugh. Only then did she pause to take stock of her body. Ailis let her head drop forward. She hurt. A quick look showed that everything was intact—at least on the outside. She sat up and took a few large gulps of air in an effort to get a handle on the pain. Thankfully, it was fading fast. Though she wouldn't forget it anytime soon.

Nothing she had read or heard had cautioned her about that. Then again, if anyone had created a doorway to another realm, they were no longer alive to speak of it. Not even the author of the book had mentioned it. That could make the case that it was a work of fiction. She ran her gaze over the violet doorway. If there wasn't a realm out there like the book described, then she wouldn't have been able to create a door to it.

Would she?

It was time to find out. Ailis climbed to her feet, testing her legs. She dusted off her hands and stood before the door. She had told herself that if she could make the doorway, she would walk through it regardless of whether it took her somewhere or gave her instant death. Yet as she stared at it now, she felt a thread of fear, troubling doubt that threatened to make her destroy the door.

Other Fae—much stronger than her both mentally and magically—had tried to create such a doorway and failed. Who was she, an unknown, a nobody, to think she could do this? And on her first attempt, no less. Her magic was adequate, but surely not enough to do something so…grand.

Ailis could almost hear Bea's laughter at her insecurity. Her aunt would've given her a wink and a little shove.

"Don't let your self-doubt ruin your life. Think you can, Ailis, and you will."

Ailis licked her lips, Bea's words making her square her shoulders. There was a chance she could die. She had no way of knowing if she'd constructed the doorway correctly or not. Creating a gateway between realms was more than baking bread. She could have all the magic in the universe and still get it wrong.

Or…she could have gotten it right.

She knew Bea wouldn't have hesitated to go through. Regardless of whether life or death waited on the other side, Bea would've greeted it with a smile.

"Then so shall I," Ailis said.

She had come this far already. She hadn't spent years searching and learning, only to turn back now. Whatever happened, she'd attempted what others hadn't been courageous enough to even think of starting.

Ailis reached for her bag and draped it across her body. She took one more look at her home world before lifting her chin.

"Here goes everything," she whispered and stepped through the door.

CHAPTER TWO

Ailis held her breath, squeezing her eyes closed as she waited to feel anything alerting her that she'd failed. Yet there was no discomfort, no ripping apart of her body. Instead, she saw a bright light behind her eyelids. It beckoned her to look, tempted her to glimpse the truth—be it success or failure.

For the briefest of seconds, she almost took a step back. Then she remembered who she was and what had driven her to such drastic actions. Ailis forced her fingers to unclench. Her eyes slowly opened, and breath rushed past her parted lips as shock slid through her. She stood on a lush mountainside, gazing at the towering peaks on either side of her, rising like titans from the craggy ground. The summit to her right had a ledge where water cascaded over the side before falling a considerable distance to a pool, mist billowing erratically from the collision.

Birds she didn't recognize with large wingspans floated on

air currents, calling to each other. Above her, thick, fluffy clouds drifted lazily across the impossibly blue sky with its bright sun. Behind her was a forest and plenty of vegetation about. Trees, shrubs, bushes. What she didn't know was if she had managed to leave the Fae Realm or if she had mangled the creation of the doorway. This could still be her world. She didn't know the birds, but she didn't know every species of animal.

A thunderous roar broke the silence, coming at her from seemingly everywhere at once. She crouched to make herself as small as possible, her ears ringing, and instantly formed a ball of magic. Her gaze scanned the area, trying to locate what had issued such a terrifying sound. It was like nothing she had ever heard before.

A *whoosh, whoosh* from overhead had her shifting her gaze skyward. Ailis fell back onto her butt, her mouth gaping in utter disbelief as she took in the sight of a…*dragon*. She blinked, afraid her eyes were deceiving her. Yet the animal was still there. It flew over her, its large body and wide turquoise wings blocking the sun and casting her in shadow. Thankfully, it didn't appear to have noticed her. She didn't want to face one in battle. She was certain she would lose.

Ailis remained immobilized by a healthy dose of dread as she watched the dragon fly to the left and soar with the birds before dipping a wing and effortlessly swinging around. She was surprised that such a large animal could move so gracefully and quickly. She didn't tear her eyes from it as it flew toward her again. She glanced around, debating whether to teleport to the forest. Maybe if she stayed still, it wouldn't see her. Her body was frozen, her mind locked until it passed overhead and flew out of sight.

Only then did it register. She had, indeed, reached another realm.

Her smile was huge as she made the orb of magic vanish and sat with her accomplishment for a moment. She looked where the dragon had gone, her grin waning. She might have reached a new realm, but she hadn't counted on dragons. Honestly, she hadn't thought about what she might encounter, which wasn't something she would admit to anyone. She had been so focused on gaining the magic and knowledge needed to cross realms that she hadn't thought of the next steps.

Ailis looped her arms around her bent knees and considered her options. She had no idea if the dragons were friendly or if her magic would be enough to protect her. Despite that, she had no intention of returning to the Fae Realm quite yet.

But her excitement at not only reaching a new realm but also uncovering so many discoveries waiting to be found soon dispelled her lingering trepidation. She was small enough that she could stay hidden from the dragons. Besides, there might only be one. She could easily hear him coming and hide.

Ailis climbed to her feet and glanced at the doorway that stood out in the open. She could close it, but would she be able to open another? Did she dare take that chance? It was better to leave it here in case she needed to make a hasty exit. She locked it to ensure no one could go through it on either side, then adjusted her bag and started toward the forest. The trees offered shelter and concealment. She could explore the woods and remain close to the doorway to return to her world should the need arise.

Once in the safety of the trees, she paused. The shade from the canopy above her made it feel like she had entered another world. She marveled at the trees with their huge, twisting trunks, roots that protruded from the ground, and gnarled limbs stretching outward as if seeking to touch each other—or maybe even the dragons. She laughed at her fanciful thinking.

Small, red, rodent-like creatures with long, fluffy tails flitting from limb to limb caught her attention as they chirped and barked loudly at each other. Ailis watched them for a bit, mesmerized by their quick scampering among the trees. She meandered through the forest, taking in everything, her senses overloaded.

She took in the ground blanketed by dead leaves and clumps of vines that went everywhere. A chorus of birds filling the silence with music. Vibrant flowers in a multitude of colors with heady fragrances drifting languidly in the air. It was amazing. All of it. She could spend hours in one spot and still not see everything. And there was an entire forest yet to explore.

Ailis dropped next to a plant similar to the giant ferns on her world. This one was much smaller, barely coming to her knees. She gently ran her finger along one of the fronds that had yet to unfurl. It even felt the same as the ones from her realm.

She removed her sketchbook from her pack and quickly drew the plant as well as the incredible tree it surrounded. Ailis rested against another tree's trunk and added the small, red animal that stared at her as it ate a nut, its fluffy tail curled behind it. She wished she would've sketched the mountains and waterfall where she had come through the doorway, but she could do that before she left. She wanted to capture everything.

Maybe she'd even draw the dragon. She hadn't gotten a great look at it since she had been too dumbfounded to take in the details, but it had been large. Very large. Threats were a part of any exploration.

Dragons, however, were not.

She laughed at herself as she put away her sketchbook and stood. How could she have known about dragons? There might even be other dangers lurking about. Though the smaller ones were sometimes the most lethal. She shuddered as she thought of the torions, the small, many-jointed invertebrates on the Fae Realm. One drop of their venom was lethal. She would meet whatever was on this fabulous new world with awe and respect. And maybe, just maybe, make an acquaintance or two.

If she were lucky.

Ailis walked up steep inclines and down even steeper ones for hours, carefully picking her way. Oh, how she wished Bea were with her—or anyone. There was just so much beauty and wonder to take in, and she didn't have anyone to share it with. Her thoughts halted when she heard the unmistakable sound of water. It didn't take long to find the source. The sight of the stream was so idyllic she decided it was a perfect spot to spend some time.

She sat and took in the water that filtered softly, dropping from level to level as it flowed southward. Moss-covered rocks, the same vibrant, striking green as the trees, dotted the shore and the tributary itself.

Everything she had seen so far on this new realm was picturesque, but this place was something more. It was serene and secluded—a hidden paradise. Ailis reached for her pad and sketched the area. She used magic to add the exact color of green because she didn't want to get it wrong. When she finished, she simply sat and allowed the mesmerizing beauty to fill her with a feeling she couldn't define. It took some time before she realized what it was: peace.

She longed to stay. In fact, she never wanted to leave this spot. But there was so much more to see. After promising herself she would return, she knelt to cup her hands in the cool, fresh water and drank her fill. Then Ailis carefully picked her way over the slippery stones to the other side, a huge smile on her face. She hesitated and looked back before continuing her journey.

When she became hungry, she used magic to produce food. She stopped many times to sketch a flower, an animal, or just a scene that caught her eye. She hadn't anticipated finding such splendor everywhere she went. The notepad quickly filled with her drawings, and she hadn't even been on the realm a whole day.

The Light Fae gloried in everything bright and beautiful. They found flowers and plants soothing. A Dark, however, scorned such things and abhorred anything that even remotely resembled something a Light would enjoy.

Ailis had judiciously kept her joy and delight for the wonders around her—trees, the black deer, the moons—to herself, hidden from everyone but Bea. She had never dared to share her thoughts with anyone else. She was already an outsider among the Dark because she didn't conform as they demanded. Which was ironic since the Dark had turned against the Light for that very reason.

She had never fit in with her people. She wasn't a Light. But she wasn't like other Dark either. It had made life impossible sometimes. In order to survive, she'd had to pretend to be something she wasn't. The only time she'd ever been herself was with Bea. Her aunt had been a safe harbor in the storm that was her life. She ran to Bea when things got to be too much.

Then, her aunt died. Leaving Ailis truly alone.

No anchor. No safe harbor. Just endless loneliness that ate at her like a cruel disease.

The edge of the forest loomed before her. Beyond it was a sizable body of water with mountains ringing it on three sides. Ailis halted at the tree line and gazed at the grandeur before her. The lake was vast, the water so still and smooth it reflected the area around it like a mirror. She put her hand against the bark of the tree, feeling it bite into her palm. She would sketch this. But the water looked so tempting. She walked from the forest, intent on taking a swim. Halfway to the lake, water bubbled in the middle, the area growing larger, the gurgles coming faster and stronger. A heartbeat later, an enormous, scaled head appeared, then the upper body.

Ailis froze. Water rolled to the shore in waves as the dragon slowly turned its head toward her, pinning her to the spot. Her stomach dropped to her feet at the sight of the silver scales glistening metallic from the sun and the water. The dragon's white eyes narrowed slightly, taking her breath. She stumbled back as the beast walked out of the lake, never looking away.

There was no hiding now. Ailis pushed to her feet and formed two orbs of magic. She held one in each hand, waiting. "I'm not going down without a fight."

CHAPTER THREE

Lennox knew every creature on the realm, and the one before him wasn't one of them. The being was small, seemingly harmless, but underestimating her would be his folly. He climbed out of the water, intending to investigate this new arrival—and what it wanted. His duty was to protect the dragons and the realm itself—from anything he deemed a threat. And until he knew differently, the newcomer was exactly that.

While he didn't know what it was yet, his magic informed him that it was female. He took in her exotic look, finding it surprisingly appealing. Her thick hair fell nearly to her hips, the black strands woven with bright silver. Her oval face was both delicate and fierce—a combination that utterly intrigued him. Her crimson eyes were ringed in black, making her thick, midnight lashes more pronounced. She had high cheekbones, a stubborn tilt to her chin, and lips that drew his gaze again and again.

She wore garments to cover herself, which he found curious. Though he had to admit he liked the way they contoured to her body, showcasing every amazing curve. The article closest to her skin was so dark a green it was nearly black. Over that was a piece of black leather laced up her front to end in a V at her breasts, showing the green beneath it and then her beige skin.

Draped across her body was a length of leather with a bag attached at the end. Her legs were encased in black with material that looked as supple and pliable as skin. Her feet were also covered in leather, albeit thicker, the material going all the way up to her knees.

His gaze moved back to her mouth as she spoke. He frowned as he listened to the inaudible words. Lennox then noticed the iridescent orbs in each of her hands. He immediately realized it was magic of some sort. So, this female had magic as dragons did. Interesting.

She spoke again, and his power began to decipher the words.

"…well? Get on with it," she demanded.

Lennox fought not to smile at her pluck. He wanted to talk to her, but dragons didn't communicate as she did. No sooner had the thought gone through his mind than pain shot through him. Bones snapped, and muscles and ligaments tore. A bellow locked in his throat at the agony. It felt like it went on forever, and then it was just…gone.

He suddenly found himself no longer towering over the female. Lennox glanced down at himself to see that he looked like her. That wasn't possible. He lifted his hands, expecting to see his long talons, but they were gone. As were his scales.

"Bloody hell," she murmured, her voice soft with surprise.

He knew *he* was stunned. This had never happened before. He swallowed and worked his mouth as she continued eyeing him suspiciously. Lennox wanted to move, but he was still testing his new body. The last thing he wanted was to fall flat on his face. The female might just use those balls of magic on him.

Lennox flexed his fingers and squeezed his toes in the rocks that lined the shore. He rotated his shoulders before stilling as something landed against his cheek. He reached up to feel it. He tugged but discovered it was attached to his head.

"That's your hair," the female stated.

He looked at her black and silver locks and tried to see his. To his surprise, he could move it around enough to see that it was a golden hue.

"You understand me?"

Lennox's gaze slid to her as he nodded. But he didn't try for words. He touched his face. His long snout and sharp teeth were gone. Once more, hands drew his gaze. He rubbed his fingers along his thumb, captivated by the feeling. This was entirely different than what he experienced in his other form. There were thousands more sensations, each demanding his attention.

Something brushed against his arm. He looked and saw the hair there stirred by the breeze. A careful look at his body showed more hair on his chest that narrowed to a line at his stomach and trailed to his manhood. At least he still had that. There was hair on his thighs that grew thicker down his legs, ending at his ankles. This form was different in nearly every way. A glance behind him showed that his tail was gone. And his wings, which he missed with a pang.

"Do you understand me?"

Her voice was smooth and melodic with an accent he quite liked. Lennox moved his mouth and tested his voice. "Aye. I do." It came out as a croak. He cleared his throat and tried again. "I do."

He marveled at the feel of the words moving over his tongue and past his lips. It was vastly different than anything he'd known before.

The female's eyes widened as her breath whooshed from her lips.

"Who are you?" he asked.

"I-I'd like to ask you the same."

He should be worried about how she'd gotten here. He should grill her on what she wanted. But all he could do was stare as a million questions ran through his head.

She wiggled her fingers slightly, and the orbs vanished. "I can bring them back in an instant," she warned.

Lennox did smile this time. He liked her spirit. "You act as if you've never seen a dragon before."

"Because I haven't." She glanced away.

Then her focus returned to him. She slowly perused his body. He watched as her lips parted slightly. She cut her eyes away again, but her attention slid back once more, lingering on his cock.

She suddenly met his gaze. He quirked a brow. Given how she shifted her feet, she liked what she saw. Yet it seemed to make her uncomfortable. "Why do you cover yourself?"

"Um," she said, swallowed, then cleared her throat. "It's just our way to wear clothes."

So that's what they were called. "And my being without makes you uncomfortable?"

Her eyes lowered to his chest. "I wouldn't say that exactly."

Lennox studied her attire for another heartbeat before using magic to create cloth that went around his legs and torso, along with some cumbersome things on his feet. He hated all of it. The garments restricted his movements. How did she wear such things? He tugged at the shirt and stretched his neck.

"Wow," she mumbled.

He eyed her. "Is there something wrong?"

"Not at all," she replied and hastily met his gaze.

"Your name." His words came out rougher than intended, but he really wasn't happy about the confinement. He appreciated being able to communicate with her, but this form was too different.

She licked her lips. "Ailis. And yours?"

"Lennox. King of Dragon Kings."

Her midnight brows show up on her forehead. "So, there are more than two of you?"

"There are thousands," he replied.

Interest tinged with a thread of alarm filled her red eyes. "Can you show me? I want to see…" She paused and looked around. "*Everything*."

"Where did you come from? I know you're no' from Earth."

"Earth?" She repeated the name carefully. "I'm from the

Fae Realm. I'm Fae. I'd rather classify myself as an explorer, though. This is my first trip to a new realm."

No one had ever come to Earth from another realm before. She wanted to learn from him, and it was a great opportunity to acquire knowledge about her people. Yet unease kept him quiet. She had come from another realm. That in itself was enough to cause alarm, but she also had magic. He knew nothing about Fae or if they were dangerous to dragons or Earth. Nor did he know how many more of her kind were already on the realm. How could he keep his world safe if he didn't know when others arrived?

"Please," she said slowly. "I only want to learn. I came alone, I assure you."

Lennox heard dragons approaching from the west. He looked up in time to see some black dragons pass overhead, but they didn't glance his way. It was a group of adolescents— getting into mischief, no doubt. Lennox lowered his gaze to her. "How did you get here?"

"Through a door."

He frowned and shook his head. "What?"

"It might be easier if I show you."

"Then show me."

"Can you teleport?"

It was a word he didn't recognize.

"I take your expression to mean you can't." Ailis shifted her weight from foot to foot. "I could walk you there, which would take some time. Or I can teleport us both."

"We could fly."

She jerked back. "In case you've not noticed, I don't have wings."

"I'd fly us," he replied.

"Ah…perhaps another time."

He fought not to smile. "You cross realms and face a dragon but are afraid to fly?"

"Aye," she stated firmly. "I am."

"I wouldna drop you, lass."

"If it's all the same to you, I'd rather not find out."

He bowed his head in acceptance. "Just as I'd rather no' find out what teleporting is."

One minute, she was before him. The next, she was gone. He heard a shout behind him and turned to find her on the opposite side of the lake. Then she was gone again. When he heard her voice, he discovered her back in her original spot.

"It's just jumping from one place to the next," she said with a shrug. "Much safer than flying."

"So you say," he murmured, unconvinced.

She smiled and held out her hand. "Not afraid are you, King of Dragon Kings? It'll get us there in a blink."

He knew she was goading him, but damn if he didn't want to prove he wasn't anxious. She didn't seem fazed by the jumping. If he could shift from dragon to whatever being he now mimicked, then he could go with her.

Just before he took her hand, a sudden, overwhelming apprehension gripped him like a vise. What if he wasn't able to return to his true form? What if he was stuck like this? What if he could never fly again? He thought of his wings, the feeling of air moving over his scales as he flew, and then heard a startled shriek.

Lennox tipped his head and found Ailis far below him. When he spotted his talons and unfurled his wings, he sighed in contentment. Maybe this was a new power. Surprisingly, he hadn't felt pain this time. To test it, he shifted again. Once more, there was no pain. Lennox chuckled to find he was naked again. He covered himself with the same clothes as before.

"I should've warned you," he said. "I wanted to test that I could return to my true form."

She nodded and held out her hand again. He was cautious about this new visitor and her motives, but he was a dragon. Nothing on the realm could compete with their magic. With one call, he could have dragons surrounding her in an instant.

He took a tentative step, learning his new body. He closed the distance between them and took her hand. The world whooshed past him almost instantly, and he found himself in the Trocana Glen. He shook his head as he fought to get his bearings.

"I should've warned you."

He looked to find her eyes twinkling with laughter. Damn if he didn't find himself liking her more and more. He should be wary, though. She no doubt hid her true motives. But he would uncover what they were.

She lifted her hands as if to showcase something. "Ta-da. Here it is."

Lennox searched the area but found nothing. "What?"

"Right here," she said as she pointed, her brows furrowed. "That's air."

Her frown deepened. "Can you not see it?"

"Apparently, no'."

Which was disturbing. There could be other doorways on Earth that the dragons weren't aware of. Ailis might not want to do anything but learn and explore, but that didn't mean others would come to do the same.

He needed to know about the Fae and what they could do so he could prepare the dragons. They were used to being the strongest, most powerful creatures on the realm. Now, there was a Fae who could create doorways to their world—ones he couldn't see. Lennox wouldn't take any chances. He had to know more to ensure the protection of his people and the realm. And if it meant spending time with the enthralling Ailis, that was a hardship he would gladly bear. "I'll show you my world if you tell me of yours," he offered.

Ailis's smile was slow as it tilted up the corners of her mouth. "Deal."

CHAPTER FOUR

Elation rushed through her so quickly that Ailis was dizzy
with it.

But another emotion swirled within her, as well. One she
didn't dare linger on—or name. Her heart raced, and her
breathing was shallow. She was suddenly all too aware of
standing on a realm that wasn't hers with a man who could
shift from mortal form to dragon. He offered everything she
wanted, but there had to be a catch.

There was *always* a catch.

She tried to look away from his pale green eyes, but they
held her captive. She had never seen such a color before. The
way he stared at her, almost daring her, made her blood
quicken. Her mind drifted to his naked body she had feasted
her eyes on. She dragged herself away from thoughts she had
no business thinking.

Ailis caught a spark of worry, a drop of fear he shuttered
quickly as he searched her face. She swallowed, feeling that

same hesitation. She didn't know if she could fight him with her magic and be victorious. She didn't want to find out which of them was stronger.

If the Dark had taught her anything, it was that only a fool put their trust in strangers.

Yet Lennox was her key to experiencing this world—and doing it safely. He could've attacked her when they first met, but he hadn't. It could have been a ruse to get her to lower her guard, but she didn't get a sense that it was—not that she was a master at that. Even with the doubt that plagued her, she didn't want to leave. Whatever awaited her with the dragons was better than the Fae Realm.

"I can mark the doorway for you," she offered. "That way, you know where it is."

Lennox's probing gaze intensified. A muscle ticked in his jaw, bringing her attention to the ruggedness of his face. She was used to her kind. The Fae were striking creatures, the males just as pretty as the females. But Lennox was all male. He wasn't pretty. He was ruggedly striking, heart-stoppingly handsome.

She tried to ignore it, fought not to drink in the sight of him, but it was like ignoring the sun. She yearned to run her hands over his hard body and the rippling muscles. Wide shoulders begged to be caressed. And his chest, with its dusting of hair, tapered to trim hips and muscular legs. He was unabashedly male, blatantly masculine.

And it made him impossible to ignore. Her knees were weak, her insides trembling. She had never felt anything like this before.

His dark golden hair was parted on the side and fell past

his shoulders. His face was all hard plains as if cut from rock. His full lips were sensual and entirely too seductive. She wondered how they would feel on her mouth. On her body.

Around her nipples.

Heat scorched her veins. Her breasts swelled, the peaks hardening at the image alone.

"You could lie about the doorway's location."

It took her a moment to return to herself and realize he had spoken. It took another second for her to compute what he had said. "I could. But I'm not. I won't."

He continued to stare, no doubt weighing his options. She didn't like that he was probably rethinking his offer. He had no reason to trust her—or her, him. But someone had to make the first move.

"I had no way of knowing you couldn't see it," she said.

"There could be hundreds more, and we wouldna know."

She looked around until she found some rocks she didn't have to dig from the earth and then set them on either side of the doorway. Ailis straightened and looked at Lennox. "That outlines the door. I've locked it. No one can enter from either side."

Lennox stared at the space where the door was. She watched as his gaze searched the area for something solid to lock onto.

"I could take you through to my world if that would make you feel better." She swallowed, shrugging. "We don't know each other. I'm a stranger to your world. There are reasons for each of us to distrust the other, but I came here simply to explore. Nothing more. I've dreamed of crossing realms. So many of my people said it couldn't be done."

"But you did it."

She smiled, still getting used to the idea. "I did."

"You could return to tell them. They would want to see what you've found."

Unfortunately, that was true. She hadn't thought about that when she stepped through the doorway. Her only thought had been getting away before the soldiers found her. "I don't want to go home." She looked out across the mountains. "There's too much to explore and too many adventures to be had here."

"There are no others like you on this realm."

Her gaze skated back to him. "You look like me now."

"Aye," he said with a sigh.

As she studied Lennox, she couldn't deny his commanding presence. King of Dragon Kings, she recalled him saying. That meant there were other Dragon Kings. He might rule over them, but could he hold them back if they went after her? Did she even want to find out?

Ailis had an adventurer's spirit, but unlike Bea, she didn't ignore warning signs when it came to her life. She had created the doorway to this realm. She could create another somewhere else. Not that she would be welcomed anywhere else, but she wasn't keen on facing one dragon, much less a horde of them.

"You're regretting your offer," she stated.

Lennox shrugged one shoulder. He walked to the doorway and moved his arm between the two piles of rocks. Then he pushed his hand forward only to be blocked. "No' exactly. I see the benefit of learning from you." He glanced at her. "There's something here."

"A doorway," she said with a quick grin. "I locked it to

prevent anyone from accidentally going through on either side. As for your hesitation, I understand it. Others might not see a reason to learn from me."

"Aye," he said with a nod. His gaze slid to the doorway. "We're protectors of this realm. I know the value of being prepared. Unless you can tell me that your people wouldna attack."

Ailis thought about the war ramping up between the Dark and Light. Conflict was a part of Fae culture—or at least it seemed that way. "I can't tell you that. And even if I did, you wouldn't believe me. But the dragons could go through and attack my world, too."

"We could. But we willna. It isna our way." Lennox shook his head. "I willna rescind my offer. I could send you away, only for you or someone else to return. That is a chance I can no' take. We will share information."

She had been so excited at his proposal that she hadn't realized the implications. But she did now. "Will you really share anything of importance? After all, I could be the enemy. What if I take what you tell me to my people, and we return in force?"

"As you said, trust has to begin somewhere. You claim to be a peaceful explorer. Prove it."

"How?" she asked, quirking a brow.

Lennox's lips curved into a small smile. "How would you want me to prove it to you?"

"A question with a question. I'm beginning to see why you're the King of Dragon Kings."

He chuckled. "Let's no' do this in the open. I'll tell the Kings about you and my ability to now change into your form, but no' until I have more information."

"Because they'll attack me?"

"Most likely."

She had said the words, but hearing him acknowledge their truth left her looking at the sky. "Where should we go?"

"The forest, for the moment."

She reached for his arm and teleported them inside the woods to the stream she had stopped at earlier.

"Warn me next time," Lennox said as he closed his eyes and took a deep breath.

"Apologies. I don't feel anything."

"It isna painful." He met her gaze. "Just disorienting."

They stared at each other. Ailis fidgeted before she lowered herself to a low-lying rock. "Since I'm the stranger in your land, I'll begin. Would you like me to start with my people or my planet?"

"Whichever you prefer."

He remained standing, which unsettled her. However, if their positions were reversed, she didn't think she would've handled things as calmly as he was. Lennox was reserved. Whether that was just his way or how he presented himself to her, she didn't know. Yet.

Now that he was in mortal form, it was easy to disregard the huge dragon that had risen from the lake. She could never forget that, though. It didn't matter that she knew next to nothing about dragons. He had magic, strength, and size. Ailis knew how to defend herself if it came down to it, but she wasn't a warrior. Lennox was all that stood between the rest of the dragons and her. She put her trust in him to keep her alive.

And they both knew it.

"I'm a Fae," she began. "I come from the Fae Realm. From what little I've seen, our world is similar to this one. We are made of magic." She paused, trying to find a way to share the next part so it wouldn't cast her in a bad light, but there was no other way to tell it. "As a race, we're divided into two groups. The King of the Light rules the Light Fae. And the Dark Fae are ruled by the King of the Dark."

Lennox leaned a shoulder against a tree and crossed his arms over his chest. "Light and Dark."

She held his gaze, knowing what he was asking. "Good and…bad." She couldn't make herself say evil, even though that's what the Light called her kind.

"In my experience, nothing is a hundred percent good or bad."

"While I agree, my people are only given two choices. All Fae are born Light. It is a…choice to become Dark."

Lennox stared at her for a long while. When he finally spoke, what he voiced wasn't the question she had expected. "Why would anyone choose to become Dark?"

"Power. It all comes down to that. As Fae, we have considerable magic, but some always crave more. Once a Fae chooses the path of a Dark, it alters more than just their magic. Their appearance changes, too."

"So, everyone knows who is Light and who is Dark?"

"Exactly."

"And that's beneficial?" he asked skeptically.

She thought about that for a moment before shrugging. "The Light and Dark have been squabbling for generations. The Light fear the power the Dark gain and wish to wipe them out, and the Dark are concerned with the purity of the Light and wish to wipe *them* out. Things are getting out of hand. I fear someone will overstep soon, and things will shift from small skirmishes to an all-out civil war."

"No doubt it will unless someone stops it."

"I don't think anyone can. Both sides distrust the other."

"Can you do anything?"

She barked a laugh. "Me? I'm nobody."

"Sometimes, the people we least expect make the biggest differences."

Ailis glanced at the stream, watching the water run over a flat rock before dropping to the next. "If I could, I would."

"You'll never know unless you try."

"A single Fae against two monarchies?" She snorted and cut her eyes to him. "But you do have a point."

One side of his mouth lifted in a smile.

She leaned forward, resting her arms on her legs. "You can ask the question."

"What question would that be?"

"If I'm Light or Dark."

"Okay."

Ailis waited for the question to come, but he said nothing. She cleared her throat and needed to fill the silence. So, she continued talking. "Because the Light and Dark can't get along, we divided the realm. The Light stay on one side and the Dark on the other. It has been that way for so long that no one remembers a time it *wasn't* like that. The land is divided into regions on my side. There are grand cities, all the way down to tiny villages and everything in between."

"Where did you live?"

"One of the large cities, though my aunt had a cottage in

the country that she left to me. I always thought of it as an escape when I visited her. Now that it's mine, I rarely go. Too many memories, I suppose." Ailis glanced at the ground. "She was the last of my family."

Ailis was overcome with emotion at missing her aunt. It had been over five years since Bea's death, but the grief still crept up on Ailis at times.

"I'm sorry."

She jerked her gaze to Lennox to find him watching her. Ailis blinked rapidly to chase away the tears. "Death is a part of life, is it not?"

"It is. That doesna mean we doona feel the loss."

She nodded and then smiled. "I try to imagine what Bea would think if she were here. She was an explorer, too. I think that's where I got my love of it. Nothing ever held her back. She always did what she wanted, regardless of what anyone said. We understood each other when no one else did. That makes missing her harder. She had a long life, though."

"How long?"

Ailis straightened her back and stretched her legs out before her, crossing them at the ankles. "Fae live for thousands of years."

"Really?"

"What about dragons?"

"Dragons also live for thousands of years. Dragon Kings live until another King kills us."

Her mouth went slack at his words. "Do you mean…are you telling me you're immortal?"

"Immortality implies I'll never die. I can be killed, but only by another King."

Which meant she couldn't do any damage to him or any of the other Dragon Kings. That was terrifying. No wonder he hadn't been concerned when he found her.

"At least as far as I know," Lennox added. "I've never fought a Fae."

She raised her brows and shook her head. "Don't look my way. I'm not about to test your theory." Ailis frowned as she studied him. "If you're all but untouchable, I imagine everyone wishes to be King."

"Many do."

"What stops them from gaining what they want?"

"The magic of the realm chooses who becomes King of their clan."

She shoved her hair away from her face. "What about you? Does the magic choose who is King of Kings?"

"Aye."

"What if someone doesn't want the position?"

Lennox's throat bobbed as he swallowed. "It doesna matter. If you're chosen, you're chosen. Tell me about your magic. What all can you do?"

Ailis wanted to get back to discussing the dragons, but by the look on Lennox's face, he wouldn't share any more for the moment. She drew in a breath and released it, letting him change the subject. "You've seen that I can teleport."

"Can every Fae do that?"

"It takes practice to master the ability. Not all Fae can do it."

"And the doorways? Can everyone create those?"

She nodded. "They can."

"Why have the doorways if you can teleport?"

Ailis grinned. "Why walk if you can fly?"

Lennox laughed, the sound bouncing around the area as his eyes sparked with humor. The way his face lit up made him even more gorgeous, if that were possible. "Tell me more," he pressed.

"I can create just about anything I want with my magic."

"Show me."

She held out her hands and made a miniature of the stream. In the next instant, a plate of her favorite dessert replaced it. Then she made it vanish.

His eyes glittered with interest. "What about when we first met? The iridescent balls you held."

"We use the orbs, along with weapons, in battle."

"Show me," Lennox urged.

CHAPTER FIVE

The new body—and assault of his senses—was playing havoc with Lennox. His palms wouldn't stop tingling. The need to touch everything was so vast and crushing that it took every bit of willpower for him to concentrate on Ailis.

Then there was the confining nature of the clothes. He despised them and their restrictions on his body. They were too tight. He couldn't understand how anyone would willingly wear them. Lennox shifted his shoulders. He stood because he hadn't gotten used to the fact that he no longer had his wings or a tail. He had always looked at the world from a certain height. Being this close to the ground brought so many things into his awareness that hadn't been there before.

Lennox swallowed hard and locked his eyes on Ailis. She helped him to focus. Grounded him when he longed to rip off the clothes and return to his true form. To stretch his wings and take to the skies so he would never forget who he was. If he could figure out how to communicate with her as a dragon, he'd do just that. But it wasn't possible. He had no choice but to stay in this form.

At least until it became unbearable.

She stood, wariness in her eyes. "Are you sure?"

His mind went blank. Why did she ask such a question? What had he said? Ah, yes. He had asked her to show him the iridescent balls he had seen in her hands. Lennox nodded. "Aye."

"You're not worried I'll attack?"

At this point, he almost wished for it—any reason to return to his dragon form. He pushed away from the tree and set his palm against it instead, gripping it so tightly the bark cut into his skin. Lennox pulled his hand away and looked at the blood welling up from the tiny pricks. Almost instantly, the wounds mended before his eyes.

He curled his fingers into a fist before spreading them wide. He was able to do the same in his true form but had talons to contend with. In this shape, he could fist his hand into tight balls. It wasn't as if he didn't feel things as a dragon, but his scales prevented the kind of contact he achieved with skin.

Lennox put his hands on either side of his face and felt his cheeks, jaw, and mouth again. Then, he slid his hands into his hair. It was smooth and cool to the touch. And long. He touched his ears and then moved to the soft material covering his chest, running his hands down his stomach as his gaze lowered to his bottom half. He lifted his toes in his boots and saw the leather move.

The sound of water caught his attention once more. He strode to the edge of the stream and peered over to look at his reflection. Instead of the white eyes he had always seen looking back at him in the water, they were a soft shade of pale green.

He didn't recognize the face staring back at him. Not the eyes, the nose, the mouth, and certainly not the hair. The absence of silver scales was as bewildering as his missing wings and tail. He knew he could return to his true form, but that didn't halt the wave of apprehension that flooded him.

He was a dragon.

Yet he was something else, too—at least for the moment.

"Lennox?"

He jerked at the sound of Ailis's voice directly behind him. He knew he shouldn't let her see his panic, but he couldn't seem to dredge up the will to care.

"What can I do to help?"

He shook his head, unable to find the words.

She lowered herself beside him. "Give it some time. Allow yourself to get used to this new body and everything that comes with it."

"I doona think I can."

"Then don't."

He swiveled his head to look into her red eyes. Dragons had all kinds of colored eyes, and he assumed the Fae did, too. "I must if we are to converse."

She gave him a soft smile. "No one said everything had to be done today."

Lennox briefly squeezed his eyes shut as he shook his head and looked away. "I can no' leave you alone. I doona know what the others will do if they find you."

"I'll stay out of sight."

He looked her way once more. "It is more than my kind you need to worry about. There are plenty of animals who would believe you food."

"Is there somewhere I can hide?"

The first thing that came to mind was his mountain. No one would dare enter it without his permission. Yet he hesitated to bring her. However, there was no other place he could ensure her safety. He could tell her to leave, but oddly, he didn't want that. There was still much more he could learn about the Fae. Much more he *needed* to learn.

His gaze returned to the water. He bent over the bank and lowered his hand into the gently flowing stream. The tiny hairs on the back of his hand swayed in the current, causing ripples of awareness to move up and down his arm. He wouldn't be experiencing any of this without Ailis. And while Lennox wasn't sure if he enjoyed the new form, he couldn't deny that it allowed him an alternative view. And all knowledge was beneficial.

He withdrew his hand from the water and watched the droplets roll across his skin and plunk back into the stream. "There is a place you would be safe."

"Then I'll go there. Tell me where it is."

"You should know it's where I live."

"So...you'll be close if something happens."

"Aye."

He sat back and spread his hands over the moss-covered rocks, the plants spongy beneath his palm. It was so different from when he had walked across them as a dragon. He had barely felt the mats then. Whereas now, it was all he could feel.

Lennox stood and faced Ailis. "It is some distance away."

"Then we'd best get started."

He watched as she turned away. "I willna be walking."

That drew her to a halt. She jerked her head around, her midnight locks fanning out as she did. "Point me in the right direction. I'll get there."

"There's an easier way."

Her brows furrowed as she shifted to face him. "I hope you aren't suggesting I ride on your back."

"I doona want anyone to see you, and they certainly would if you did that."

"Then what do you propose?"

He wondered if being in this new form had addled his brain. He couldn't imagine himself ever making this plan otherwise. "I can carry you there. In my hand."

"Your…hand." She looked away, considering.

He watched her and tried not to think about tangling his fingers in her hair to see if it was as silky as it looked. He fisted his hands when his mind wondered what her skin might feel like beneath his palm. Or her lips against his.

Lennox nearly touched his mouth. He pressed his lips together. It was a peculiar sensation. Much different than when he had a mouthful of razor-sharp teeth.

His eyes raked down her body. His blood heated as he imagined pulling her against him. He could hold her as he'd never held a dragon. His cock hardened as desire engulfed him. It was swift and overwhelming. And he was thankful that Ailis's attention was elsewhere. Lennox quickly adjusted himself and thought of anything but the Fae before him. Not that it did any good. The image was in his head, and it wouldn't leave.

"I asked for trust. Now, you are offering it," she said before turning her head to him. "And I shall give it in return."

"I willna harm you, Ailis. No' unless you attack me."

"I have no intention of attacking anyone. I meant it when I said I'm a peaceful explorer."

He nodded. "Then let's do this. The longer we're out in the open, the more opportunities there are for dragons to see us."

"We could hear them coming."

"Dragons come in all sizes."

Her eyes quickly scanned the area. "So, they could be near?"

"They could be. But they're no'. We are not so plentiful that we take up every space on the realm. Each clan has a territory. Only a handful of dragons live in some portions, while more congregate in others. Much like your cities."

"You were listening," she said with a smile.

"Aye." Though not as well as he should have. "The dragon who lives in this area tends to stay on the far end of the forest." He began walking toward the lake, and she fell into step with him.

"Were you visiting him?"

Lennox shook his head. "I was flying. It's good to stretch my wings and check on the clans. Each of the Kings is responsible for their clan."

"And you're responsible for them."

"In a manner, aye. I'm also accountable for my clan."

She used her hand to vault over a fallen tree. "That seems like a lot for one individual—one dragon—to handle."

It was. Some days, he didn't think he could do it all and questioned the magic's decision. "It willna be forever. The magic will find another to take my place."

"For which position? King of your clan or of the Kings?"

He glanced at her to see her frowning. "Both."

"That hardly seems fair."

Lennox shrugged. "It is our way."

"I don't like it."

He smiled at her tone that hinted she was appalled on his behalf. "I'll do the duty I was chosen for."

"That's right. You don't even get a say in being King. On top of that, you don't get a say in whether you remain one."

Lennox chuckled. "As I said, it is our way."

"And I repeat, it's not fair."

"When is anything in life fair?"

She shot him a dubious look. "We were having a nice conversation. You didn't have to spoil things by being rational."

He threw back his head and laughed. When he looked her way, Ailis was smiling. They shared a look as they reached the tree line. Beautiful, clever, and witty. It was no wonder he was drawn to her. She would make a great mate. Except for one glaring problem: She wasn't a dragon. He would do well to remember that she was a visitor. They could be friendly, but at the end of the day, she was a Fae and not of his world.

Lennox halted and turned to her. "Once I'm in my true form, we willna be able to communicate."

"I know."

"Remain here until I shift. I'll come for you. Curl yourself into my hand. Mind your hair. I doona want it spotted."

She reached up and touched her head. "I can do that."

"I'll fly as quickly as I can. If I stop, it's because I doona have a choice. Stay as you are until I release you."

"Right. I need to play dead so dragons don't discover me."

"Something like that," he said with a grin.

Her red eyes met his. "I trust you."

He wasn't prepared for the words. They struck him hard, shifting something within him. Here was this Fae, this outsider, who was willing to put her life in his hands. "I willna let any harm come to you."

"I believe you."

Lennox glanced over his shoulder at the lake. With one last look at Ailis, he turned on his heel. As he left the forest, he thought about returning to his true form. It happened just as quickly as it had before. One moment, he was something, and the next, he was something else.

He paused before slowly turning toward the woods. It was easy to locate Ailis. She stood next to a tree, her eyes lifted to him. There was no fear on her face—at least none he could see. Lennox extended his hand until it was beside her. She paused for only a heartbeat when her gaze landed on his talons.

She climbed into his palm and sat, drawing her knees up to her chest. Her gaze lifted to him once more, and she gave him a tentative smile as she gathered her hair to one side. He slowly closed his hand, careful that his talons weren't near her. Then he launched himself into the sky.

CHAPTER SIX

Ailis sucked in a breath at the jolt that knocked her back against Lennox's palm. The force was enough to keep her there for a few moments. It was only when she was able to right herself that she swallowed and tried to find the calm from before.

Which was difficult since a dragon held her in his palm. He could drop her at any moment. While she had never tried to teleport after falling, there was no reason it wouldn't work. At least she hoped it would. She could do it now before he had a chance to harm her.

Her gaze landed on one of his very long, very black talons. They surrounded her like a cage and looked as sharp as any Fae blade, which was saying something. The claws made her nervous. Flying made her uneasy. Yet she remained. Mostly because she wanted to learn, and the best way to do that was through Lennox.

What awaited her on the Fae Realm would be worse than

whatever happened to her here. Besides, there was nothing for her on her world. She had always known that, but now she admitted it. She had acquaintances, but no close friends. Being a Dark tended to make her wary and distrustful of everyone. With no family left and no one else she missed—or would likely miss her—adventure beckoned.

Well, that wasn't exactly true. While she *had* sought adventure, it was more than that. Something had always tried to lure her away from her realm. Her gaze was always on the stars as she wondered about other worlds and the beings that lived on them. She had daydreamed of exploring those realms and meeting others. It had felt like it was always just out of reach.

Until it wasn't.

She still couldn't believe she had crossed to another world. In the back of her mind, she had never actually thought her magic would allow such things. Keeping an eye on her goals and learning had helped her in the months after Bea's death. She had poured everything she had into it instead of properly grieving her aunt.

Ailis felt the wind in her hair and noticed that some of it had found its way between Lennox's large digits. She winced and hurriedly gathered it in her hands again. She rested her chin on her knees and closed her eyes. She heard the steady sound of his wings flapping over the rush of wind. Light filtered through Lennox's fingers, but the slight movements up and down as he flew made her stomach churn. She decided to keep her eyes closed just in case.

Her mind wandered, jumping from thought to thought while trying not to linger on the growing nausea. A roar that didn't come from Lennox made her eyes fly open and her heart jump into her throat. She clutched her legs tighter but didn't feel Lennox slow. Ailis leaned to the side and looked out through a gap in his fingers to see the feet of another dragon before they moved out of view.

A deep rumble went through Lennox, causing the air around her to vibrate. It didn't sound angry or threatening. Could he be trying to tell her to remain calm? Ailis rolled her eyes and shook her head at trying to decipher a dragon.

She had just settled again when she began tipping forward slightly, alerting her that Lennox was descending. Ailis braced herself as she tried to imagine what he might look like if she were watching. She did a poor job of it. In fact, she couldn't pull up a description of him even after seeing him twice.

To be fair, the first time had just been a glimpse before he shifted. The second time, she had told herself she would look closer, but his white dragon eyes had hypnotized her. They were different from his mortal eyes, but there was no denying it was Lennox watching her. Then he had held out his hand. Or was it a paw? Claw? What did one call parts of a dragon? Whatever it was, she had seen it and immediately climbed inside while trying not to notice just how large that hand was. Or how deadly the talons appeared.

Then she was flying and forgot all about what Lennox looked like. But now that they were headed back to the ground, it was all she could think about. She looked at his hand where the sunlight struck the beautiful silver scales.

Her thoughts halted when the flapping of his wings shifted to beat in quick, short bursts. A moment later, he landed. It was softer than she expected. She readied for him to open his palm so she could climb out, but nothing happened.

She released her hold on her hair. As she leaned forward, she heard a loud thump. She moved onto her hands and knees and peered through Lennox's fingers to find the ground was still quite a ways down. From what she could see, the area looked much like what they had left. While she was looking around, she caught sight of another dragon's legs and tail, this one with lavender scales.

It stood before Lennox. Neither of the dragons moved. She craned her neck to see more of the newcomer, but she couldn't see more than the edge of a wing tucked against a large body. And it was just as big as Lennox's.

Ailis slowly returned to her sitting position to wait. She didn't want to give herself away and put either Lennox or her in a difficult situation. He hadn't moved his hand since before they landed. Was it odd for a dragon to hold one hand closed? Or did he hold both like that? Did he walk on two legs or four? She had no idea what to expect, and that ratcheted her nervousness.

She might be an adventurer, but only the smart ones who recognized danger and avoided it returned home. Bea had been reckless to a fault and had many scars to prove it. Ailis might have gotten the same explorer spirit as her aunt, but she wasn't nearly as cavalier.

Until she opened a door to an unknown world and stepped through.

Ailis grinned. Bea would've loved this adventure. *She* was loving it. There was always a measure of danger when investigating. Ailis had held some of herself back before, allowing Bea to rush headlong into things. Now, she had the opportunity to give it her all. There was no reason to hesitate or restrain herself.

This was her quest. This new realm and all it held were hers to discover.

The unmistakable sound of flapping wings broke through her thoughts. It was loud at first but soon diminished. Then Lennox turned and began to walk. She watched the grass as they moved, noting the rocks that protruded from the ground. The light dimmed, and then it was gone. Lennox kept walking. Darkness soon bathed Ailis. Her unease grew the longer it lasted. Lennox didn't seem to have a problem moving about. Either he knew where he was going by heart or could see in the dark. She had put her trust in him, and it seemed it would be stretched to its limits.

She tapped her leg with a finger in a bid to keep her fretfulness to a minimum. Unfortunately, it wasn't working all that well. Just when she was about to try to get his attention, he finally halted. Ailis didn't let out a sigh of relief until he lowered his hand and spread his fingers. More inky darkness met her. It didn't matter how adjusted her eyes were, there was nothing for her to see but a wall of black. She had no idea where she could step. For all she knew, there was a cliff she could topple off. Or a wall to run into.

That same low rumble sounded from Lennox again.

Ailis lifted her face to where she thought he might be. "I can't see. Is it safe for me to light the area?"

Another rumble.

She took that to mean she could. Ailis crafted a small light no bigger than her palm. She threw it up into the air where it hung above them and spread its luminosity. She found herself staring at rock walls that domed above her. A few boulders of various sizes were pushed to the side to leave the middle clear.

Ailis unfolded her legs and scooted to the edge of Lennox's hand before standing. The size of the cavern was mindboggling. She turned in a circle to take it all in until she faced him. "Wait," she said, just in case he was about to shift. "I want to see you."

White eyes locked on her, and he nodded once.

She moved back a few steps to take him in. Lennox stood on all four legs. There were several feet between the top of his head and the ceiling of the cavern, with plenty of room for him to move around. It might even be wide enough for him to spread his wings.

Ailis then took a deep breath and looked him over, the King of Dragon Kings. His large white eyes sat delicately within his bony, horned skull, giving him a daunting appearance. Five large horns spiraled up from atop his head, the center being the tallest. Along his jawline were two rows of small crystal growths. He had a round nose with two narrow, slitted nostrils and small tendrils hung from his chin.

The sharp teeth poking from the sides of his mouth were a reminder that he was a predator. As if she could ever forget. Her gaze drifted to his long neck covered in thick scales, then to his colossal body. Rows of spikes dotted with crystals ran along his spine. She lowered her eyes to find his scales curved on his stomach, their color lighter than the rest of him.

While Lennox's scales gleamed, his wings seemed to soak up the light, even folded against him. They were thick and had the appearance of finely tooled leather. Their edges were rounded slightly on top, but sharp tips grew from the bottom of each wing. She spotted a few holes in his wing, though it obviously didn't prevent him from flying. Finally, she came to his long tail covered with more crystals along the top. It ended in a sharp point that resembled a spear.

She had never seen anything so magnificent or frightening. She would've been duly alarmed even if he didn't have magic. When she first saw him, she had been so terrified that she had thought to fight him off simply because of his size and chilling appearance. But then the dragon had transformed into a male who stole her breath and made her ache for his nearness.

Lennox shifted his head to the side. Somehow, she knew he wanted to know what she thought of him. Should she be honest? Lying might gain her a slight advantage, but only briefly. A being didn't become King of Kings without intellect and cunning. He would sniff out her falsehood soon enough.

"I've never seen a dragon before." Ailis heard the tremor in her voice and tried to squash it. "Your size alone is enough to give anyone pause. And yet," she said, running her gaze over him once more, "I've also never seen anything so stunning."

In a blink, the dragon was gone, replaced by Lennox in his mortal form—dressed. His green eyes held hers. "But you know about dragons. How is it you know of us but have never seen one?"

"Books. And trust me, those looked much different than you."

His brows furrowed.

Ailis pulled the book from her bag. "A written account of

things. We have buildings full of these, all with different subjects."

"Books," he repeated while staring at the volume in her hand.

She held it out to him. "How does your kind keep records?"

"Each clan has a group who collects and passes down stories. None have ever spoken of any beings like you."

"They will now. At least you'll have the story."

His shoulders lifted with his breath. "I'll be able to share it once you're gone."

She didn't like the churn of feelings his words caused. It wasn't as if she could stay here forever. She didn't belong.

She didn't fit anywhere.

CHAPTER SEVEN

"Do you want to look?"

Lennox studied the small item in Ailis's outstretched hand. He would rather touch her, but at least the thing she called a book would give his hands something to do and his senses more to soak up. He closed the distance between them and took the item, his fingers brushing hers. The shock that went through him made his lungs seize. It was by sheer will alone that he didn't let it show.

He took a half step back just to put some space between them so it wouldn't be so easy to reach for her. Lennox drew in a breath, feeling it shudder through him. Ailis watched him closely. Did she see what their brief contact had done to him? He wasn't sure he wanted to know. Instead, he turned his attention to the item in his hand. It was dense, the leather binding smooth to the touch. Cool and solid at the same time. He turned the book over, looking at it from every angle. He stilled when the top fell open to show the inside.

"Those are pages," Ailis told him. "What you see is our written language."

He was stunned. And obsessed. Here, in his hands, was a story. No need to have dragons who had the gift of remembrance to recall new and old tales to share with the clan. If they could create such symbols for their language, they'd never need to worry about forgetting their history. "And you have many of these?"

"Countless titles."

His gaze jerked to hers.

She grinned and nodded. "It is a little hard to comprehend, but it's true. Some contain works of fiction—that's what we call stories made up to entertain."

"We share such tales."

"Really? How interesting. We also have those that hold accounts of the Fae. There are others, like the one you hold, that share knowledge someone has gained so others can learn."

He leafed through the pages. "What is this one about?" No sooner had he asked than his magic allowed him to understand the words. He read a few lines before her voice reached him.

"How to open a doorway to other realms."

Lennox wanted to devour the entire book. "And you say you're the only one who has done this?"

She shifted nervously. "It's only been a theory until now. It's about more than just the knowledge to craft such a door. It's also being able to muster the magic needed. I worked months to be able to do this."

"You expect me to believe you're the only one who has?"

"Of course not," she said with a shake of her dark head. "There were others. Some tried and failed. Some never tried, believing it was out of their reach. The author of that book vanished before anyone could ask them if it was true or not. Hundreds of Fae attempted to create a doorway and died. The rulers of the Light and Dark demanded that the books be gathered and burned. That is the only known copy to still exist."

He snapped the book shut. "When you return to your world and tell others, they will then attempt such an endeavor."

There was a slight pause before she said, "Probably."

"Undoubtedly."

"I won't tell them about this realm."

"That doesna mean they willna come. How did you find it?"

Ailis's gaze dropped to the book.

Lennox grunted. "That's what I thought. How did this author know about it?"

"I don't know. As I said, they disappeared."

"You really believe this is the only copy?"

Her throat moved as she swallowed. "There's a good chance. I searched for some time to find a copy. In the end, I had to steal it. Well," she said with a twist of her lips, "I borrowed it. I planned to return it."

"How did you know you could come here?"

"I didn't. I took a chance."

His brows rose at that. "You could've died."

"I could have, but I didn't."

"Why?"

She shrugged. "Why not? I'm an explorer, and in order to find new things, I must seek them out."

"Even if it ends your life?"

"Even if it ends my life."

Lennox handed her the book. "How many Fae are there?"

"Millions. How many dragons are there?" She returned the book to her bag.

"Millions," he replied.

He stared at her for so long that Ailis returned her attention to the cavern. His home. Or at least the cave he had used since becoming a Dragon King. He wondered what she thought of it. He had been surprised to learn she couldn't see in the dark. Seemed that was one advantage dragons had over the Fae.

"What is this place?" she asked.

"It is my mountain at the capital. Each King has one."

She looked at him over her shoulder, their eyes meeting. "Do you get much time on your own?"

"No' really."

She continued her exploration along the edge of the cavern. "We're inside a mountain?"

"Aye."

"How far down?"

"No' verra."

Her lips were turned up when she glanced his way. "I like your accent. Especially the way you roll your *R*s."

"You have an accent, too." He crossed his arms over his chest and widened his stance. It felt odd not having something in his hands. And it wasn't as if he could grab hold of her— even though he wanted to.

"Do I?"

"Aye."

Ailis halted and turned to him. "Do you like it?"

"I do." Maybe too much.

"You don't have to lie. My self-esteem can take it."

He grinned, glancing at the ground. "I've no need to lie, lass."

"Lass?" she repeated, her brows drawn together. "What does that mean?"

"Girl."

She pressed her lips together. "Hmm. Where are we exactly?"

"Every clan has an area they control, but one section of our realm is only for the Dragon Kings. It is our capital. That is where we are. It is where the magic of our world is the strongest."

Ailis sat on a low rock near her and removed the bag to set at her side. "So, all of you come here?"

"Sometimes, to hash out issues or discuss problems we see rising. Other times, to get away."

"Like now," she said with a grin.

Lennox nodded. "Aye."

"This place isn't controlled by any one King, right?"

"Correct. It is the seat of our power, for lack of a better term."

She folded her arms around her legs and raised her gaze. "You mean the seat of your power."

"I suppose." It was true, but he had never thought of it that way.

"Is the lavender dragon I saw around?"

"He's gone. He just needed to tell me about an upcoming

mating ceremony.”

"You spoke?" she asked in surprise.

He dropped his arms and chose a rock to sit on near her, carefully keeping his distance. "We doona communicate as you do. We speak through a mental link."

"That's incredible. You hear voices in your head?"

"Aye," he said, trying to hold back his laughter.

She rolled her eyes. "Of course, you do. I just can't imagine someone's voice in my head. Doesn't it get annoying to have all of them coming at you?"

"I can choose whether to hear someone or no'. We all can. We say the dragon's name we want to talk to, and they can decide if they wish to talk."

"If someone is standing before you, I'm sure it's difficult to ignore them."

"Before me?" he repeated before he realized what she meant. "We can communicate over vast distances."

Her mouth formed an *O*.

"I gather yours can no'?"

"No. Now, someone *could* call for me. A Fae can hear their names over very long distances and know who called for us and where they are. We can ignore them or jump to their location to see what they want."

He leaned forward, bracing his forearms on his thighs. "Similar to us, then."

"A little. When you say vast distances, how far?"

"I can speak to anyone around the realm."

"The entire world?"

He nodded once. "Aye."

"Wow."

Silence stretched between them, and he found himself thinking of her words after she'd scrutinized him in dragon form. He liked their easy exchange, but he had seen her trepidation. "I doona want you to fear me."

"We're getting to know each other. I'm a stranger on your world. You could've killed me but chose to talk to me instead. We're developing trust."

"I saw the look in your eyes when you saw me."

She pressed her lips together. "Your size alone is frightening, but you haven't given me a reason to fear you."

"And the other dragons?"

"I'm not getting to know them as I am you," she said with a grin.

It didn't quite reach her eyes. Though, he didn't blame her. He wasn't sure he would handle being on a strange world as well as she was.

Ailis cleared her throat. "If things get out of hand, I'll jump to the doorway and leave."

That meant she could depart anytime she wanted, and he could do nothing about it. He should be happy there was a way for her to get free if any dragons came upon her. And he was. Sort of. It would be better if she left and none ever knew she was here. But there was no going back. Lennox had grasped that immediately. Ailis was here. More Fae could come.

There was something magnetic about Ailis that had nothing to do with the fact that she had magic or was an outsider from another realm. It was all her. Her voice, her smile, the way she looked at everything with delight.

"How long will you stay?" he asked.

She shrugged. "Until you tell me I've overstayed, or I feel threatened."

"My realm is large. There is much to show you."

Her lips curved into a bright smile. "I can't wait to see it." The grin vanished almost instantly. "Tell me there's another way to get around than in your hand."

"Did I hurt you with my talons?" Lennox hadn't smelled blood, but that didn't mean he hadn't harmed her.

"It's not that at all. It's just…" She paused and rolled her shoulders.

"Was it too cramped?"

She shook her head. "I became nauseous from the slight up and down movement."

"I see. The only other option would be for you to climb onto my back."

"I don't think that would work either since others could see me."

"There's no guarantee how they would greet you."

"Trust me, I understand. I'm here befriending the King of Dragon Kings. You've flown me to safety in your private mountain. I've come so much farther than I ever dreamed."

He liked how she found the upside to things. "Do all Fae think as you do?"

"Few. The Light are so fixated on eradicating the Dark that they don't know how blurred the lines are from them to the Dark. And the Dark split their time between wanting to wipe out all traces of the Light dond betraying each other to gain more power."

"You said all Fae are born Light. The Dark could never wipe them out."

Her lips twisted as she nodded. "Nor could the Light get rid of the Dark. Where there is one, there is the other."

"There's always balance. It's everywhere."

"Even with dragons?"

He sighed and nodded. "The magic chooses us, but it is always looking at others to see if someone is stronger. There have been a few occasions when a King has lost his way. That's when the magic chooses another."

"For Kings or the King of Kings?"

"Both," he replied with a shrug.

"I get the feeling that what happens after the magic chooses another isn't simple."

"Hardly. It's insistent when it picks someone. For me, it was like a churning within me." He rubbed his chest, remembering how it had consumed him, the feeling crushing and unrelenting. "There is no ignoring it. One way or another, the magic always gets what it wants."

"What did you have to do?"

He looked into her red eyes, letting his thoughts drift back to that time. "I challenged the current King of my clan. A King can no' decline such a petition. It doesna matter who issues it. Once the words have been spoken, there's no taking them back." He lowered his gaze to his fisted hands. He forced his fingers to unfurl before flexing them. Lennox remembered the blood that had coated his talons. "It is a fight to the death. Mine lasted for two days."

"Why a battle?"

"To prove to the clan who is the strongest. Some claim to hear the magic, but those are the dragons who want power so badly they either lie or allow their minds to create a scenario

that causes them to believe they've been chosen. The King
will end their lives easily and quickly." He looked at her. "One
the magic has chosen is another matter."

A small frown puckered her brow. "Did you like your
King?"

"I didna know him. He had seemed like a good King. It
wasna until I took his place that I discovered he'd allowed
several of our dragons to be killed by a neighboring clan. He
also put us at great risk and on the verge of war by stealing
from other clans. I spent the early part of my reign sorting out
that tangle. Only a few instances resulted in battles."

"Did you win?"

"Does anyone ever win in a fight?"

She shrugged. "Some would say yes."

"I doona see how death can ever be claimed as a victory."

"I take it you don't like warfare."

He blew out a breath. "I loathe it. But I'm good at it."

CHAPTER EIGHT

Ailis regretted bringing up how Lennox had become King. She was insanely curious, but it would behoove her to be more aware of how her questions affected him. Lennox's entire body radiated tension. He was careful to keep emotion from his face, but it was just another clue to how much the current conversation bothered him, that there were memories he would rather not dredge up.

All the Dark she had known would shout to the world if they had Lennox's abilities. They would sweep across the land, facing both Dark and Light until they had bested everyone. Then, they would rule with an iron fist.

But not Lennox. He had the ability, but he didn't use it. Ailis was beginning to understand what the magic of his world looked for in the dragons—and why it had chosen him. Lennox would only unleash his skills if he had no other choice. But if it happened, if he had to go to war, then she had no doubt he would win.

At least for a while.

If what he said was true, then he would only be King until the magic found another. Upon which time he would fight to the death. Seeing his power and command, she couldn't imagine that day would ever come. All she had to do was look into his eyes to see the truth, though. He was ready for it. He bore the weight of responsibility easily but not willingly.

She needed to change the subject—for both of them. She wanted that smile back on his lips, for his eyes to crinkle as he fought not to laugh at something. She needed to see him relax and forget the worries that plagued him. And she didn't think too hard about why it was so important.

"Do all dragons live in mountains?" she asked.

He blinked as if her words had dragged him from his thoughts. Then he eagerly turned to the new subject. "Mostly. Is it…different from your home?"

"A bit. My aunt left me her cottage, but my main home was in the city, in a building several stories high. One floor can have up to several flats—that's what we call small homes in these structures. Then there are several floors, one on top of the other." At his confused look, she used her magic to create a replica of her building. "Like this."

He leaned forward, tilting his head to look at the model in her hands. "Your kind build these?"

"Aye. There are those who specialize in architecture."

"Some of the cave network is similar. We doona build the mountains, but we do carve out the tunnels and some of the caverns."

Her eyes widened at that. "How? With your talons?"

"Those and with dragon fire. There's nothing hotter on the realm."

She whistled softly as the replica vanished. It must be as hot as lava in order to carve out rock. "We have doors with locks to keep others out."

His shoulders loosened as he grinned. "A dragon wouldna dare enter another's cave without permission. Though, there are younglings who slip away from the adults to have a peek inside. Mine especially. They never get far, however."

"Ah. Sadly, Fae have no such compunction. Hence the locks. And sometimes, even that's not enough. We need to add wards to the deadbolts."

"Wards?"

"Magic that prohibits others from entering."

"The point of our clans is to have those who watch our backs. Do the Fae no' do the same?"

She wrinkled her nose. "Not as a general rule, no."

He grunted, his brow furrowing. "Do you no' have anyone watching out for you?"

"Nay."

His green eyes held hers as he softly asked, "No' even your family?"

Ailis had known the question would come, but she still wasn't prepared for it. She was *never* ready for it. Even after all this time. "When I was small, one of the skirmishes I spoke about happened near us. It spilled over into our town. My parents shielded me with their bodies. It's the only reason I survived. Aunt Bea took me in after that and raised me."

"I'm sorry."

"It was a long time ago."

"The pain of losing family never really leaves, does it?"

She shook her head and leaned her arms on her legs once more. "You say that as if you know loss."

"Aye."

One word. But there was so much pain in it that her chest constricted. She wouldn't pry. How could she after hearing his anguish? She had hoped to change the subject into a happier one, and she had only made it worse. Her mind raced to find something else to speak about when Lennox raked a hand through his hair.

He blew out a long breath. "My father was a great warrior, but it doesna matter how good you are. Eventually, a mistake is made. Sometimes little, sometimes big, but the result is always the same. Death. I was just a hatchling when it happened, but I remember the day the King told Mum the news. She did the best she could, but I believe a part of her died that day. I lost her a decade later. She went into her cave and never came out. I was the one who found her."

"What happened to you after?"

"Both of their families always kept in contact with me. They were there. They still are. But…"

"You still felt alone."

He nodded slowly. "Aye."

"Even as King?"

"The Dragon Kings are a close bunch. No one understands the responsibilities we bear other than another King. I think that's why this place was founded."

A dragon from a different world was across from her, and

yet they had so much in common. She hadn't expected that. Or to feel such a connection to him. If she weren't careful, it would be hard for her to leave when the time came. Because, for the first time, someone truly understood things about her that she had never shared with another. Not even Bea.

Ailis cleared her throat. "Tell me about this realm. Does everything look as green and mountainous as what I've seen so far?"

"Far from it. We have vastly different areas around the realm."

Her excitement was so great it was difficult to contain. "Deserts?"

"Aye."

"Snow?"

"Aye. Does yours no' have such?"

"Not the places I've seen. I heard there are snow-capped mountains, but it is in the other section of the Fae Realm where I'm not allowed."

He grunted in response.

She knew the longer she waited to tell him she was Dark, the worse it would be. But she couldn't just come out and say it. However, she couldn't fathom why. Perhaps it would be better to tell him now. "You can ask which I am."

"Describe your area."

"We have a moderate climate where the temperature stays the same nearly all year. We have a few days where it might rise, and there's a lot of excitement when it drops a few degrees."

Lennox lowered his gaze to his feet and rotated his ankles.

"We have four seasons here. Spring, summer, autumn, and winter. And there is lots of snow in the winter months."

"I've read about snow, but I've never seen it."

"If you could handle the flight, I could take you to such an area now."

She bit her lip, debating if she could handle such a journey. "Let me think on it."

He bowed his head. "There will be dragons there."

"Dragons live there?"

"Dragons live everywhere. Some choose the frozen places, their caves deep in the ice-covered mountains. Some choose the deserts, burrowing beneath the huge sand dunes. Some prefer the water and live in caves deep beneath the surface. Some like tropical areas and live behind waterfalls. We have adapted to all regions."

She closed her eyes, imagining each place in her mind. "I've seen pictures in books and paintings of such things."

"Then we will find a way for you to see it for yourself."

Her eyes opened as she looked at him. "Why would you risk so much for me? You don't know me."

"I'm beginning to. You're an explorer. Should you no' be able to see things with your own eyes instead of what's in a book?"

What he offered was more than she could've hoped for. But there were hazards. "Just because someone wants something doesn't mean they should have it."

"You gambled with your life to come here. You would be out there exploring now if I hadna encountered you."

She rose to her feet and moved around in an attempt to dislodge the knot of worry that had begun to grow. "Maybe."

"Are you afraid for yourself or for me? If it's me, doona concern yourself."

Ailis whipped her head to him and came to a halt. "Why don't you want me to worry about you?"

"Because I can take care of myself."

She almost asked if he wanted death to get out from under his responsibilities, but she couldn't quite bring herself to do it. Mainly because she feared what his response might be. "So can I."

"How long do you think you can remain in this cave before you leave? How long can you listen to my descriptions of things before you must see them for yourself?"

He spoke with such certainty, as if he had known her for years instead of a few hours. Was she that easy to read? Or did he have magic that enabled him such insight? Ailis wanted to tell him he was wrong, but he wasn't. Instead, she turned away and wrapped her arms around her middle.

"I'm no' trying to anger you, lass. I'm pointing out facts. Ones I didna consider before bringing you here. It wasna fair of me to agree to show you my world only to stick you in a cave."

"I'm not angry." She glanced at him, their eyes meeting. "You're right. About me not staying in here."

"What will you do?"

That was the question of the hour, wasn't it? She knew what she wanted to do, but she couldn't. She wouldn't put Lennox in a position where he had to either protect her or defend his decision to allow her to remain. But neither could she return to her realm. How could she after seeing this new world? That meant other worlds were out there. Maybe even one where she could set down roots and make a home.

Her gaze was drawn back to Lennox. She turned to face him, only to find his eyes locked on her. Out of her three options, she crossed off returning home. That left remaining or going to a new world.

Lennox stood and calmly waited for her decision. The male—no, the *dragon* who had offered her a glimpse into not just his world but also himself was unlike anyone she had ever met before. Though she hadn't spoken to any other dragons, she was confident that none would've befriended her as he had.

They'd established the foundations of trust. It was something different than she was used to, something new and unique. And she wasn't quite ready for that to end.

She dropped her arms to her sides. "I'm not ready to leave."

He took a half step toward her. "I gave you my word that I'd protect you, but if another dragon comes upon you when I'm no' around—"

"I won't leave the cave. With or without you."

His brows snapped together. "Then how will you explore?"

"I won't put you in a position where you need to defend yourself about me. I won't be the reason you fight anyone."

"Being here without seeing anything is no different than looking at your books."

Ailis smiled. "Oh, it's much different. For one, I get to know a dragon. If I see nothing else of your realm, that is enough."

He took another half step, his eyes intense as they bored into hers. "Ailis…"

"I left my world looking for something. I thought it was an adventure, and I suppose it still is. But I was also looking for…" She paused, trying to find the right word. "A friend. I found you, Lennox. I don't think it was by accident."

CHAPTER NINE

Fate had brought Ailis to Earth. Lennox was certain of that. He didn't want her to leave, but he also couldn't ask her to remain hidden. Essentially, it would make his cave her prison.

"Can we be friends?" she asked.

He moved closer to her without realizing he had done it. He had to stop himself from touching her hair. It wasn't as if he didn't have friends, but Ailis was distinctly unique. There was a connection between them from the very instant they met. Their shared pain of losing their families was only one part of what bound them.

"Aye," he said. "I'd like that."

Her smile was soft as it curved her lips. "Good."

Lennox rubbed his hand down his arm to stop himself from reaching for her. He felt everything twice as much now. He craved to touch everything—but especially Ailis. The scrape of the air across his forearm beneath his palm sent prickles of awareness over him. He shifted his shoulders.

"Are the clothes bothering you?" she asked.

He nodded and yanked at the collar of the shirt. "They're confining."

"Then change them."

"Everything will feel this way."

Lennox took a step, and pain radiated from his foot. He sat and yanked the offensive boots off. The cool stone beneath his feet made him sigh. He put his hands on his knees and scrunched his toes before spreading them. He repeated the movement over and over, relaxing more each time.

"I'm sorry we can't communicate in your true form. I know you'd rather be in that one."

He caught her gaze. "The first time I shifted, it was painful, but I doona mind this form. Things are…different."

"What do you mean? Do you see things differently?"

"I see the same. Dragons have exceptional eyesight."

"You can see in the dark. I can't."

He nodded as she resumed her seat. "It's more than having a different vantage point since I'm closer to the ground. It's everything else."

"Like what?"

Lennox held out his hands, palms up. "I feel things I doona feel in my true form."

"Oh," she said as realization dawned. "You also now have hair."

"Without a tail or wings."

Her eyes lowered to his hands. "Do you not like how things feel now?"

"That's the problem." He paused, wondering if he should

tell her more. Then he decided he had come this far. He might as well say the rest. "I like it too much."

"Does that mean you cannot feel things through your scales? Did you not feel me when you held me?"

He felt her, all right. He experienced every movement, every breath. It had been nearly unbearable, but only because he had wanted to touch her with his mortal hand to sense even more. "We feel through our scales. It's just no' as..." Heady? Potent? "Strong."

"What do you want to touch?"

"You," he said before he could stop himself.

She stood and crossed the short distance between them. He fisted his hands when she dropped to her knees before him. Her scarlet eyes held his, unflinching. "Then touch me."

"Nay." She didn't know what she offered. If he put his hands on her, he wouldn't be able to stop. His need to feel mixed with desire, and he could no longer tell them apart. And the closer she was to him, the harder it became.

Ailis placed her hand atop his fist. He flinched at the unexpected contact, but he couldn't pull away. She held his gaze, refusing to let him look away as she used both hands to gently unfurl his fingers. She brushed her fingers across his open hand. Her soft touch sent chills racing over his skin and blood straight to his cock. He fought for breath as he put every sensation to memory.

Then she brought his palm to her face.

Lennox's heart skipped a beat as he took in her smooth skin. He cupped her cheek, and to his surprise, she closed her eyes and leaned into his hand. The weight of her head and the teasing caress of her hair against the back of his hand left him dizzy for more. He couldn't look away from her.

His other hand slid along her jaw to cup her face. He used his thumbs to stroke from her chin up to her mouth. His heart skipped another beat when her lips parted at his touch. Her long lashes lifted, and her crimson eyes met his.

"Don't stop," she whispered.

It was all the push he needed. He slid his hands into the thick, cool strands of her midnight and silver hair. Her eyes closed once more, and her head tipped back. His gaze lowered to her exposed neck, where he saw her pulse, and he had the overwhelming desire to place his lips there. Touching her wasn't enough. He wanted to taste her.

To be inside her.

He couldn't believe he was thinking of claiming her. Yet there was no denying the need thrumming hotly through him. It ran through his veins, searing and demanding.

His hands caressed her neck and over her shoulders. Her fingers dug into his arms. He didn't know when she had taken hold of him, but he yearned for her touch as much as he needed to feel her.

Lennox scooted closer, his legs on either side of her body. Her head lifted, and their eyes met once more. The desire he saw reflected in her gaze took the last of his willpower. He wrapped one arm around her while his other moved to her waist. Her hands skimmed up his shoulders, setting him ablaze.

Her skin beneath his palms was a heady sensation, but her touch left him undone.

His eyes dropped to her mouth. She was breathing as

harshly as he was. His thumbs still tingled from touching her lips, and that urge to put his mouth on her escalated, this time much more insistent.

He pulled her closer until their bodies fit against each other. He had never held anyone like this. It was incredible and intoxicating. He wanted more, *needed* more.

A groan left him when her nails softly scraped against his scalp.

"Lennox," she whispered as her eyes drifted shut.

He lowered his head to press their lips together. Just one touch. That's all he needed.

"Lennox."

The sound of his name in his head had him rearing back as if struck.

Ailis opened her eyes as a frown formed. "What is it?"

"Hide," he urged as he set her aside and stumbled to his feet.

He had to get himself together, but how could he when he was on fire? Lennox didn't dare glance toward Ailis as he shifted. The pain had him stiffening. It was the first time he had felt anything since the original shift. He wanted nothing more than to return to his other form and have her back in his arms.

"Lennox?"

He pushed aside the riot of emotions and the desire that licked at him. Everything he felt had to remain in the cave. He couldn't allow anyone to see anything. They might understand, but he couldn't take the chance that they wouldn't. He didn't want Ailis to leave, and if anyone found out about her, she might have to.

Lennox walked from his cave. Each step became a little easier. He left a part of himself in the cavern with Ailis, and he feared that she would always hold a part of him. He halted his thoughts. By the time he exited the mountain, he had control of himself.

Osric stood in the valley, waiting for him. The King of Blacks wore a smile as Lennox approached. *"Did I catch you napping?"*

"Verra funny. Do you need something?"

"Can a dragon no' look in on his friend?"

Lennox gave him a dry look. *"No' you. No' wearing that look. What's going on?"*

"Heller said you didna seem yourself. I thought I'd check on you."

Lennox shook his head. *"Everything is good. I just needed some time to myself."*

"You may no' have wanted your position, but we all know you're the right dragon. I've told you that for three thousand years. I'll keep telling you that."

Lennox chuckled. Of all the Kings, Lennox was closest to Osric. He had been the one Lennox had confided in about not wanting to be King, much less King of Kings. *"Rest easy, brother. Heller wanted to gripe about his sister's upcoming mating ceremony, and I wasna in the mood to hear it all for the thousandth time."*

"I can understand that. Heller doesna like his future brother-in-law. But a dragon always knows his mate."

An image of Ailis filled Lennox's mind. He thought of her on her knees before him as she'd brought his hand to her cheek. That moment was now burned into his memory for eternity. Just as she was.

Something bumped into Lennox. He came back to himself to see Osric folding the wing he had knocked him with.

"You seem preoccupied," Osric said. "*Anything the Kings need to be concerned about?*"

"Nay."

Osric's red eyes narrowed on him. "*If I didna know better, I'd say a female was to blame, given that absent look on your face a moment ago.*" Osric perked up. "*Please tell me one has finally caught your attention.*"

"*You're the one with female problems. How many are after you now?*"

"*You're no' going to get out of answering the question. Spill, brother.*"

Lennox almost ignored his friend's plea, but in the end, he realized he needed to say something. He just couldn't tell Osric everything. "*This needs to stay between us.*"

"*I knew it,*" Osric said as he moved closer, his eyes glittering with eagerness. "*Tell me everything. Who is she? I want to get a look at her.*"

"*Nay. We've no' progressed that far.*"

"*Lennox, you're King of Dragon Kings, you could have the pick of any female in any clan, and you know it.*"

He eyed Osric. "*We mate within our clans. You know that.*"

"*It doesna have to be that way.*"

"*It doesna, but it always has been.*"

"*Be the one to change it.*"

Lennox fought not to look back at his cave as his mind filled with thoughts of Ailis. *"I'm no' sure."*

"So she isn't in your clan. Interesting."

It felt wrong to talk about Ailis as his mate. She wasn't a dragon. He couldn't… Could he? Lennox shook his head. Desire ruled him right now. He couldn't think clearly past his need for her. Once he had her out of his system, he wouldn't be so confused about things.

"Bloody hell. You have it bad," Osric said. *"I'm no' the only one who thinks we should be able to find a mate outside our clans. I'll back you on this. So will others."*

"You make it sound easy when it willna be. We would be without a clan."

"You'd make your own."

Lennox looked away from his friend. *"My clan wouldna accept her, and hers wouldna accept me."*

"As I said, you're King of Dragon Kings. No one would turn you away."

The Fae might. Lennox inwardly winced. He hadn't meant to think about Ailis, but he couldn't get her out of his mind. He continued the conversation with Osric to keep his friend from looking too closely at him, but now he realized it had been the wrong thing to do. Because Lennox was actually trying to imagine what life would be like if everyone knew about Ailis.

"Is she your mate?"

Lennox swallowed. *"I desire her more than I've ever wanted another."*

"But is she your mate?"

"I doona know."

Osric grunted. *"We all know when we know. Maybe there's just an intense attraction. There's nothing wrong with exploring that. I never turn a female away."*

"And we all know it," Lennox teased.

"I can no' help it if I'm irresistible."

Lennox laughed, but it died quickly. *"This stays between us."*

"Always. I'm here if you want to talk. Or if you need a second opinion on whether the female would measure up to be your mate," Osric said with a grin. He jumped into the air. *"Talk later."*

CHAPTER TEN

Ailis sat on the cavern floor as she sucked in large mouthfuls of air. Yet she couldn't get her heart to stop racing.

Or her mind to stop thinking of how she had been about to kiss Lennox.

Her eyes slid shut as the scene replayed in her head over and over. She put her hands on her stomach as a peculiar sensation developed. Her lips parted, and her ragged breathing intensified whenever she thought of how his eyes had darkened with intense longing right before she placed his hand on her face.

That simple touch had rocked her to her very foundation. The warmth of his palm, the way he'd so tenderly held his large hand against her cheek, had made her melt. It'd felt so good, so *right*. She had been drunk from his touch, and when he cupped her face, she never wanted him to let go.

She had felt *everything*. His curiosity, his hesitation.

His craving for more.

Ailis brushed her fingers over her lips when they tingled from remembering his touch. She had sensed that he was about to withdraw. It was why she'd asked him not to stop. Such simple, innocent caresses had made her tremble with burgeoning desire. She was on fire, and it raged even now.

Her breath was ragged as it passed her lips, and ripples raced over her skin when she recalled his fingers delving into her hair. His touch was light and inquisitive, but for the first time, she felt truly seen. And he didn't stop there, thankfully. His hands slid down her neck and over her shoulders. She'd gripped him, ready to beg him for more, when he moved closer. She needed to see him, to know if he was as affected as she.

The hungry, ravenous look in his eyes had her heart tripping over itself. She had known he was about to kiss her. She wanted to grab his face and press her mouth to his, but her body had been flooded by hunger that'd kept her locked in place.

Every second that passed between them had more flames of need licking at her. She bit her lip at the memory of how he had pressed her body to his. There was no mistaking his hard arousal—or her throbbing sex. Even now, she ached to have him sliding inside her.

Then he left. And she had fallen forward, barely catching herself on the rock as he hurried away. He had mumbled a request for her to stay hidden—as if she would leave. She hadn't wanted him to go, and had been sitting in the same spot ever since, reliving the encounter in her mind. Ailis turned to recline against the boulder she had been sitting on and leaned her head back.

Her eyes were trained above her as she tried to come to terms with the unfathomable attraction. Lennox was a dragon. He had never been in mortal form before. Maybe he was just curious about sex with a Fae. She hadn't asked if he had someone in his life. Surely, he would've told her if he did. She knew from experience that not everyone was forthcoming with such information if it got in the way of something they wanted. And now she didn't want to ask.

Ailis tried to shake off the desire, but it wasn't going anywhere. That could be a problem. How could she ever look at him the same now?

The ground trembled beneath her as he approached. She hurriedly sat up, her eyes locked on the entrance. She didn't know what she would say to him. Would they pick up where they'd left off? She'd be lying if she said she didn't want that.

The slight tremors halted. Ailis frowned as she rose to her knees. Maybe Lennox had shifted again, and that was why she couldn't feel him approaching. But as the seconds lengthened into minutes, she knew that wasn't the case. After a long while, the ground vibrated again as he walked away. Then there was nothing but silence and stillness.

She sighed and sank backward. If she needed confirmation that he regretted what had transpired between them, his retreat gave that to her. Ailis thrust her hand into her hair and shoved it back as she tried not to take offense. They were different species, after all. He was a dragon who happened to be able to shift into her form to converse. That didn't make them similar. Even if she wished it did.

Ailis brought her legs up to her chest and wrapped her arms around them. She rested her chin on her knees and closed her eyes. She was exhausted. Running from the guards, using more magic than she ever had to build a doorway to another realm, crossing into that new world, and then encountering such wonders—as well as dragons—combined with her near kiss had left her drained.

She eyed the hard ground before crafting a bed with her magic. Ailis kicked off her shoes and climbed into the softness. She was asleep before her head hit the pillow.

Lennox climbed high into the sky. He flew through the clouds, pushing himself higher than ever before, but nothing he did pushed Ailis out of his head. His hands still tingled from touching her, his body still ached.

He hadn't been able to go back inside the cave. He would've gone straight to her and dragged her against him if he had. He would've given in to his need, the yearning to join their bodies. He might be able to shift to look like her species, but he wasn't a Fae. Why delve into something that could never be? His mate—if he ever found her—was somewhere among the dragons. It wasn't fair to Ailis, or himself, to give in to such desires.

Yet he couldn't stop thinking about her—how she'd felt in his arms, and the desire that'd filled her gaze.

She had wanted him as much as he craved her. It had been so unexpected he hadn't thought it through as he usually did.

If he had, he never would've let it slip that he wanted to touch her—or allowed himself to make that contact.

But the damage had been done. There was no going back now. Ailis had intrigued him at first sight. Her arrival worried him because he feared she would be the first of many. He'd done what any King in his place would have and decided to learn about her kind. He rarely second-guessed his decisions because he went through alternatives before he did anything. With Ailis, he had acted quickly.

More than once.

What was it about her that made him forget who he was? Even now, knowing there was no future for them, he wanted to return to her side. He didn't know what he would say, but her time wasn't unlimited. He was surprised that she had decided to stay at all, and that could change at any moment.

It became difficult to breathe. Lennox glanced down but couldn't see the ground through the clouds. He stopped climbing. Instead, he tucked his wings and flipped around so his head was lowered. The air zoomed past him with such speed he had to squint. As he burst through the last cloud and spotted the ground rising quickly, he spread his wings. His descent halted instantly as he soared through the air.

Lennox kept his speed by flapping his wings. When he reached the mountains, he descended until he was close to the ground. He zipped through the peaks, tilting from side to side to keep his wings from slamming into the rocky mountainside. He zigzagged until he was winded, and his thoughts were clear.

Then he swung around and returned to his mountain. He

landed and started through the entrance. Once he was concealed within the mountain, he shifted. For a moment, he remained naked. He called clothes to himself but left his feet free of confinement.

He hesitated only a heartbeat before walking the descending tunnel to his cavern. He expected to find the light Ailis had created, but darkness met him. His heart fell. She must have left. Without a farewell. His steps slowed. Had she been upset that he hadn't returned? Or worse, offended by how he had held her?

They were questions he'd likely never get answers to, but perhaps that was for the best. He had learned a lot about the Fae. They were powerful, and he had no idea whether the dragons could stand against them—he hoped they never had to find out.

Lennox reached the doorway to his cavern, and his gaze went to the rock where he had sat with her in front of him. Suddenly, he saw something off to the side. He approached and found Ailis on top of whatever it was, asleep. She was on her stomach, her head turned to the side, and her black and silver hair spread out behind her. She had one hand near her face and the other tucked under her.

He placed his hand on the long, flat surface she slept on and was surprised to find it soft and pliable. Almost as if it cradled him. Whatever it was, it wasn't something a dragon would ever use. No matter how similar he and Ailis were, too much proved how different they were.

She shifted in her sleep, turning onto her side. He slowly straightened and decided to let her rest. Lennox took one more look at her before silently walking out of the cavern and deeper into the mountain.

Whatever kept Ailis in his mind didn't let him get far from her. If he felt that way now, what would he do when she left? Because she *would* leave. She couldn't remain on Earth. Even if he managed to convince the dragons that she meant no harm, there were no others like her on the realm. He might be able to shift, but would that be enough?

And how would the dragons take to that?

Then there was another issue, one he hadn't wanted to consider. What if other dragons could shift? What if all the dragons changed into forms like hers and forgot who they really were? Right now, the biggest issue the dragons faced was whether to mate outside the clans. Ailis's arrival could change all of that. Was that what needed to happen?

Lennox paused and pressed his back against the wall. He dropped his chin to his chest and sighed. He should urge her to leave. Even as he thought it, he realized he wouldn't be able to. He lifted his hands and gazed at his palms. He still felt her. No matter how long he lived, he would never forget her.

His search for a mate would never go anywhere. He would never find a female who measured up to what he'd experienced with Ailis. Maybe that was why he hadn't found a mate yet. Fate had known he would meet Ailis. If he belonged to another, he wouldn't have had the interaction with the Fae.

He lowered his hands and stared at the opposite wall. What was he still doing in this form? Ailis wasn't here to talk to. He had no reason not to return to his true self. That question hung above him, but he did nothing about it.

Lennox pushed away from the wall and started back toward Ailis. When he reached the cavern entrance, he lowered himself to the ground. He had never been one to lie to himself, and he wasn't about to start now. He wanted to be near her—for however long she was on Earth. Their destinies were intertwined for this moment. Who was he to question that?

CHAPTER ELEVEN

The darkness that greeted Ailis when she rolled onto her back was disorienting. There was no light coming through the curtains of her bedroom window. A shiver raced across her skin, making her pull up the covers. The air was much cooler than usual. She yawned and rubbed at her eyes, wondering about the quiet around her.

As she shook off sleep, things started coming back to her. Creating the doorway. Meeting Lennox. Nearly kissing him. Either she had actually crossed to a new realm, or she'd had the most vivid dream of her life. She had to know if it was real or not. She had to know if Lennox was real.

Ailis sat up and created the light in her palm before tossing it into the air. A sigh of relief left her when she saw the cavern. It had been real. All of it. The dragons, the world. Lennox. All the wonderful and terrifying emotions from the previous day slammed into her like a tidal wave. She squeezed her legs together as her sex throbbed, remembering the delicious, wonderful feel of his touch.

Cold reality hit then. She was alone. She had no idea how long she'd slept, but there was one thing she couldn't deny — Lennox hadn't returned. He hadn't handled the transformation well. Or the clothes. Perhaps she had pushed him too far. Ailis dropped her head back and squeezed her eyes closed. Why had she done that? Why hadn't she given him the time to come to her? She may have ruined everything.

She threw off the covers and swung her legs over the side of the bed. After tugging on her boots, she got to her feet and took one more look around the cavern. A dragon's home. Nay. A Dragon King's lair.

She was about to take a step to…she wasn't sure where. That made her hesitate. Where would she go? Lennox had asked her to stay concealed. This place was the center of the realm's magic. It was also where the Kings gathered. She didn't want to meet any dragons without Lennox, but especially not another King.

She bit her lip and ran her fingers through her hair to detangle it. As she worked her way through the long strands, she weighed her options. Remaining where Lennox had left her was prudent for a number of reasons. While she wanted to see more of the world, she realized the threat to not just her life but also Lennox's. However, that didn't mean she couldn't look around the mountain.

Ailis blew out a breath and straightened her shirt. Then, she decided to change into fresh clothing and clean herself with just a thought. She immediately felt better. Just a quick exploration. She wouldn't go too far. The mountain was

Lennox's home. Surely, he wouldn't mind her seeing what else was around.

She walked across the large cavern to the exit with her head held high but her stomach in knots. She ensured the light followed her so she could see. The size of Lennox's home reminded her how immense he was as a dragon. When she reached the door, she paused and looked the way they had entered. Then she turned her head the other way and drew up short. Lennox sat against the wall with his legs outstretched and his ankles crossed. His arms were folded over his chest, and his eyes were focused on her.

He was here. It didn't even matter that he hadn't been in the cavern. She had honestly thought he had deserted her, and that'd hurt worse than it should for someone she'd just met. But she wouldn't think about that now. Because he hadn't left.

She swallowed as they stared at each other. There was so much she wanted to say, and it all nearly spilled from her mouth in a rush. Somehow, she held back. He was silent, still. Not at all the male—or dragon—from the day before. Was it even the next day? She couldn't see the sky to tell.

"I wondered where you'd gone," she said, needing something to say.

"I didna want to disturb your sleep."

She glanced over her shoulder at the bed. An image of him sliding in beside her before pulling her against him made her heart trip over itself. "You should've woken me."

"You looked as if you needed the rest." He got to his feet in one fluid motion. "What was that you were on?"

"A bed. I can sleep without one, but it's much more comfortable to use it."

His gaze briefly skated away. "We must live verra basic to what you're used to."

"That doesn't mean one of us lives wrong. Just differently."

"Aye."

She shifted her feet, suddenly nervous as the conversation lagged. He wasn't as open as before. Or perhaps *she* was the one who'd closed herself off. What could she say after the passion that had kindled between them? "Um…should we perhaps…well…I mean, before—?"

"I take it you were about to leave?"

"Not out of the mountain," she hurried to say. "I just wanted to have a look around while I waited for you to return."

His pale green eyes studied her for a moment. "What makes you think there is more?"

"Because I'm coming to learn there is a lot more about dragons than what one sees on the surface."

His face eased as a small smile formed. "There is more. Would you like to see?"

"Very much."

"Come. I'll show you."

He turned to go deeper into the tunnel, and she fell into step with him. She didn't say more about earlier as the tunnel took them even deeper. Her attempt had been disastrous, and he obviously didn't wish to speak of it. She tried not to think the worst, but the ease that had been between them was gone. Things were strained now, the tension hard to ignore.

"How often do you rest?" he asked.

She inwardly sighed with relief when he found something for them to discuss. "Every night."

"How long do you sleep?"

"Bea used to be fine with about five hours, but I do better with eight or more."

His surprise was evident in how he glanced at her, his brows raised. "Really?"

"I take that to mean it isn't the same for you."

"We do sleep, but it's the dragon sleep. Centuries can pass when we go that deep."

She tripped over a rock she hadn't seen. His hand shot out to right her and then immediately fell away once she had regained her footing. "You don't sleep daily, then?"

"We rest when we need it, but I can go days without. Sometimes weeks."

"That's incredible. When you say *rest*, what do you mean exactly?"

His lips twisted. "What I was doing while you slept. I closed my eyes."

"And that's not sleeping?"

"I was still conscious and aware."

"Astonishing."

Lennox chuckled. "There are many differences between our kinds, lass."

And many similarities, but she didn't point that out. She wasn't sure he would take too kindly to that now. She missed the relaxed air they'd had before but didn't regret what had transpired between them. The passion had been intense, the desire tangible. Like a living, breathing entity. It had swept through them both, seizing and consuming them.

No one—*ever*—had made her *feel* like that.

Wanted. Needed. Desired. As if he couldn't go on without her.

Ailis glanced at Lennox, but he stared straight ahead. She should apologize for pushing him. Nothing would have happened if she hadn't put his hand on her face. Then again, he could've pulled back anytime he wanted. He hadn't. Because he had wanted to touch her. He'd said as much.

She opened her mouth to say something when she heard a drip. She cocked her head and listened closely.

"You hear it," Lennox said with a smile.

She quickened her pace, eager to get to the water.

"Careful," he cautioned, right behind her.

Ailis barely registered his voice as they came to a wide, low-arched entrance. Her light lit up the archway before it moved over the water. She gasped at the sight of the pool. The water was a shade of blue she hadn't known existed. Bright and clear, a color somewhere between cerulean and turquoise. The light allowed her to see the various rock formations below the surface. She saw the water moving and followed it to find there was a narrow exit where it flowed out. A quick glance to the other side showed a wider part where the water entered.

"And underground river," Lennox explained as he came to stand beside her. "It flows through several mountains on either side."

She squatted near the edge and put her fingers into the water. Almost immediately, she yanked them out at the cold temperature.

"Too cool?"

"I'm afraid so. That's too bad. I wanted to swim."

Lennox dropped to one knee and put his hand in the water. He remained there for a few moments, his brow furrowed.

"Is it different?"

"Aye," he said softly. His eyes lifted to her before he stood and shook the water off his hand. "I swim here often. The water is cool, aye, but nothing I couldna handle."

"And now?" He had the most beautiful eyes. She didn't know which ones she liked better. The green in his mortal form, or the white dragon ones. She wanted to touch him, to feel the flames of passion once more.

He looked away. "It is chilly, but it wouldna bother me."

"Then swim."

He slowly turned to her, a brow quirked. "Why?"

"Why not? Experience more of the differences between your two forms. Earlier, you wanted to touch things. Water on your skin can be relaxing or exhilarating. Or both."

The heat that flared in his eyes nearly made her knees buckle. Ailis had no idea how she managed to stay standing. He might not want to talk about what happened, but it was there, waiting to be reignited.

"I can do that anytime."

She caught him when he started to turn away. "I'll leave if you wish to be alone. Don't let me stop you."

"I doona want you to go."

Ailis hadn't realized she needed those words. She forced her fingers to release him when all she really wanted was that strong arm around her. "I won't go."

"Swim with me."

She would likely freeze, but how could she refuse such an

offer? Besides, she had magic. She could think of something so she could join him. Ailis nodded. "All right."

Neither of them moved for several heartbeats. She was the first to begin undressing. Ailis took off her boots, then her vest. Lennox's eyes followed her movements. Her pants were next, followed by her tunic, leaving her in only her underthings. She reached for the waist of her lace drawers. He made a sound that was half moan, half growl—and all desire.

Their eyes met as he yanked his shirt off so hard he tore it. Her gaze dropped to his impressive chest. She had run her hands over him through his shirt, but she wanted to feel him, skin-to-skin. To have his hard body and warmth against her.

"Ailis."

Her breath locked in her lungs at the sound of his passion-roughened voice. She couldn't get enough oxygen into her lungs. He stared at her hands. She hooked her thumbs in the lace. He clenched his jaw, a muscle jumping as he did. She slid the garment over her hips and down her legs, never taking her eyes off him.

There was another half moan, half growl that made her sex clench in need. She straightened and reached between her breasts to unhook the material that held them. Ailis didn't do anything until his gaze met hers. Then she released the hook and shimmied her shoulders so it fell down her arms to the ground.

Lennox's nostrils flared. She stood still while he raked his gaze over her with the same hunger as when he'd first touched her. No longer did she feel the cool air of the cave. Heat suffused her now.

He mumbled something incoherent and ripped off his

pants. Her mouth went dry as she took in all of him. Nothing she had ever seen could come close to the perfect specimen before her. It was as if he had been honed from rock. His strength showed in his muscles, his command. In the way he held himself.

The fire in his eyes revealed his supremacy.

She ran her eyes down his chest, corded with sinew, to his trim hips. Then lower to his arousal that stood thick and hard between them. She squeezed her legs together as need pooled at her center. She had to touch him or go up in flames.

Ailis took a step. Then he was there, his arms gathering her close as he held her tightly.

"I need you to kiss me," she said in a hoarse whisper.

His brows drew together briefly. She grabbed his face and gently pulled his head to her. His body was rigid until their lips met. Then, a low moan rumbled through his chest, and his body eased. She moved her mouth over his, alternating between short and lingering kisses. Then she ran her tongue along his lips.

A jolt went through him. A moment later, he tangled his tongue with hers. It was a kiss to end all kisses. It was fiery and all-consuming, scorching and passionate. He stole her breath, her very will. All while spreading fire and need through her until she burned with it.

His cock pressed into her stomach. She sank her nails into his skin when he ground against her. His hands moved over her, seeking and learning. When he cupped her sex, and she rocked against the heel of his hand, the pleasure that shot through her was so intense that she cried out.

Instantly, he was gone. She opened her eyes and found him standing a few feet away with his chest heaving.

"I didna mean to hurt you."

She shook her head. "I hurt without you. Please. Don't stop."

He searched her face before once more coming to stand before her. His touch was tentative, almost reverent, as his fingers caressed her face. "I ache for you."

"Take me. I'm yours."

His green eyes flared with passion as he claimed her mouth once more.

CHAPTER TWELVE

His senses were on overload. Lennox had never known such need or felt such longing for another. He couldn't stop touching Ailis. Or kissing her. He wanted to know every inch of her. The softness of her curves and the silkiness of her skin were almost too much to endure. And yet there was no way he could stop.

He stroked down her slim throat to her narrow shoulders. He kissed the erratically beating pulse point in her neck. She sucked in a breath when he ran his tongue down the middle of her chest and paused in the valley of her breasts.

Lennox watched as her head rolled back. A soft sigh fell from her lips as he bent her over one arm. He flattened his hand against her stomach and moved it upward. Her breathing quickened the closer he came to the rounded globes. He cupped one breast and gently rolled it in his palm. Her nails dug into his skin. It was the pert nipple that grabbed his attention. The dusky tip strained toward him.

Ailis's back arched when he ran his thumb over it. He bent and wrapped his lips around the peak. The low, pleasure-filled moan she emitted made his balls tighten. He suckled the nipple until her hips rocked against him steadily. He fought against the need to bury himself inside her. He didn't want this over too quickly. He wanted to savor every second as he discovered more of her body and the wonderful, wanton passion between them.

He shifted his mouth to her other breast and swirled his tongue around the turgid peak. Small cries fell steadily from her lips, but he didn't relent. He smoothed his hand down her side to the indent of her waist and then over the seductive swell of a hip before moving around to cup her arse.

"Lennox," she whispered as he suckled her nipple.

He lowered his hand to the back of her thigh and lifted her leg. She wrapped it around his hip, bringing his aching cock against her soft center. It was his turn to groan as his arousal throbbed with a need so great he knew he would never be the same again. He was ablaze, the desire scorching his veins hotter than any dragon fire.

His hand holding her leg slid toward the junction of her thighs. He curved his hand around the back of her leg until he brushed her sex.

"Aye," she cried.

He tenderly stroked the folds of her sex, his fingers dampening with her need. Then he slipped a finger inside her. Her hips bucked against him as her nails drew blood. He became lost in her tight, wet sheath. He stroked her, moving his finger in and out in time with his mouth pulling at her nipple.

Her cries grew louder. Her hips met his thrusts. Then his thumb found her pleasure point. She issued a soft exclamation when he brushed it, shifting his focus to that part of her. He teased the tiny numb mercilessly. And then she stiffened in his arms.

The walls of her sex clenched around his finger as the climax rippled through her. He lifted his head and watched the pleasure fill her face. He slowed his ministrations as her body went slack. Only then did he release her leg and pull her against him. She rested her head on his chest, her breathing ragged.

Lennox closed his eyes and put to memory the feel of them, skin-to-skin, her body flush against his, and the long drape of her hair brushing his side. He didn't want this to be the only time he held her thus, but he was afraid it might be.

The moment was too beautiful to let dark thoughts mess it up. He shut them away and returned his mind to memorizing the blue of the water, the coolness of her hair, the warmth of her body, and the brush of her breath over his chest. She fit perfectly against him, allowing him to rest his chin atop her head. As wonderful as all of that was, it didn't compare to her arms holding him. She gripped him as if she feared he would release her at any second. He wanted to tell her he would never let go, but would such words be welcome? Did he dare voice the tumultuous feelings that had bombarded him since her arrival? Things that continued to grow and evolve into emotions he feared putting a name to.

Ailis finally lifted her head and met his gaze. She smiled at him and slowly shook her head. "That was incredible. No one has brought me to orgasm so quickly before. Or made me come so hard."

Lennox smoothed her hair away from her face. He never wanted anyone else to touch her again, but he couldn't ask that. She was a visitor, an explorer on Earth only briefly. But he had her now and would make the most of it. "I'm no' done with you yet."

Heat flickered in her red eyes. "Don't tease."

"I mean every word."

His gaze dropped to her lips. He could spend eternity kissing her. Dragons didn't kiss. How in the world would he survive once she left? A tightness crept up from his gut and encircled his chest. It threatened to squeeze the life out of him if he allowed himself to continue that train of thought.

"You're something special," Ailis said as she moved her hands softly over his chest.

"As are you."

"I don't know if we've made a colossal mistake or not, but I don't regret what has happened." She met his gaze. "Or what will happen."

Before he could ask what she meant, Ailis began placing kisses across his chest. She paused at his nipples and flicked her tongue over them before continuing. Her lips were soft and warm as she left a trail down his torso.

He loosened his hold as she shifted lower. Her hands caressed his sides to his hips and then roamed back up his stomach. She used her tongue to trace the line of hair that traveled from his naval to his cock.

Lennox held his breath as he watched her. She glanced up at him as she knelt, a smile curving her lips when she wrapped her fingers around his arousal. He fought to remain standing at the heady sensations that swarmed him.

Slowly, Ailis began pumping her hand up and down his length as she continued kissing his hips, coming closer and closer to his rod each time. He closed his eyes as everything fell away but her. She knew just where to touch him, just *how* to touch him. He moaned when her lips pressed next to his cock, so close he felt her breath.

His eyes flew open when she wrapped her lips around him. His breath caught, his limbs locking at the unbelievable pleasure that ripped through him. Her hands and mouth worked him expertly, quickly bringing him to a tipping point. He fisted his hands in her hair to pull her away, but he couldn't. It felt too good.

He moaned as she took him deep before rolling his balls in her palm. Lennox clenched his teeth together as the orgasm rushed toward him. He tried to hold it back, to experience more. He wasn't ready for the incredible rapture to end. Not now.

Not ever.

She pumped her hands faster as her head bobbed up and down his length, her warm mouth and tongue sending him spiraling. He watched her lips on him. Then she met his gaze and swirled her tongue around his sensitive head. The orgasm slammed into him. Lennox bit back his bellow as he squeezed his eyes shut when ecstasy flooded him. He threw back his head, his seed coming hot and fast. He came harder when he realized Ailis's mouth was still on him.

Then she had her arms around him, holding him as he had held her moments earlier. He buried his face in her hair, still floating from the incredible pleasure. This wasn't the first time he had been with a female, but it was the first time he had ever experienced anything as mindboggling as that release.

"Come," Ailis said.

He didn't want to move, but he allowed her to take his hand. When he turned, he saw the bed nestled against the wall. He followed her to it. She climbed in and held up a thick cloth before patting the spot beside her. Lennox slid in next to her and let her cover him. He rested back on the bed and the extra bit of softness that cradled his head.

"You may not need the blanket. We can always throw it off," she said as she leaned on an elbow to look at him.

Lennox smiled at her. "After what you just did, you can have anything you want."

That made her laugh. "All I want is this moment."

"It's yours."

She scooted close to him. Lennox moved his arm out of the way and waited as she snuggled next to him. Once she was settled, he draped his arm around her and gazed up at the ceiling. He used the river to swim, but he had never looked at the cavern as he did now. Nor would he ever look at it the same again.

"Is the pillow all right? Do you need more?" she asked.

"Pillows?"

"What your head is on."

He liked the way it cradled him. "It's perfect."

She placed a hand on his chest and looped her leg over his. "I don't think I'll be the same after this. After you."

"I know I willna be," he admitted. There was no reason to

lie or hide anything from her. Not that he could if he wanted to.

"I never asked, but do you have someone?"

He moved his other arm behind his head. "I'm no' mated, nay. If I were, I wouldna be with you."

"You sound very sure of that."

"I am. Dragons mate for life."

She glanced at him. "Seriously?"

"Aye. I gather the Fae doona?"

Ailis grunted. "Not hardly."

"Are you…with someone?" It was harder to get the words out than he thought. He worried what her answer might be. The thought of sharing her with anyone made his heart hurt.

"Nay."

He couldn't hold back the sigh. "Good."

"How do you know you aren't choosing the wrong mate?"

"We know it. It's a feeling each of us gets."

"Has no one gotten it wrong?"

He shook his head. "No' that I'm aware of."

"And you've not found yours yet? I can't believe you're single."

"I could say the same."

She laughed, her lashes fluttering against his chest. "I'm not in a position of power as you are."

"I didna say females doona seek me out, but none have claimed my heart." And none would now. Not after Ailis.

"I'm sorry to hear that, but I'm glad for me. This…well, it wasn't something I expected to find here. Anywhere, for that matter."

He flattened his hand on her back. He hadn't either.

"Is it…?" She paused. "Is it because you've shifted, and everything is new?"

"Perhaps, but I think you've played a major role. It was you I needed to hold."

She was silent for a long moment. So long, he worried he might have said too much. Then she spoke. "Do you mind if I ask you a personal question?"

"Ask anything you want."

"Do dragons have sex like we just did?"

He drew in a deep breath and thought of the lovers he'd had. "Nay. We do pleasure the females before we join, but there is no kissing."

Her head jerked up to look at him. "None?"

"I've never kissed anyone before you." Nor would he kiss anyone else.

Ailis smiled softly and resumed her position on his chest. "I have to admit, I like the idea of being your only kiss."

"And the only one who has put their mouth on my cock."

She laughed. "A lot of firsts, then."

"Aye." More than she would ever know.

"I meant what I said earlier. I don't regret this. I hope you don't either."

"Never."

She rubbed her cheek against him. "Neither of us considered the consequences during the heat of it all."

He had, but it had been brief and easily snuffed out by his craving for her. "This is between us. No one need know. No' while you're here, and no' even after you've gone." The words nearly stuck in his throat.

CHAPTER THIRTEEN

"No' even after you're gone."

His words hung in the air, affecting Ailis deeply. It was a reminder that she didn't belong, that she would never belong, which didn't make her want to leave. In fact, it was the furthest thing from her mind. How could she contemplate such a thing after such an intense and wonderful interaction with Lennox?

Ailis swallowed past the lump of emotion in her throat. Never in her wildest fantasies had she ever imagined someone like Lennox could exist anywhere but in her dreams. Maybe that was all this was. Things were too perfect to be real. She must have crossed the doorway, but she wasn't in a new world with dragons. She was caught somewhere between worlds, her mind refusing to admit the truth and creating Lennox for however long she had left to live.

That sounded plausible. And entirely more realistic.

Not some Dragon King who could shift into a mortal who

wanted *her*. There was nothing extraordinary about her. Quite the opposite, in fact. And only someone truly exceptional would catch the King of Dragon King's eye. She hadn't been able to find anyone among the Fae, which put her squarely in the ordinary column.

She listened to his heartbeat as his chest rose and fell with each breath. He was warm and solid. Everything around her appeared tangible, but the mind was a powerful organ that could do astonishing things. She wanted to believe that Lennox was real, and that what she had experienced at his hands was genuine. But she couldn't. It wasn't in her nature to believe she deserved anything good. Her past was proof enough of that.

Her eyes closed as Lennox's large hand moved into her hair. He splayed his fingers on her scalp and gently rubbed. Chills prickled her skin at his touch. He could elicit responses from her that she hadn't believed herself capable of. How many Fae had told her she was cold and unfeeling? How many had claimed she was meant to be alone?

Lennox rolled her onto her back and leaned over her. He searched her face as his brow puckered. "What is it?"

"Just thinking."

"Trying no' to feel regret?"

She gaped at him. "Never. I didn't lie about that." She glanced away and shrugged. "I was thinking that this can't be real."

He arched an eyebrow. "You doona believe I'm here?"

"It sounds crazy, I know, but it makes sense."

"Explain it to me."

She licked her lips and flattened her hands over the thick

sinew of his shoulders. As soon as she started to form the words to tell him, she shook her head. "I don't want to say it out loud."

"You can tell me anything, lass."

There was such certainty and assurance in his gaze that she knew he meant it. "You're perfect."

"Hardly," he murmured.

"To me, you are. You aren't just a dragon, you're a Dragon King. The King of Kings, I might add. It's inconceivable that we would meet or you would wish to talk to me—or allow me to remain."

His brows rose on his forehead as he asked flatly, "You doubt my decision-making?"

Ailis sighed and briefly closed her eyes. "Never, Lennox. I doubt myself. I doubt this," she said and waved at the cavern. "Things like this don't happen to me. The odds of me being able to create a doorway between realms is infinitesimal when others have never succeeded. And on my first try?" She rolled her eyes. "Real life doesn't happen like that."

"Sometimes, it does."

She shook her head and tucked a thick blond strand behind his ear. "Not in my world. Not to me. Someone like you would never pay me even the slightest bit of attention."

"Then everyone else is blind."

"I want you to be real. With all my heart, I want all of this to exist."

"It does," he insisted, his gaze refusing to let her look away.

"On my realm, I'm rejected. Alone. I don't fit in. I never have."

He brushed the backs of his fingers along her jaw. "Because you were meant to come here. If you had found someone, you wouldna have wanted to leave."

His words held truth, but that was precisely what her subconscious would want her to believe. "Maybe."

"It's true, and you know it. You say you doona belong on your realm, and I think it's because you were fated to come here. Our paths were destined to cross. I've fought the confines of being chosen as King from the verra beginning. If the magic hadna chosen me, I wouldna have left my clan's lands. I wouldna have been at the loch to meet you. I would never have shifted and discovered what a kiss is. I wouldna have known the ultimate bliss of holding you in my arms. I'm verra real, Ailis. So are you. And I'll prove it."

A tear fell, weaving a trail to her brow. His thumb caught it, and he brought it to his lips. Real or imagined, she never wanted to leave this world—or Lennox. But she was reminded that she hadn't been entirely truthful with him.

"Why haven't you asked if I'm Dark or Light Fae?"

"Because it doesna matter."

"It does."

He drew in a long breath and then slowly released it. Then he bent and lightly pressed his lips to hers. "I base my decisions on someone by getting to know them."

"Fae lie, and I'm sure dragons do, as well."

"Aye."

She didn't want his perception of her to change, but she couldn't keep this from him any longer. "I could be lying."

"I'm good at reading others. Some can deceive for a wee bit, but they eventually slip up. I've sensed nothing but the truth in you. The only time there was any doubt was when you spoke about your people. You were careful in the things you said. I believed that was because you wished to put them in a favorable light so I'd allow you to remain."

"Nay," she said with a small shake of her head. "It was because I didn't want you to know what I am."

"You're Fae. That is enough."

If only it were. She pushed at his shoulders until he rolled away. Ailis sat up and tucked her legs against her as she faced him. "You need to understand that the Fae are dangerous, Lennox. The Dark are conniving liars who will do anything for power. And I mean anything."

"Some dragons do the same."

"Light and Dark are distinguishable by their coloring. The Light have black hair and silver eyes."

His expression remained neutral. "All have the same coloring?"

"Aye. The Dark have…" She paused. He was smart enough to deduce what she couldn't say, but that didn't make things easier. "We have red eyes and silver in our black hair."

Lennox simply watched her.

The silence grew uncomfortable, and she had to fill it. "The eyes are the first thing to change. The more silver in the hair, the more…evil has been done."

He reached up and fingered the silver strands but said nothing.

"There are only a select few places on our realm where the Light and Dark mix. It's considered neutral territory. It's where the Light go to walk on the dangerous side. The Dark go to conduct illicit business with the Light, and well, to see if they can get one of them to become Dark." Ailis looked at Lennox reclining on the bed, his hard body stretched out in all its glory. "I've never understood what drew my parents to each other until now. Mum was from a powerful Dark family. She had visited a club to find a Light to have a fun night with. My father, from just as prominent a Light family, had gone to see what the fuss was all about. They found each other and fell in love that night. Dad gave up everything to be with Mum. As for Mum, she was expected to marry another. When she refused, her family disowned her—all but her sister, Bea."

Ailis looked out over the water. She hadn't thought of her parents in a long time. She barely remembered them. Bea had kept their memory alive for her, but her parents were figures from a past that faded with each year.

Ailis cleared her throat and returned to her story. "Bea was all I had. She was both mother and father, and I would've done anything to make her proud."

"Becoming a Dark was part of that."

She slid her gaze to Lennox, but there was no censure on his face or in his words. "Aye. I would've had to go to the Light side if I hadn't. I couldn't bear the thought of losing her. Of being alone without anyone."

"Even with your father's family waiting?"

"We discussed it. It was possible they would've taken me in, but in the end, it was my decision. I couldn't chance it, knowing what they thought of my mother."

Lennox rested his hand on her leg. "Do you regret becoming Dark?"

"I thought once I embraced the darkness that I would

finally fit in, but it didn't happen. I bemoan that decision now because I know it'll change how you view me."

He grunted and put his other arm behind his head. "I willna. We have every color dragon you can think of. There are as many different-colored eyes—even red ones. I never thought the shade was anything more than your color."

"You don't seem to understand what I had to do to become Dark."

"I can guess."

She looked away. Should she press the issue? Why couldn't she be content with the way things were? He didn't seem fazed by her revelation. Was she trying to sabotage things? That was exactly what she was doing—because she didn't think she was worthy of anyone, much less someone like Lennox.

"I've killed, too, lass," he said.

Her gaze jerked to him. "You didn't want to do it, though."

"Did you enjoy it?"

She pressed her lips together and shook her head. Ailis wiped away a tear that spilled. "I had decided to become Dark, but weeks passed without me doing anything. Finally, a female who had harassed me for years confronted me one night. I learned a handful of years later that Bea had set everything up. I came out the winner that night. I could've let her go, but I didn't."

Lennox pulled her back down to lay beside him. He brought her close until she rested her cheek on his chest. "We've all done things we regret. You've done nothing since you arrived that would make me question you. But let me ask you something. Would you have found the answers you needed to build the doorway to my realm with the Light?"

"Doubtful. The Dark are always looking for ways to enhance their magic."

"Then it was all meant to be exactly as it is."

She lay there for a few moments, then asked, "Has this changed your view of me?"

"As I said, I base my decisions about someone through actions and evidence. The past forms us, but it shouldna decide our future."

"I like that. I get to decide who I am."

He kissed the top of her head. "You've always been able to decide that. It's difficult to discover that when others are telling us what we should be."

She rose onto her elbow to look at him. "If you're right, and we were destined to meet, then I've never had the ability to make any decisions myself."

"No' true, lass. We have a path, and our choices will eventually lead us where we need to go. Sometimes, it's an easy route. Other times, it's difficult. All I have to do is look into your eyes to know that it was written in the stars for us to find each other. You've changed everything for me."

Lennox could've stayed there with her for eternity. Even with the weight of knowing her stay was temporary, the contentment he found was staggering. All the centuries of dealing with loss, loneliness, and confusion melted away. It was almost as if he were seeing the puzzle of his life with all the pieces finally fitting together.

Her red eyes were still filled with doubt. He understood her thinking that he couldn't be real. In fact, he had wondered if she was flesh and blood. His realm was made of strong magic, but there had never been anyone like Ailis before to prepare him for…well, her.

He touched her face, mesmerized by the softness of her skin. He wasn't sure he could ever keep his hands off her. Or his lips, for that matter. Kissing was his new favorite pastime.

"You've changed things for me, too," Ailis admitted. Then she sat up and flashed him a smile. "I didn't mean to turn things sour. My thoughts sometimes take me to places I'd rather not go."

"You're no' alone in that."

She shrugged one shoulder. "I'm famished. Are you up for tasting some of my favorite Fae dishes?"

"I am."

"Perfect." She rubbed her hands together, then shivered. "It's rather cool without your body heat."

Lennox grinned and raked his eyes down her body. "You could lie back down."

"Oh, I definitely will," she replied with a wink. "For now, we're going to see how different your taste buds are."

In a blink, a fuzzy charcoal-gray top covered her. It had a wide neck and hung off her left shoulder. On her legs were loose-fitting pants in a silky material with a thick band around her ankles. He wasn't sure how she could look as good in clothes as she did without.

He sat up and fingered the fuzzy garment to discover it was soft to the touch. "What is this?"

"A sweater made from an animal from my realm with long hair," she explained.

"Interesting."

"I wish you could see my realm."

He dropped his hand. "I would like that, but I can no' leave Earth."

"I understand. Since I plan on sharing the meals I love, tell me which ones you like, and I'll try to create them with my magic."

"I could use mine."

Her brows knitted together. "Then why don't you?"

"Why do you use yours so often?"

"Because I have it," she said with a laugh.

He slid one leg off the bed to let it dangle. "As do we. But as a rule, dragons use magic frugally."

"That's…" She stopped and pressed her lips together.

"Go on. I doona want you to stifle yourself with me."

Ailis blew out a breath. "That's senseless. Why not use what you have?"

"What if there comes a time we can no' use magic?"

"Why would you think that would happen?"

"Why would you think it wouldna?"

She opened her mouth to answer, then closed it. After a moment, she asked, "Are there other beings with as much or more power than the dragons?"

"Nay."

"Then there is no reason for you not to delve into your power."

"I didna say we didna know how to use it. I said we used it sparingly."

She leaned her head to the side, causing the curtain of her hair to slide over her shoulder. "Fae are magic. It's in every aspect of our bodies, our lives, and our realm. I think the same applies to dragons. There's no reason you wouldn't be able to turn to your magic."

"It is our way. Maybe you're right, and nothing will ever disrupt our lives. Then again, perhaps a stranger from a different realm will arrive and change everything."

"Point taken," she said with a grin. "I might not agree with you, but I do understand. Now. Back to the food. What is your favorite?"

"You willna want to know."

"Sure, I do. You intend to try all of mine, right? I'm up for the challenge."

Lennox bit back a grin. "Is that so?"

"Absolutely."

"I'm no' so sure."

She lifted her chin, displaying a stubborn streak. "I can handle whatever you bring."

"I suppose I could bring it to you."

"Please. I'm eager to try your food."

Lennox rose from the bed and stretched. He turned to walk to the water when he heard her gasp. He spun around to find her eyes wide. "What is it?"

"Your back."

"My back?" he repeated with a frown. "What about it."

She motioned for him to return to the bed. She crawled to the edge and rose onto her knees as he reached her. She then turned him around. He stood silently as her fingertips lightly stroked over the expanse of his back.

"Ailis?" He tried not to be alarmed, but he couldn't dismiss the fact that something had startled her. His back didn't feel any different than the rest of him. However, that didn't mean something wasn't wrong. She had touched him all over, so obviously it was something that could be seen. "What is it?"

"Your back is marked," she said in a whisper.

His brows snapped together. "Marked? How do you mean?"

"I've never seen the likes before," she continued as if he hadn't spoken. "It's...beautiful."

"What is it?" he pressed.

Both of her hands were on him now. "A dragon."

"A what?" He must have misheard her.

"A dragon. Your skin isn't raised, but it's as if the marking has penetrated it. I don't feel anything, but there's no missing it."

He wanted to see it. "Describe it."

"I'd rather show you."

"How?" he asked and turned to her.

She held out a round object with a handle. He could see his reflection like he did in the water.

"It's a mirror," Ailis said. "Hold it up and maneuver it until you see the big mirror behind you."

It took a couple of tries before he found the mirror behind him that stood as tall as he did and was several feet wide. He then moved the glass in his hand until he could see his back. He could only stare in shock at the design. The color was a mix of red and black, not one or the other but a combination of both.

The dragon stood on its hind legs near his waist. Its wings were spread wide, reaching from the tip of one shoulder to the other. The dragon's head was turned to the side, fire billowing from its mouth. Its tail lay curled near its back feet. But the craziest thing about the dragon was that it looked like him. From the horns to the crystals to the shape of the scales.

Lennox slowly lowered the hand that held the mirror and rotated his shoulders to see if he could feel the design, but he still didn't sense it. He thought there'd be no more shocks after shifting, but he'd been wrong.

"Are there more?" he asked.

Ailis shook her head. "Just the one, as impressive as it is."

He handed her the mirror and ran a hand down his face. "What does it mean?"

"You're a dragon. I think it's just confirming that. Or perhaps it's to show your kind when you're in this form. To prove to them you're who you say you are."

He sank onto the bed once more. "There has to be a reason for it."

"You may never know what it is."

That simply wouldn't do. If there were questions, he sought answers. Always.

"Talk to the other Kings."

He shook his head. "I never intended to let them know I could shift."

"It might be something all of them can do. Don't you want to prepare them for what might happen and how?"

Lennox squeezed the bridge of his nose between his thumb and forefinger. "I doona know. Maybe."

"You're worried about how they'll view you if they find out."

He turned his head to meet her gaze. "Aye."

"You're their King."

"Who can be replaced anytime."

"Is that what you're really afraid of?"

Lennox blew out a frustrated sigh and looked back at the water. "I doona know."

Ailis moved to sit beside him. "I'm sorry. I shouldn't have pushed. Again. You've had a lot of change in a short amount of time. You need to process everything. Do what you think is important. Only you get to decide what, if anything, to tell the others."

He put his hand on her leg. "Being a Dragon King doesna automatically grant me wisdom and the right answers to everything."

"You've known exactly what to say to me." She rested her head on his shoulder.

"I like being in this form with you."

"But?" she pressed.

He leaned his head against hers. "What if this is the start of something? What if all the dragons shift to this form? And… what if they can no' return to being dragons?"

"I was too wrapped up in you and this world to think about that. Obviously, it has weighed on you."

"A wee bit."

There was a long stretch of silence before Ailis asked, "Should I leave?"

"Nay," he answered immediately. He wasn't ready for that.

"What if I'm the cause? If I leave, things will return to normal."

He snorted. "Lass, nothing will ever be normal after you."

She raised her head, and he met her gaze with a smile. Her lips curved briefly. "I want your word that you'll tell me if I need to leave."

"I give it."

"Good," she said with a firm nod. "I want more time looking at the dragon on your back, but for now, can we get back to the food?"

He chuckled and shifted to face her. "You were asking about our food."

"I was."

"You're no' going to want it."

"I might like it," she said, affronted.

Lennox grinned and shook his head. "Think about it, Ailis. You wear clothes, and we doona. Your words are vocal, while ours are telepathic. You sleep in a bed, and we take whatever is available."

"And your food will be different. I get it."

"I doubt it. When I get hungry, I hunt."

She shrugged. "There are Fae who do the same."

"I dive from the sky, scoop up my prey, and eat it. Right then."

"Oh." There was a pause. Realization dawning in her crimson eyes. "I see."

He gave her a pointed look. "Shall we skip my favorites?"

"If you don't mind," she replied, her nose wrinkling.

Lennox couldn't contain his laugh. She was so eager to explore his realm and his culture that she didn't always consider what the differences could be. And he adored her for that. She didn't see him as some unsophisticated animal. He'd felt like it a few times when they compared their worlds, but he had to remind himself they were different species. No matter how they looked at things, there couldn't be an accurate comparison.

"Laugh it up," she said with a smile as her eyes twinkled. "I'll get you back."

He held up his hands. "I was hoping you'd come to the conclusion on your own."

"I'm too hungry to think straight."

"Then eat."

She tapped a finger on her chin and then held out her hands. Two dishes filled each palm. She set them down between them before producing a thin metal object. "A fork to help gather the food."

He eyed the utensil as he accepted its light weight. There was little time to inspect it before Ailis handed him a plate. He inhaled, and a riot of smells filled him.

"Fire-grilled ginger mussels with igorula bread. My favorite dish of all time."

Lennox raised the plate and took a deeper sniff. He caught a whiff of the ocean. He had to admit it seemed appetizing.

"The mussels come from our seas and are seasoned with a bit of a kick, and the bread is perfect for soaking up the sauce."

He watched her spear a mussel with the utensil and take a bite. Her eyes closed with enjoyment as she chewed. Lennox stuck his fork into the mussel and brought it to his mouth. He bit into it, noting the firm and slightly chewy texture combined with the hint of heat from the spices. It was a curious—and appealing—flavor. He definitely wanted more.

CHAPTER FIFTEEN

Ailis had known watching Lennox taste the food would be exciting. The surprise that flashed over his face at his first bite had her grinning. He followed that forkful with another before tearing off some bread and sopping up the sauce.

"I doona have words for how delicious this is," he said between mouthfuls.

"Which is why it's my favorite." She nibbled on the bread, her hunger forgotten as she turned her attention to him.

Lennox greeted every encounter with gusto. He didn't hold anything back, no matter how different it was from what he was used to. He devoured the food quickly. She pushed her plate between them and shared.

"I wonder if these ingredients are here," he mused.

She swallowed her last bite of mussel. "It wouldn't matter if they were. I can't cook."

"You use magic for all your food?"

"There are places called eateries where Fae create such dishes by testing out different ingredients."

Lennox shook his head. "Truly?"

"Truly. I'm a horrible cook. I can follow the directions of a recipe to the letter, but it never turns out. I've learned not to try."

"We must appear verra primitive to you."

"Not at all. As you pointed out earlier, we're different. It doesn't make either of us better than the other. Which brings me to my next question. Do you want more food or dessert?"

He raised a brow. "What's dessert?"

"Well, that settles it then. Get ready to fall in love. If there's one thing I can't do without, it's an elderberry and vanilla pastry. It's divine. The pastry is light and fluffy, and the inside is moist and full of flavor."

"Are you going to keep teasing, or do I get to taste?" he asked with a grin.

Ailis rolled her eyes but soon had two plates of the pastry before her. She handed one to Lennox, but she didn't wait for him to try it before taking the round dessert in her fingers and bringing it to her mouth. Her eyes closed with bliss as she bit into it. She licked her lips and savored the earthy, tart flavor of the elderberry mixed with the vanilla. She didn't open her eyes until she swallowed. That's when she found Lennox's gaze locked on her, the pastry halfway to his mouth.

"I'm no' sure whether I want to taste the dessert or you," he said in a husky voice.

"Why not have both?"

"Oh, I will have you again, lass," he vowed, his pale green eyes filled with promise.

She had to squeeze her legs together at the surge of need that shot straight to her center. He didn't let her look away as he sampled the pastry. He groaned, his tongue snaking out to lick up a bit of elderberry and vanilla that stuck to his lip.

"That's the most delectable thing I've ever tasted," he said and ate more.

"I know."

"How do you no' eat only these?"

She laughed and readied herself for another bite. "I have."

He chuckled in response. There were no more words as they finished the pastries.

"There's so much for you to try," she said. "I don't know what to serve you next."

Lennox got to his feet and held out his hand. "How about you think on that while we take that swim?"

"You're already full?"

"For food. I'm famished for you."

His cock stood hard and waiting. Her knees were weak as she took his hand, and he brought her to her feet. He was still naked. Fae were sexual creatures, but they didn't hold a candle to the dragon before her. Lennox dominated more than the cave. He governed her thoughts and tempted her beyond measure. No one would be able to deny him.

But it wasn't denial she was after. It was the carnal decadence she had found in his arms.

"You willna be needing those clothes."

The husky tenor of his voice sent shivers over her skin. She snapped her fingers, and the clothes vanished.

A slow smile spread across his face. "I'm coming to reconsider my stance on no' using magic."

"It does come in handy." She barely recognized the breathlessness of her voice. But that's what he did to her.

His large hand gripped her hip, and he dragged her to him. His other arm wrapped around her as he lowered his head. Their mouths met for a lingering kiss before his tongue sought entry. She parted her lips and tasted the dessert on him.

"You taste so damn good," he murmured between kisses.

She tried to respond, but her mind couldn't form the words.

His mouth moved to her jaw and then up her neck to her earlobe. She gasped at the tingles that shot to her sex when his lips brushed the top of her ear.

"Doona be afraid of the water. I'll keep you warm," he whispered, his breath fanning her neck.

So much heat was flowing through her that she didn't think she would ever be cold again. It took her a moment to realize his mouth was no longer on her. She blinked open her eyes to see him grinning, a knowing look on his face. He had done that on purpose.

He turned, took two steps, and dove into the pool. He entered so elegantly, there was barely a splash. The water rippled outward. She could see Lennox clearly as he dove deep before angling his body upward and resurfacing. He shook the water and hair from his face as he turned to her while treading water.

"Are you coming?"

She walked to the edge. "I'm enjoying the view."

"You can do more than look."

The temptation was too much. Ailis dove. The shock of the cold water was instant, but it didn't last. She didn't plunge nearly as deeply as he had, and when she broke the surface, Lennox was there. He brought her against him.

"I fear I'll never get enough of you," he said before claiming her lips.

Whatever response she might have had vanished at the ardent kiss. His desire enflamed hers, setting them both ablaze—the flames hotter and stronger than ever before.

She wound her arms around his neck. He deepened the kiss, stealing her breath. She was vaguely aware of water moving around her, but her thoughts didn't linger on it. He lifted her legs to wrap around his waist. That put his arousal against her.

Ailis needed him inside her. She had to be connected to him, needed to join their bodies as only two people could. When she attempted to adjust to do just that, he stopped her with his hands on her hips. His fiery kisses kept her mind whirling and her body buzzing as need built to a frenzy. Her body was his to do with as he pleased.

Something brushed against her lower back. In the next moment, she found herself sitting on a smooth rock near the edge. Lennox raised his head and caught her eyes. That same hunger from before was there, making her heart trip over itself.

"Lie back," he urged.

She didn't hesitate to do as he asked. She reclined and found herself staring at the ceiling as the water reflected the light and danced in beautiful, seductive waves. The water lapped at her ears. He loosened her legs until they hung beside him. Then he lifted her hips until her entire body floated.

His hands caressed from her ankles up her legs until he

held her hips. His grip was firm. The water gently lapping at her most sensitive places heightened her arousal. She heard her breaths in the water as she waited and waited and…

She cried out when his mouth found her sex. He licked along her vulva in a slow, steady glide. There was nothing but water for her to grab. She tried to squeeze her legs together, but his hold was secure and firm. He found her clit and circled the tiny, throbbing bulb. Desire, thick and hot, stole through her. She was already on the verge of climax. She tried to shift her hips, seeking more. He only doubled his ministrations. The more she moved, the more the water shimmered on the ceiling.

And the closer Lennox brought her to her peak.

She turned her head, only to have water fill her mouth. Ailis spat it out and fought for breath. She had to stay perfectly still, which was nearly impossible in her present state.

"Please," she murmured. "Please, Lennox. I need you."

Her voice was muffled in the water. She didn't know if he had heard her. Her sex clenched. She had never been so needy or desperate for release. He expertly teased and tormented her aching flesh as desire built in a tangled throb low in her stomach. Her breathing was so harsh that the water rose and fell over her chest, coming to her nipples before rolling away.

Then he slid two fingers inside her and found that special spot. He rubbed it twice before the orgasm claimed her. Her body jerked as pleasure rolled through her again and again. He kept stroking and licking, prolonging the climax until she was limp, her body spent beyond thought or reason.

Lennox slowly removed his fingers and gently pulled her

to him. She lay against him, feeling boneless as her body quivered from the aftershocks of such a powerful orgasm.

His mouth moved to her ear as his hand went to the back of her head. "We're just getting started. I had to know the taste of you. Och, lass, I didna know pleasure could taste so good."

Somehow, she managed to lift her head. "I guess it's only fair since I know what you taste like. But I need you inside me."

"Aye, beautiful. I crave that, too."

"Don't make me wait."

He lifted her hips until the blunt head of his arousal brushed against her. Ailis bit her lip, lost in his pale green eyes as he slowly lowered her onto his shaft. Her body adjusted for his girth. She moaned at the friction as he moved, entering her inch by inch. Then, finally, he gave a final thrust of his hips and seated himself fully within her.

The muscles in his neck stood out, his chest rising and falling quickly. "You feel so damn good."

"Lennox," she whispered before bringing her mouth to his.

The kiss was slow and sensual, filled with passion and a hunger like no other. He began moving his hips, the length of him sliding in and out of her in a steady rhythm. She clung to him, desperate to meld their bodies.

He tore his mouth from hers. "Ailis," he ground out.

She understood. She felt it, too. The pleasure built swiftly, the desire tightening rapidly. Her entire body tingled with awareness from the water, from his body moving against her —in her. He began to thrust hard and deep, stroking against her sensitive flesh.

Suddenly, his hand was tangled in her hair as he pulled her head back and seized her lips. That's all it took for the climax to sweep over her. Her body clamped around him. He raised his head and cried out as he buried himself deep, pumping once, then twice before stilling.

CHAPTER SIXTEEN

The only sounds in the cavern were the water lapping and their harsh breaths. Lennox loosened his hold on Ailis's hair. Her eyes opened and met his. In that instant, he knew without a doubt that she was his mate. A part of him must have known from the moment he laid eyes on her. It explained his decisions.

But how could they be together? A Fae and a dragon. She didn't belong in his world, and he didn't belong in hers. There would be adversity wherever they turned. He couldn't think about that now, not after such a mind-blowing joining.

They reached for each other simultaneously. It didn't matter that he was still inside her. He needed them heart to heart. She must have felt the same given the way her arms gripped him. They remained locked together, neither speaking as they got lost in their thoughts.

When Lennox felt her shiver, he knew it was time to get out of the water. With her legs still locked around him, he swam to the opposite side. Once there, he gently pulled out of her. She leaned back and met his gaze. He desperately searched for words to contextualize his emotions, but none could accurately describe his feelings.

One moment, Ailis was in his arms, and the next, she was out of the water and dry. She smiled and motioned for him to follow as she climbed into the bed. Lennox braced his arms on the rocks and pulled himself out of the pool. For once, he turned to his magic and used it to dry himself. Ailis lifted the covers, waiting for him. He strode to the bed and slid in beside her. Once he was settled, she snuggled against him. Skin-to-skin. Heart to heart.

"One more thing," she said as she lifted her head.

The light over the water blinked out, only to be replaced by dozens of tiny, flickering lights scattered throughout the cavern.

"We call them candles. Their light isn't nearly as bright," she told him.

Beds, pillows, blankets, desserts, clothes, and candles. What else would he learn from her? She seemed to adapt on Earth, but that was only because of her magic. If she didn't have that to turn to, she likely wouldn't remain. There were no buildings for her to call home, no beds for comfort, and then there was the matter of food.

But she did have magic. His mind focused on that because he didn't dare contemplate his life with her next to him—even though he wanted it with every fiber of his being.

"Ailis," he began. He wanted her to know, *needed* her to know his feelings.

"Aye?" she whispered.

He released a long breath and tightened his arm around her.

"I know." She placed a soft kiss on his chest. "I felt it, too."

Lennox could tell her she was his mate. It was the perfect time, but he chose not to. He wanted to shout her name to everyone. If he knew she would be accepted, if he knew the dragons would consider his ability to shift beneficial, he'd do just that in a heartbeat. Yet he couldn't be sure of any of it, and he refused to put Ailis in danger. She might have magic and be able to teleport, but he had no desire to pit her against his kind. Right now, they had peace and each other. He wouldn't upset that.

"What aren't you telling me?" she asked.

He had delved into her thoughts earlier. It was only fair for him to share as she had…at least as much as he dared. "I've never experienced anything like that before."

"Me neither."

Lennox rubbed his fingers over her back. "Does that… change things for you?"

"Aye. You?"

Very much so. "Aye, lass."

She linked her fingers with his on his chest. "This complicates things."

"It does." In ways she couldn't begin to fathom.

"We could pretend none of this happened. I could dress and leave through the doorway right now. You could forget about me."

"I would remember you a thousand lifetimes from now."

He looked at her as she raised her gaze to him. "I doona want you to leave. No' now. No' ever. And that's the problem."

"Because I don't belong."

He wanted to deny it, to tell her they would find a way. But he would only be lying to them both. "Aye."

"I've been thinking the same thing. I even contemplated having you come with me. You look enough like a Fae."

"It wouldna work."

She sighed and looked away. "Not for me here or you with me— even if you could leave, which you can't." She paused. "Well, now that we have that covered, what do we do?"

"I wish I knew."

"I'll stay. You said no one enters a dragon's cave without permission. None of the dragons will find me."

Lennox shook his head against the pillow. "It isna fair to ask you to remain in the mountain."

"You aren't asking." She rose onto her elbow and looked at him. "It's my decision."

"Ailis," he began.

She put a finger on his lips to silence him. "We may get tired of each other in a few days. I may fret at not being able to see the sky. You may get weary of keeping me a secret. Anything could happen, but we don't know all the outcomes. Why not let things play out?"

It was the simplest solution. He hadn't made any decisions, and the one she had was no different than what she had endured for the day. A single day. She was right. She would probably chafe at being confined to the mountain and return to her realm. He wouldn't suffer long without her because a dragon who found—and lost—his mate withered away. But she didn't need to know that.

"The brunt of this decision is on you," Ailis continued. "You would have to keep me and your ability to shift a secret from your clan and the other Kings. That may be easier than I think, but you told me the Kings are close."

He gently kissed her fingers before returning their linked hands to his chest. "I could only keep you a secret for so long."

"And you have no idea how the dragons will react to me."

"Some will believe I have things under control. If I didna, the magic would replace me. Others will fear you and what your arrival means. A few will be eager to get to know you and ask questions about your world."

A quick grin curved her lips. "What of the Kings?"

"Our duty is the protection of this realm and our clans. I have the additional responsibility of the Kings."

"Which means you have to think about them in whatever decisions you make."

Lennox blew out a breath. "Aye."

"They will see me as a threat, won't they?"

"Maybe."

"Lennox, let's not lie to each other," she chided. "It's better to be truthful and lay it out."

He ground his teeth together. "Aye. They will most likely see you as a threat."

"Well, I can't say I would blame them. I'd probably do the same thing in their place."

"I would stand with you," he began.

"Nay," she stated firmly. "You won't do any such thing. They'll turn on you."

He gaped at her. "You expect me to leave you on your own against them?"

"I do. In fact, I demand it."

Lennox rolled to his feet and paced a few steps away, his hands raking through his hair. "You ask the impossible."

"Tell me you wouldn't do the same if our roles were reversed. And don't you dare say it's different because I'm female."

He spun around to her as he dropped his arms to his sides. "But it is."

"Were you happy before I came?"

The change of subject threw him. He blinked as he tried to decipher where she was going with the question. "I was as content as I could be."

"My arrival has shaken your world."

"That isna a bad thing."

She smiled sadly and sat up, tucking her legs against her. "I think it is exactly that. I'm putting you in a tenuous position. I can fix that by leaving."

The distress that gripped him was so strong he couldn't breathe. "Nay, Ailis. Please."

"I didn't say I wanted to go, but it's the right thing to do. For both of us." She waved her hand around the cavern. "I've been here only a few hours, and in some ways, it feels as if I've been here for decades. But as we've both pointed out, I don't belong."

"You belong with me, and I with you."

She looked down at her hands in her lap. "It isn't meant to

be, Lennox. I don't want to admit it, but it doesn't serve either of us to lie to ourselves or each other."

"You're my mate." He hadn't said the words earlier, but they burst from his lips now in a desperate attempt to keep her from leaving.

Her head slowly lifted, her scarlet eyes meeting his. "I used to rail against my parents' decision that pitted my father against his family. I couldn't fathom the kind of feelings that would make someone give up everything they knew for another. Then I met you. I shouldn't feel the depth of emotions I do for you, but there's no denying what's inside my heart. I yearn for the impossible."

Lennox searched her face, hope springing anew within him.

"You say that destiny brought us together. I wanted to doubt you, but I can't. The proof is all around us. I just can't see how so many things had to go right for us to meet, only to realize we can't have a life together."

"No' here or on your world. But we could find a place on another realm."

She shook her head. "I can't let you do that. You're the King of Dragon Kings. Your clan looks to you. The other Kings look to you. The magic of the realm saw your potential, just as I do. You're not the type to shirk your responsibilities —no matter how much you may want to."

"I would for you." And there it was. The truth he hadn't wanted to admit. He would give up his world, his responsibilities, and everything he knew. For her.

Ailis climbed from the bed and walked to him. She put a hand on his jaw and looked deep into his eyes. "I know you would, and you'll never know just how much that means to me."

"You're my mate. There's no ignoring that fact or disregarding it." He wrapped his arms around her. "You feel it, too. I know you do."

"I do, but it doesn't change things."

He brought her to him, resting his chin atop her head. "Nothing has happened yet. We doona need to make any hasty decisions now."

"Won't it be worse the longer I remain?"

Maybe, but it was a chance he was willing to take. "You're already in my blood. Parting with you will be tantamount to ripping out my heart."

"You think it would be easy for me to leave?"

"I doona wish to find out."

She sighed softly. "I don't have the will to leave."

That was all he needed to hear. Lennox lifted her in his arms and carried her to the bed. As soon as he laid her on the mattress, she pulled him down for a kiss. His body ignited with the first press of her lips against his. She slid a hand between them and wrapped her fingers around his cock. It hardened in her grip.

She spread her legs and brought him to her entrance. He was inside her in one thrust, their bodies moving together in a sensual, carnal dance. Within moments, he was lost in her—his body, soul, and heart given to a Dark Fae he couldn't get enough of.

CHAPTER SEVENTEEN

Ailis woke to find herself alone. She felt the side of the bed, finding the covers cool to the touch. She sat up and looked around for Lennox, but he was nowhere to be found. With a thought, clothes covered her as she stood. The candles still burned. She took one near the entry and carried it with her as she made her way through the tunnel to the front cavern Lennox used to rest. He wasn't there either.

He had duties as a Dragon King. That was probably where he was. She just wished he had woken her to tell her that so she didn't search for him. Ailis stood in the tunnel and faced right, in the direction of the outside. While she didn't dare venture out alone, she wanted a quick look. It had been hours since she had seen the sky. She didn't even know if it was night or day.

She slowly crept toward the entrance, keeping close to the wall, though she wasn't sure why. She planned to teleport to the water cavern if another dragon appeared. And if they pursued her, she would go to the Fae doorway. But that was a last resort.

The conversation with Lennox from earlier reared its head. She knew leaving was the right thing to do for him, but she couldn't bring herself to do it. She had been working up the courage, but his words made it much more difficult. The longer she stayed, the harder it would be for her to go. *If* she ever left.

He had called her his mate. She had wanted to deny it, but the truth was in his eyes. The Fae couldn't sense their mates. In fact, when beings lived as long as they did, they rarely stayed with the same partner the entire time. It seemed unimaginable that dragons, who lived even longer, did.

Yet it was something she yearned for. A secret she kept in the darkest recesses of her heart and brought out only occasionally.

With Lennox, she had found someone who accepted all of her—the good and the bad. Her admitting she was Dark hadn't repelled him. He had *understood*. Even now, that floored her.

Ailis spotted the fringes of the cave and saw the shadow the mountain cast across the ground. It was either sunrise or sunset. She sat and leaned against the rocky wall. The candle was on the far side of her, away from the entrance. She breathed in the fresh air and observed the bright green grass growing among the gray rocks. What she had seen of Earth was wild and fierce. Its untamed beauty touched a place deep inside her.

As an explorer, she had never been content staying in one place for too long. Or maybe she had just been looking for Earth and Lennox because she no longer felt that impulse to see something different. However, had she not felt that drive to explore a new realm, she wouldn't have made it here.

Despite the reasons she should've stopped and the ways she could've failed—she hadn't. She was on a new realm. With dragons! She smiled thinking about it. She was just getting to know Lennox but couldn't wait to hear all his stories. She wanted to know everything. Her knowledge of dragons was nonexistent, but what she had learned so far was astonishing.

They had a civilization that rivaled the Fae's. Some might think differently because the dragons didn't live in conventional homes, but that didn't make them any less intelligent or sophisticated. They took pride in their land and their families. They looked out for each other, and while there were skirmishes and battles, the clans stuck together. It was something the Fae could learn from.

Not that they would.

She knew exactly what would happen if any of the Fae, Light or Dark, came to Earth. They would attempt to dominate the dragons. Because the Fae saw themselves as superior. Ailis almost wished it would happen, if only to see her people taught a thing or two. Because she had no doubt the dragons would triumph for one simple reason—they fought together.

The Fae were fractured in so many ways, she was amazed they still existed. They were headed toward a civil war, and with the way the Fae fought, they could tear their realm apart. It probably wouldn't come to that. Or so she hoped. The Fae were reckless, but they weren't that rash.

She wondered what Bea would think of Lennox and Earth. As much as Ailis had loved her aunt, Bea was a true Dark. She always believed that gaining power was worth anything. In Bea's eyes, the only way to survive was with magic.

What would Lennox have thought of her when she was younger? Would they have gotten along as they do now? Ailis tried to imagine Lennox as a young dragon. She couldn't quite picture anything but what he was now. Yet that made her wonder what baby dragons looked like. Maybe he could show her one. Just so she could see if they were as adorable as she imagined.

Thoughts of babies suddenly made her consider her own. With Lennox. Her hand immediately went to her stomach as she realized they'd had sex. Twice. All it took was a little magic to prevent a pregnancy, but her mind had been on other things. It was careless and thoughtless. Though the likelihood of her getting with child was slim. Lennox might look like a Fae, but he was all dragon.

Still, it gave her pause. Ailis had never been in this position before. She could be pregnant now, but did she take that chance? If they couldn't agree on whether she should stay or leave, adding a child into the mix wouldn't help matters. Ailis sent a shot of magic through her stomach from her hand. She couldn't take the chance. As wonderful as it would be to have Lennox's child, things were too precarious for everyone. Why increase that a hundredfold for a baby? Then she used more magic to ensure she was protected from future pregnancies.

The ground trembled beneath her. It jerked her out of her musings to see a large shape at the cave's opening. The sight of Lennox's silver scales calmed her. He walked into the mountain and then shifted.

"Is everything all right?" he asked with a frown when he spotted her.

She got to her feet, dusting herself off. "Of course. I just wanted to see what time of day it was."

"Night is falling. I had a matter to take care of. I didna want to wake you."

"Wake me next time, please."

He nodded and walked to her side, then took her hand. "The cave getting to be too much?"

"Not at all. I was just looking for you and thought I'd get a glimpse of the outside."

"There's no' much to do within my mountain."

"I beg to differ." She tugged at him to follow her after she grabbed the candle. "You never thought about it in your true form, but there are smaller openings all over. Look."

She paused beside a pile of rocks. Above them was an opening large enough for her to get through. "There are many of these. Who knows where they lead?"

"You could get stuck."

Ailis chuckled. "I've magic, remember? It'll get me out of any trouble."

"I suppose you're right."

Her gaze moved around him to the opening of the mountain. "I don't suppose I could see the stars, could I? I want to see how different the constellations are here from what I'm used to seeing. You could be in your dragon form. I'll hide in your hand or next to you. No one will see me," she hurried to say. "And if another dragon comes, I'll teleport back here."

His pale green eyes studied her for a long moment. "We wouldna be able to communicate."

"I think I can decipher your grunts."

Lennox let out a bark of laughter. "Is that right?"

"It is. Besides, we can come up with a way for you to answer *aye* or *nay*. I'll make sure to only ask questions that require that kind of response."

"We can try it. I know you want to see my world, and I want to show it to you. There is so much beauty."

She grinned and gave him a quick kiss. "I found a treasure of my own right here."

"Och, woman. You're going to drive me mad with wanting."

"That's the plan," she said with a wink.

He glanced behind him. "Once I shift, climb onto my back, but lie down. You can get down once we're on the top of the mountain."

"The peak?" Now she was really excited. "I'll be able to see so much."

"I thought you'd enjoy that."

"Wait," she said when he went to turn.

He quirked a brow at her.

"What about your *aye* and *nay* responses?"

"Ah. For an *aye*, I'll tap a talon."

"And I assume your rumbling growl will be a nay?"

He flashed her a smile. "It will."

"Good. Now we can go."

They returned to where she had been sitting. Ailis set aside the candle as Lennox shifted. He lowered himself to the ground and looked at her. She began to teleport to his back but then stopped, thinking about how she always reached for her magic. That was when she decided to climb up, only to realize she hadn't asked how. He probably didn't know either. It wasn't as if he had others crawling all over him.

He jerked his chin toward his front leg as if reading her mind. Ailis walked to it. She put her foot on him and pushed herself from the ground. As she made her way up his arm and shoulder, she hoped she wasn't hurting him. Which almost made her laugh. His scales were hard beneath her, warm but very dense. It wasn't anything like skin. He might not even feel her. She hesitated when she reached his back. The spikes and crystals made it difficult to get settled, but she eventually managed it.

"I'm ready," she told him.

She firmly gripped one of the spikes and looped her leg around another. Smaller crystals dug into her stomach and hips, but she ignored them as Lennox stood. She noted that he was careful in how he got to his feet. Thankfully, he didn't jar her too much.

Ailis got a different perspective of dragons when he began walking from the cave. There wasn't much space between her and the top of the tunnel, but that wasn't what made her suck in a breath. It was how his body moved from side to side, shifting her to such a degree that she might have fallen without the spikes to hang onto.

It wasn't until they were outside that she realized she hadn't asked him how he planned to get to the top of the mountain. The thought barely went through her head before he was in the air. She bit her tongue to keep from making a sound. There was no reason for her to be afraid. It wasn't as if she could fall to her death. Then again, this was only her second time flying.

The ride was over quickly. Lennox landed so gently she barely felt it. Then he lay down and turned his head to look at her with one white eye. Ailis glanced at the sky. She could see dragons in the distance. She didn't waste time climbing down, preferring to teleport instead. He had curled a hand in such a way she could sit within it to look at the sky without being seen.

Ailis got comfortable and leaned back as the dark blue skies gave over to a blanket of darkness. The quarter moon hung just over Lennox's back, and the sheer number of stars that began to twinkle was worth any amount of flying she had to bear.

"Oh, Lennox," she whispered. "It's so beautiful."

He tapped one of the talons on his other hand. He faced the opposite direction, his eyes moving constantly, no doubt looking for dragons who might come near. She wasn't worried, though. This was their moment.

They sat in silence for the first hour until the sky was pitch black. Ailis noted the stars were completely different than hers. She began pointing out the brightest of them while musing about what dragon would someday name the constellations.

"Thank you," she whispered as she stood and touched his jaw. "We can go back inside now."

A low rumble was his response. Ailis chuckled and returned to his hand to continue her exploration.

CHAPTER EIGHTEEN

Ailis's excitement was infectious. Lennox watched her, only occasionally looking to where she pointed when her gaze darted to him. He had never thought too much about the stars. He paid more attention to the moon. Always had. But the realization that there were other realms in the universe made him reconsider the dots in the night sky. Was one of the tiny pinpricks of light Ailis's realm? She'd said that none of the constellations looked the same to her. How far did she travel? He couldn't answer that because he didn't know how big the universe was.

After gazing at the night sky for hours, she had risen and taken a look at the world bathed in moonlight. She couldn't see the mountains in all their glory, not like she would during the day, yet her soft sighs and whispered *ohs* told him she saw enough.

It hadn't bothered her that he couldn't converse with her. She talked enough for both of them. He loved getting insight into her thoughts. She was witty and had a deep connection to new things he had never seen before. She was also brave. It took great courage for her to leave her realm—regardless of the reasons—and go somewhere without assurance that she could get there. Even when they'd first met. She hadn't run. She had stood her ground.

Lennox wouldn't have thought to bring her up here if she hadn't mentioned it. He was glad she had, but it brought the things they had discussed earlier back to the forefront of his mind. He didn't want her hidden away. She posed no threat to the dragons, and he could ensure that. His first step would be to speak to the other Kings. All he needed to do was convince them. It would be up to the Kings to get their dragons to understand. Lennox wasn't fool enough to think any of it would be easy. There would be pushback from at least some of the Kings. None of them blindly accepted anything. It was why they were Dragon Kings.

They would worry about Ailis's intentions, and that other Fae might come after her. He wouldn't lie to his brothers. He had nothing to give them that would assuage their concerns. The biggest threat was that they couldn't see the doorway Ailis had created. But she could.

Lennox smiled inwardly. *That* would be his rationale for allowing her to remain and explore Earth. She could see if other doorways existed as he took her around the realm. There would be skepticism that she would actually tell him, but he knew Ailis would. His brothers trusted him, and he trusted her.

Eventually, he would tell them she was his mate. He was still coming to grips with that himself. It'd never occurred to him that his mate wouldn't be a dragon. Why would he think that? They'd had no other visitors to their world—at least as far as he knew.

The dragons had ruled over Earth for generations. Many things could've gotten lost or forgotten in their retelling of stories. He thought of Ailis's book. If they wrote their stories down, the dragons could have access anytime they needed it. That meant coming up with a written language. Which was hard to do in dragon form.

Then again, they had magic. Their stories were already kept with the help of magic. He had always thought nothing could be left out, but that was another misconception. If he didn't tell the Kings about Ailis, there would be no record of her anywhere in their history. It would be his secret.

And if he had a secret, others did, as well.

There was so much to consider, so much to speculate. He had to take into account the Kings' responses. Then there were the dragons. And he couldn't forget the magic. He had many to answer to. The burden of his position was a heavy one. Many thought the King of Kings' station meant unlimited power. It actually confined.

The Kings accepted his title because the magic had chosen him, but that didn't mean he unconditionally had their respect and trust. He had to earn it, and he had done it gladly. Lennox never wanted blind support. Each King was powerful in his own right. He urged them to speak their minds when they came together to sort through issues among the dragons. He wasn't one to decide things without discussing it with all the Kings and hearing their thoughts and opinions. Not all Kings of Kings had been so open.

He realized that Ailis had been quiet for some time.

When he looked down, he found her asleep in his hand. Lennox slowly stood and flew them to the ground. He carried her to their bed and carefully laid her on it. After he shifted to mortal form, he removed her boots and crawled in beside her. She turned toward his warmth, making him smile.

His decision was made. He would tell the Kings about her.

Lennox got his chance three days later when Darald, King of Yellows, asked for a meeting. Lennox had cautioned Ailis not to get too close to the opening of his mountain. He didn't want anyone seeing her until he'd had a chance to talk to them. The meetings could sometimes go on for days, and they usually happened very close to his mountain.

Lennox looked around at the Kings. They sat in a large circle with the smaller dragons situated in front of the larger ones. He had always loved the camaraderie they experienced as a group. None fully understood what it meant to be a Dragon King until the magic bestowed the mantle on them.

Some Kings had wanted the position. Others didn't seek it but accepted it gladly. Not many were like him, those who hadn't wanted anything to do with the title. He had gotten to know each of the Kings well. Though he wasn't around them all the time, he tried to keep an eye out if one ventured from the path the magic had put them on so he could be prepared for a change of King.

Less than a year ago, they'd gotten their newest King. Zeff, King of Emeralds, had joined them. Change was a way of life. No one, not from the lowliest dragon to the King of Kings, ever forgot the impermanence of their role.

"Darald," Lennox said, bringing the meeting to a start. *"What do you bring us?"*

Darald breathed deeply and then released it. *"I have a situation in my clan that is dividing us. One of the females claims to have found her mate with a Copper."*

Lennox glanced at Osric to find his friend staring at him. This wasn't the first time such an event had arisen. But it didn't happen often. It was so uncommon, in fact, that it was rarely discussed. Before Lennox could respond, the other Kings began to talk over each other with their opinions. He listened as they argued for each side until it began to dissolve into a yelling match.

He slammed his tail down, shaking the ground to get everyone's attention. Once all eyes were on him, Lennox refocused on Darald. *"Why do you say* claims?"

"She's young."

"As if that means she can no' sense her mate," another King stated.

Lennox lifted his hand to halt any more outbursts. *"There must be more to it than that for you no' to believe someone in your clan."*

"She's doesna understand what she does." Darald bared his teeth. *"She would disrupt two clans with this nonsense."*

Lennox found Rolf, the King of Coppers, who had yet to say anything. The Yellows and Coppers bordered each other, and it was conceivable that the couple in question interacted. Lennox asked Rolf, *"How do you feel about this?"*

"I've looked at it from both sides. Who are we to say mates

can no' be together?" Rolf questioned. "It isna our way. We are meant to find our other halves. The male in question is my cousin's son. He's a good, decent dragon. He's no' prone to fanciful thoughts or actions."

"That doesna make this right," Darald said.

Lennox glared at Darald. "No' another word. You had your chance to speak, now it's Rolf's."

Darald bowed his head, but the anger didn't leave his gaze.

This was a prelude to what Lennox might expect when he told them about Ailis. The Kings' reactions about mating outside a clan were just as he had expected—all over the place. Which would make things much more difficult.

And that didn't bode well for his announcement.

"Rolf," he said, turning back to the King of Coppers. "Continue, please."

Rolf flapped his wings in agitation. "I want the best for everyone in my clan. Each of us understands why the clans are in place. We know who we can turn to, who to trust, and who will be there for us. To mate outside the clan begs the question of which clan would take them in. One would never quite fit. The verra things that make our clans so beneficial wouldna be there for one of this pair. Of course, neither clan might take them. Then they would have nothing and no one. They would be on their own, defenseless against anyone who attacked. And once they had children…" Rolf paused as if the words were too difficult to say. He sighed loudly. "If these two are mates and we keep them apart, we know what we'll be sentencing them both to."

"Aye. A slow, painful death." It was something Lennox thought about now that he had found Ailis.

A low rumble of talk began among the dragons before Osric's voice broke through, loud and clear. *"This isna the first time this has happened. It willna be the last. In the past, the couples were kept apart. My clan had to watch one of ours suffer horrendously before succumbing. We can no' keep two dragon mates away from each other. The magic picks us for these positions. It's the magic of this realm that grants us our abilities and power. There's no doubt in my mind that it also chooses our mates. We must* accept *the truth."*

"And where would these couples go?" Darald demanded. *"Will your clan welcome them?"*

Osric's red eyes turned to Lennox. *"You have the power to carve new territory. Grant this couple—and any others—the ability to live in a place of their own."*

"Any others?" someone asked.

A loud snort from another. *"Osric, you make it sound like couples would want to leave their clans. I doona know what happens with the Blacks, but my people are happy."*

"That's exactly what I'm saying," Osric declared forcefully. *"Dragons should have options."*

"That isna our way," someone stated.

Osric's lip lifted in scorn. *"Change is around us in everything but the obvious. We can no' speak to the magic. We can no' ask if it set up the clans or if it was our ancestors. If everything else shifts and revolves, why no' our ways?"*

Lennox was impressed by how well Osric laid things out. He'd agreed with his friend, even before he found his mate in a Fae.

"It would create chaos," Elstan, King of Pinks, stated. He

turned his silver eyes to Lennox. *"Clans are the one constant we have."*

"They wouldna go away. A new clan would be created," Lennox explained.

Darald slammed his hand into the ground. *"And which King will rule it?"*

"Maybe the magic will give them their own," Osric replied. *"Maybe that's why dragons are finding mates outside their clans. Did you ever think of that?"*

As Lennox had expected, Darald and his supporters took offense, and the talks dissolved into more arguing. He had to slam his tail down again to get everyone to be silent. Then he looked around the circle of Kings, meeting each of their gazes. *"This isna a decision to be made lightly. I want to speak to the couple in question. Meanwhile, I want each of you to think about what it might feel like to find your mate outside your clan. For those who have a mate, you know the strength of the bond and the surety of what you feel. Keep that in mind. For those who doona have a mate, we've all been told about the feeling we get when we meet them. We know without a doubt. Age and clan shouldna bring doubt to any dragon who says they've found their other half. Seriously consider everything that has been said here. We'll reconvene soon."*

Lennox looked pointedly at Darald. *"Every point of view should be weighed, no' just what each of us wants or believes. Does everyone understand?"*

There was a round of ayes before the dragons began to disperse. Lennox released a sigh and started to leave when he spotted Osric coming his way.

CHAPTER NINETEEN

Over half of the Kings headed back to their clans. Those who remained either went to the Dragonwood, their mountains, or took to the sky, soaring over the range. Lennox waited for Osric. Despite their close friendship, Osric never took advantage or asked for favoritism. Not that Lennox would give it. Osric was steadfast and loyal, but he didn't pull any punches when giving Lennox his opinion.

"Well. That went about as good as it could," Osric said.

Lennox looked in the direction Darald had gone to return to his clan. *"Aye."*

"A decision will have to be made this time."

"I'm all too aware. It's astonishing that no previous Kings did anything."

Osric grunted, his exasperation clear. *"Because they didna want to take a stand."*

"So, it rests with us."

"Unfortunately, brother, it rests solely on you."

"That kind of decision shouldna rest with one dragon."

"But it does."

Like it or not, Osric was right. And Lennox didn't like it. What if he made the wrong decision? His thoughts turned to Ailis. If they were mated—which he intended—his clan wouldn't accept her, no matter how much he wished otherwise. She wasn't just from a different clan. She wasn't a dragon. Once his clan rejected them, he would be without a clan and therefore no longer King of Silvers. Another dragon would come to claim that title, as well as that of King of Kings. Lennox could take Ailis as his mate, only to turn around and be killed, dooming her to a short life. He doubted very much that they could join this new clan—if he created it — and have him remain a King. Or King of Kings.

No matter how he looked at it, he would lose everything.

All because of love.

"Are you ready to tell me her name?"

Lennox jerked his gaze to Osric. He almost played dumb, but he couldn't find the strength. Not to the dragon he thought of as a brother. *"Ailis."*

"And she's no' of your clan."

It wasn't a question. *"Nay."*

"Then creating a new clan could benefit you. Why did you no' push for that?"

Lennox fought not to look at his mountain, wondering what Ailis was doing. Probably exploring the tunnels. Maybe laid out on the bed, naked, waiting for his return. *"Of course, it crossed my mind."*

"But?"

"It would condemn her to a quick death."

Osric's brow knitted before realization dawned. *"You'd no longer be in your clan, and you think that means the magic would choose another."*

"It absolutely would."

"What if you're wrong. What if the magic keeps you as a King?"

Lennox snorted and shook his head. *"The likelihood of that is slim. One of the Kings will probably come for me, solving two problems with one battle."*

"If you doona claim your mate, brother, then you will die anyway."

"But I wouldna take her with me."

Lennox knew he'd slipped up as soon as the words were out. Osric's gaze intensified. He was one of the most intelligent dragons Lennox knew. Few things got past the King of Blacks.

"What are you no' telling me?"

Lennox blew out a breath. *"Doona ask that."*

"Too late."

"Brother," Lennox began.

Osric stepped closer, his tail twitching indignantly. *"You began it. Tell me. Whatever it is, you know I'll have your back. That should never come into question."*

"I'd rather no' test that."

Shock slackened Osric's visage. *"Lennox, you're my brother. I doona care what color scales you have or what clan you hail from. You can trust me."*

"I want to tell you."

"Then what's stopping you?"

"Your reaction. And what you might do."

"Do?" Osric repeated, jerking back his head. *"You think I'll attack? Or worse, turn on you?"*

Lennox was exhausted from keeping Ailis and his love for her a secret. And it had only been hours. How did he think he could do this alone?

"Whatever is going on is taking its toll on you. You can no' keep it to yourself because you need to be entirely focused on this current issue."

"I'm aware."

"Then talk to me," Osric beseeched.

If any might understand and give Ailis a chance, it was Osric. Or Lennox could get this entirely wrong, and his best friend—his brother—could go after her. Which would send Ailis to the doorway and out of every dragon's reach. Including his. Forever.

"Lennox."

He took a deep breath and released it. *"I need to show you something first. In your mountain."*

"Of course."

Lennox followed him the short distance to Osric's mountain. The entry was halfway up the side of the peak. The cavern wasn't the size of his. It was a tight fit, but they managed. It wouldn't be for long, anyway.

"No more delaying. What is it?" Osric pressed.

Lennox didn't say anything. Instead, he shifted.

Osric jerked back in surprise so hard that he crashed into a wall, sending rocks cascading around them. *"What the bloody hell?"*

"It's still me, brother," Lennox hurried to say as his magic kept the debris from crashing into him.

Osric stared at him for a long moment before leaning close and eyeing him. Shock and wariness vibrated off him. *"But…how?"*

"That, I can no' explain. It just happened."

"When?" Osric asked, relaxing.

"A handful of days ago."

"And you're just now telling me!?"

Lennox winced at the shout in his head.

Osric walked around him, his curiosity piqued. *"And you can still converse with dragons?"*

"I wasna sure until I tested it with you."

"What is this shape you're in? And what is covering you?"

Lennox looked down at the pants. It was the only garment he had called. *"They're trousers,"* he answered, deciding not to answer the first question.

"Lennox, have you seen your back?" Osric asked in a soft voice.

That was the reason he hadn't clothed his top half—that and because he hated the restriction. *"Aye."*

Osric walked back around to face him. *"What does all this mean? And what does it have to do with your mate?"*

Now came the time for Lennox to decide what, if anything, to tell Osric about Ailis. He had already come this far. Why not go all the way? *"Again, it's better if I show you."*

"There's more?"

"Oh, aye. If you're up for it."

Osric grunted, giving him a flat look in answer.

Lennox returned to his dragon form and launched himself from the mountain. He and Osric flew to where Ailis had marked the doorway. They landed in the Trocana Glen.

Lennox faced the doorway and waited. Osric came to stand beside him.

"*What are we looking at?*"

"*You can no' see it either?*" Lennox asked.

Osric looked around. "*See what?*"

"*Those rocks there. They mark a doorway.*"

"*A what?*"

Lennox tried not to take offense at the doubt in his friend's voice. "*An opening created by another being called a Fae from another realm.*"

Osric's head swung to him, his gaze searching as uncertainty tightened his face. "*You're no' joking.*"

"*Nay, I'm no'.*"

"*I'm guessing Ailis is a Fae.*"

Lennox nodded once.

"*This is how she got here?*" Osric asked as he gazed at the space where the doorway was marked.

"*It is.*"

"*How many Fae are here?*"

"*Just her.*"

"*Are more coming?*"

"*She locked the door. No one can use it either way.*"

Osric walked around the rocks, sniffing the area. "*We only have her word about that.*"

"*Aye.*"

"*You mean we could go through it to her world?*"

"*I believe so.*"

"*I doona like that we can no' see it.*"

"*That is a major concern.*"

Osric stood in front of him, then raised his head and asked,

"Obviously, you believe her."

"I do."

"Because she's your mate?"

Lennox hesitated for only a moment. *"She is."*

"Do Fae look like what you turned into?"

"They do."

"Shite. This is a lot, brother."

"Now do you understand why I was hesitant to share?"

Osric poked a finger between the rocks and met resistance. He grunted in surprise. *"I do."*

"You didna believe me?"

His friend gave him a sheepish look and shrugged. *"Difficult to believe what I can no' see."*

"Point taken."

They shared a grin. Osric's faded. *"I take it Ailis is here. Now."*

Lennox almost lied. Osric wasn't giving his thoughts away, and Lennox didn't want Ailis to leave because Osric went after her. Like before, he had come this far. There was no turning back now. *"She is."*

"Can I meet her?

"You willna be able to communicate with her. I found that out when our paths crossed. That's when I shifted."

Osric drew in a long breath and released it, nodding slowly. He looked at the doorway and was silent before he turned back to Lennox. *"Does it hurt when you change?"*

"Initially."

Osric hit his wing against Lennox. *"You found your mate. That's cause for celebration, and yet I see my friend weighed down with worry."*

skull to its shoulders, where the enormous wings began. They were folded neatly, the tail lying still behind him.

"Osric, this is Ailis," Lennox said. "Ailis, Osric, King of Blacks."

She licked her lips. "Hello."

Osric shook his head and made a sound that could only be described as a pain-filled rumble. His black talons cut into the rock floor as a shudder ran through him. And then the dragon was gone, leaving a male on his hands and knees.

Lennox released her and rushed to his friend. Ailis stared in shock as Osric wobbled when he got to his feet. No words passed between the two Kings, and she never wished to hear telepathic voices more than she did at that moment. Instead, she remained rooted to the spot, noting the differences between the two Kings.

Where Lennox had long, blond hair, Osric's was black as night and fell thick and straight to the middle of his back. Where Lennox had sun-kissed skin, Osric's was a warm brown. Lennox had pale green eyes, and Osric's were a deep, rich russet. Ailis also caught sight of the same red and black markings on Osric's right chest and arm. She couldn't make out the design, but she had a feeling it was a dragon.

Lennox shot her a quick look as he steadied Osric. Ailis recalled how confused Lennox had been after he shifted. He had touched his face and hair while trying to figure out what had happened. Osric had the same confused look while doing the same. She might have helped Lennox by telling him what his hair was, but she hadn't fully understood the changes in him. At least Osric had Lennox to aid in the transition.

"This is Ailis's language. It'll take a moment, but you'll get it," Lennox said.

Osric's dark eyes moved around Lennox to spear her with an unfathomable look before he returned his attention to Lennox.

"I can no' explain how I understood her words so easily," Lennox continued. "But you'll pick it up just as quickly."

"Aye. I understand."

Osric's voice was just as rough as Lennox's was the first time he spoke. She had never asked Lennox what had gone through his mind after he shifted, but now she wished she had. Maybe then she would have an idea of the direction of Osric's thoughts.

Lennox turned to Ailis. "Is it your magic causing us to shift?"

"Not that I know of." She briefly looked at Osric, who now stared openly at her. It would be easier if she knew whether he would be hostile toward her. At the moment, he showed nothing. And that was so much worse.

Lennox walked to her. "He wanted to see you. I thought I'd have to be the go-between for any conversations. But now…" He swung his gaze to Osric, who stood naked, slightly apart from them.

"I'm sure you have many questions," she told the King of Blacks.

Osric's gaze moved between her and Lennox, then down to their joined hands. But he said nothing. At least not out loud. For all she knew, he and Lennox were communicating.

Lennox jerked his chin to Osric. "You asked about the

dragon marking on my back. You have one of your own, brother."

Osric looked down at his body. He flexed his right arm, testing it. Then he smoothed his left hand over the dragon on his chest. "I doona feel anything."

"Neither did Ailis," Lennox said.

At the mention of her name, Osric's gaze returned to her. Standing still under his scrutiny was the hardest thing she had ever done.

"She covers everything while you only have one item," Osric said to Lennox.

Lennox chuckled. "That's because I hate the confines of clothes. I tried them all, including the boots, but it wasna to my liking."

"Why do you wear such things?" Osric asked her.

Ailis shrugged. "It's what my people do. It's a form of fashion. There are different styles and colors of clothing."

"But…why?" Osric asked, his face creasing in confusion.

Ailis chuckled as she glanced at Lennox. "I don't have an answer."

Osric didn't say more as he looked at Lennox's trousers. A moment later, a pair covered him. He grimaced as he moved around. "I doona like these."

"They're easier than the rest," Lennox told him.

Osric hesitantly took a few steps before he got the hang of walking in his new form and moved toward them. "This is verra strange."

"Indeed," Lennox murmured.

Osric sighed and pinned Ailis with a look. "Lennox shared

some of your culture with me. My greatest worry is also his. We can no' see this doorway you came through."

"I wish I knew why. For me, it stands out like a beacon," she said.

"How soon will more Fae come?"

She shook her head. "I can't say. No one knows I'm here."

"But when you return and tell others?"

Ailis met Lennox's gaze. "I don't intend to tell anyone. Ever."

Osric grunted. "You can no' promise that."

"She can, and she has," Lennox stated, a hard edge to his voice that she hadn't heard before.

Ailis slid her gaze to Osric. "I left the Fae Realm because there is nothing there for me. I attempted what others long believed was impossible. I learned for months, strengthening my magic and studying everything I could get my hands on to achieve the unfeasible. I had nothing to lose. I even stole a book to get here."

"A book?" Osric repeated.

Lennox spoke before she could. "It's their language in written form."

Ailis held out the book in her other hand to Osric. He took it, running his fingers over it almost exactly as Lennox had done. He looked at his fingers before spreading his entire hand over the book.

"Look inside," Lennox urged.

Osric did as instructed. His eyes widened at what he saw. "This is your language?"

"It is. We have hundreds of thousands of books," she explained.

Lennox motioned to the tome. "Some with facts, and others with made-up stories."

"I can read this," Osric said in a voice edged with excitement.

Lennox's grin grew. "Aye."

"This is incredible." Osric flipped through pages, pausing to read a few lines before he flipped some more. Suddenly, he snapped the book shut. "You stole this?"

Ailis nodded. "Not that one. It was another one."

"The Fae could guess what you've done, then," he stated.

She flattened her lips and sighed, realizing the truth of his words. "They could. They probably will, but they have no idea where I've gone. Nor can they follow me. Most likely, they'll assume I failed and died, caught somewhere between realms where I'll remain forever. Even if they find my doorway, nothing they do will unlock it."

"Fate brought her here, brother," Lennox said.

Osric grunted. "It certainly appears so."

Ailis might no longer feel that Osric would lash out at her, but she also didn't think he had completely accepted her. Which she understood. She was a stranger in their land, and her arrival had caused disruption among the Dragon Kings. Lennox had once said he feared all dragons would shift as he had and never be able to return to their true forms. What if he was right? What if she was the catalyst that altered their very way of life? Could she really stay knowing that? Could she do that to Lennox?

"I know why you kept all this a secret," Osric said to Lennox. "I would have, as well. But she willna stay concealed forever. Someone will see her."

"I don't plan on leaving the mountain," she stated.

Osric's dark eyes cut to her. "You came to explore, and you're satisfied with one mountain?"

"The last thing I want is to cause any kind of trouble—"

"Too late," Osric replied.

Lennox glared at him, but Osric didn't seem to notice.

Ailis tightened her fingers around Lennox's. "I'm sure you have many concerns. How can a Fae know they've found their mate? Do we know ours as dragons do? I can say that we don't. I know the right thing to do would have been to leave as soon as I came upon Lennox, but I didn't. Knowing him and learning about the dragons and this world…it has left a mark on me that will remain for the rest of my life. I don't belong here. I doubt any dragons will accept me." She looked at Lennox. "We've discussed this."

"You wanted to leave," he said.

She shook her head. "I don't want to leave. Ever. But I fear it will be the only solution. Osric's right. You can't hide me forever. Nor can you tell your realm about me. That leaves us where we've been from the start."

Lennox pulled her to him, his arms going around her in a tight embrace. "There has to be a solution."

"Agreed," Osric said. "We'll figure something out."

Ailis leaned back to look from Lennox to Osric.

It was Lennox who answered her silent question. "The Kings met earlier to discuss a mating of two dragons no' from the same clan."

"You and Lennox are no different," Osric added.

She flattened her hands on Lennox's chest. "But I'm not a dragon."

"It's still the same issue." Osric grinned as he looked between them. "My brother has found his mate, and that means we need to figure out a way for the two of you to be together."

CHAPTER TWENTY-ONE

Lennox sagged with relief. The interaction between Osric and Ailis could've gone a hundred different ways. He'd held out hope, but when Osric shifted, Lennox had been worried things would go sideways.

He met Osric's eyes. The color change was different. He looked nothing like the black dragon Lennox had always known, but then again, Lennox also appeared different from his true form. And while he liked that Osric and Ailis could speak directly to each other, it didn't alleviate his growing concerns that all the dragons might shift around her.

Because it was Ailis that'd caused the change. It had to be. She was the only common factor.

Lennox held Ailis's gaze as she searched his face. She looked from him to Osric. Lennox wished he knew what she was thinking. She kept it to herself. Neither speaking her mind nor posing questions. And that worried him.

"What is it?" he pressed.

She sighed as she dragged her gaze back to him. "How long have dragons lived on this realm?"

"Eons," Osric answered before he could.

Ailis red eyes briefly lowered to Lennox's chest. "In all that time, you're saying no dragon has mated outside their clan?"

"Aye," Lennox reluctantly replied.

Ailis smoothed her hands down his chest and pulled out of his arms. "I'm happy that Osric is willing to help, but I fear nothing will change."

"It's time for a change," Osric stated. "It's been time. Other Kings in Lennox's position have no' had the courage to put anything in action. Lennox is motivated like none before him."

Lennox nodded. "He's right."

"How resistant will the other Kings be?" she asked.

Lennox shrugged. "We're divided. I've sent them back to their clans to think about both sides. In the meantime, I'm going to talk to the two who wish to be mated."

"The best option is for Lennox to create another clan. One where any dragon from any clan can join if they wish to mate outside their clan. Or if they just want to leave their clan," Osric explained.

Ailis's brows snapped together. "I thought the clans took care of their own."

"They do, for the most part," Lennox told her.

Osric shrugged. "The clan is a large family. At times, someone doesna feel as if they fit in, or there is an argument. It doesna happen often, but it does occur."

"My father left his family because he fell in love with my

mother." Ailis sat on a rock. "Mum's family banished her. They had no one."

Osric's brows rose as he nodded. "Exactly! Things happen. Another clan is the best solution."

"Can you make a new clan?" Ailis asked Lennox.

He shrugged as he crossed his arms over his chest. "I have the power to do it, aye."

"You might have the authority, but so did other Kings of Kings. Why didn't they set something up?"

He glanced at Osric. "There are many reasons."

"Lennox," she said softly when he didn't explain.

She would keep pushing until she got an answer. There was no use beating around the bush. He might as well tell her now. "Because it would disrupt the order of things. Because there will be many who fight against it. Clans will erupt into chaos as soon as someone leaves."

"Change in any form is always difficult, but the end result can be beneficial in many ways."

"I know." And he did—more than most.

Osric cleared his throat. "This may take some time. None of it will happen quickly. Even if Lennox decides to create a new clan right now, the transition will take many, many decades."

Lennox tried to imagine Ailis's life stuck in his mountain, leaving only occasionally as they had done the other night.

Her mouth softened into a grin. "I would get to remain with you, though?"

"Aye." He'd make sure of it.

"Then I don't see a problem."

Lennox dropped his arms and closed the distance between

them. He cupped her face in his hands, her fingers gently wrapping around his wrists before he pressed his lips to hers.

"As happy as I am for you both, I think it's time I left," Osric said.

Lennox chuckled and released Ailis. "Understandable."

"So, how do I…?" Osric's lips twisted. "How do I change back?"

"All I did was think about it, and it happened. Just be mindful of where you are. I've hit my head a few times."

"Good advice." Osric turned to Ailis. "It was nice meeting you. I hope we get to speak again soon."

She smiled and nodded. "Agreed. And thank you for being such a good friend to Lennox."

Osric met his gaze before stepping back a few paces and returning to dragon form. *"Walk with me,"* he bade Lennox.

Lennox turned to Ailis. "I'll return shortly."

"Of course," she replied.

Lennox waited until Osric left before walking to the center of the cavern and shifting. Then he trailed behind his friend out of the mountain. *"What is it?"*

"Do you…feel things…differently in the other form?"

"Aye. The skin is much thinner than our scales. There seem to be many more nerves than what we have with these," he said as he lifted his hand.

"The hardest part was no' having my tail or wings. How do you get used to that?"

Lennox shook his head. *"I'm no' sure I ever will."*

"Do you think I'll be able to shift without being in front of Ailis? I didna get to spend as much time with the new body since my thoughts were on the two of you."

"*Maybe. You can try. Just make sure no one is around.*"

Osric shot him a flat look. "*As if you need to remind me. I willna do anything outside my mountain.*"

"*It's a lot to take in all at once.*"

"*It made it easy to communicate with her, but I honestly can no' say that I would've done it had I been given a choice.*"

Lennox grunted in agreement. "*It happened without any warning for me, as well.*"

"*You were right about the initial pain. It was intense but left almost immediately. What I'm really curious about is the dragon markings on us both.*"

"*On different areas of our body.*"

Osric's red eyes narrowed slightly. "*You really doona believe Ailis caused the shift in us?*"

"*She was as surprised as I was. Same with you. If she's doing it, she isna aware of it. The magic of our realm is powerful, brother. There's a real possibility that it triggered the change in our appearance so we could talk to Ailis.*"

"*Aye,*" Osric murmured. "*I had that same thought. It would be easier if it was Ailis. If it is the magic, we may never figure out the why.*"

"*The why is obvious. Ailis was a stranger. A different species to our world. How else were we to know what she wanted?*"

"*You know if any other dragon had found her—King or no'—they probably would've killed her on sight.*"

Just the thought of that made Lennox's gut clench. "*I know.*"

"*Yet she came upon you.*" Osric shook his head in bemusement. "*It's as if the two of you were meant to meet.*"

"*Fated.*"

"*Your mate.*" Osric paused, his gaze moving to the side and going distant. "*I meant what I said. We will figure out a way. It's time for change. We both know it.*"

"*Do I? Or am I deciding based solely on my own desires?*"

Osric's gaze slid back to him. "*We both know the magic would replace you if it thought for an instant that you were no longer the right dragon.*"

"*I wish we could talk to the magic. It would make things easier.*"

"*Ha,*" Osric said with a roll of his eyes. "*There's nothing easy about being a King. I've never envied you as King of Kings. You have double the duty. Triple, actually, because corralling other Kings is much more difficult than a clan.*"

Lennox laughed. "*It certainly is.*"

"*When are you going to talk to the couple?*"

"*Soon.*"

"*You'll be gone at least a day.*"

He looked back at his mountain. "*Ailis can handle herself. She crossed realms, remember?*"

"*I'll remain at the capital. Just in case. I want some time alone anyway. I need to process Ailis, the Fae, and my change.*"

"*You're handling things remarkably well.*"

Osric snorted loudly. "*Would you rather I rail about it? Ailis is here, and you've fallen for her. There's no changing that. You're my brother, and I've always believed we should get to be with our mates, whoever they may be. However, I'm concerned about the shifting.*"

"That's been on my mind from the beginning. More so now that you changed. We're dragons. What if we all shift? And what if we can no' return to our true forms?"

"I thought about that, too. We could test the theory. Bring Ailis around other dragons and see if they shift."

Lennox shook his head. *"I doona think it's time for that."*

"We need facts."

"We do, but I have another matter that takes precedence right now. Ailis wants to stay. If she feels threatened, she'll leave."

Osric's nostrils flared as he drew in a breath. *"I see your point. One step at a time, then. I'll be here. Go take care of business."*

"Contact me if there's a problem. I'm sure Ailis wouldna mind answering any questions you might have."

"That would require me to enter your mountain. I'd rather no' until you return."

"Fair enough."

"Good luck, brother," Osric said before flying to his mountain.

Lennox turned and made his way back to his. Once he was inside, he shifted and found Ailis standing in the doorway of the cavern.

"How did he take the shifting?" she asked.

Lennox shrugged. "He didna have time to really process things since we were discussing us. He needs time."

"I don't think I'm responsible for it, but I was around both of you when it happened."

He reached for her, taking her hand and pulling her toward him. "We'll sort things out somehow."

She gave him a soft, lingering kiss. Then she looked into his eyes. "Will we?"

"Why do you ask that?"

"Because I know what you didn't say."

He should've known she would piece things together.

"If you leave your clan, you won't be a King."

Lennox released a long breath. "Nay."

"Do Dragon Kings step away from their roles?"

"There's only one way a King leaves his position."

Concern clouded her face. "Death."

"Aye."

"If things remain as they are, no one has to know about me. We can live in secret just as we have been."

Lennox tightened his arms around her. "That isna a life for anyone. And it isna just us."

"I forgot about the dragon couple." Sadness filled her eyes. "If I wasn't here, if you found your mate with a dragon, what would you do?"

"The same thing I'm doing now. I need to consider all sides. Darald brought the complaint to the Kings. I'll leave shortly to talk to each of the dragons separately and then together. I also plan to have a conversation with the respective Kings."

She smoothed her fingers through the hair at his temples, moving it from his face. "You're going to the clans, right?"

"I am."

"Talk to some of the dragons there. Away from their Kings. Get their thoughts."

"That's a good idea."

She grinned, shrugging. "It's what I'd want someone in

power to do for me. Their lives will change with one decision. For some, things will get better. For others, they'll get worse. If you don't do anything, the reverse is true."

"No matter what I choose, there will be anger and resentment."

"That is the way of things."

He pressed a kiss to her forehead. "Osric was right. Everyone should be able to be with their mate, regardless of who it is."

"Then you've already made your decision?"

"I know what should've been done ages ago."

She cupped his face and tilted it down until he looked at her. "Knowing what should be done and doing it are two different things. The magic chose you as King of Kings because it knew you were the right dragon. You'll do the right thing."

CHAPTER TWENTY-TWO

Ailis's words stayed with Lennox as he made the trip west toward the Yellows to speak to the female first. He flew for hours, crossing many territories. As he did, Lennox looked down at the land and wondered about the workings of each clan. The magic ensured that the clans had the fiercest, most powerful dragon as their leaders. There were no Queens, simply because the males were much bigger, and that automatically made them physically stronger.

He wondered at the dynamics of each clan. His was far from perfect, but none were. There was always a hierarchy in the clans, and that could make life for those on the lower end of things particularly challenging. He should know.

But would changing things be better?

No decision would solve everyone's problems. There would always be those who got the raw end of the deal. As much as he wished otherwise, there was no getting around that fact.

When Lennox approached Darald's territory, the King of Yellows flew to meet him. They had a quick greeting that was far from pleasant before Darald led him to the clan. He didn't need Darald for that. It was Darald's way of stating his authority. As King of Kings, Lennox couldn't be turned away from any clan. Ever. That didn't always mean he was welcome, though. And by the stony looks of those coming out to see him, most weren't pleased by his arrival.

"I've come to speak to the female. What is her name?" Lennox asked Darald.

"Noma. I'll have her brought to you."

"I'll go to her," Lennox replied evenly. It was time Darald realized who was in charge. *"I wish to speak privately."*

Darald's orange eyes narrowed slightly before he gave a serene nod. *"Of course."*

Lennox didn't let his guard down. Darald was vexed, but he hadn't questioned Lennox. No doubt it would come when they spoke later. *"Point me in the direction. I'll find Noma."*

Darald did as requested, and Lennox quickly left to seek out the female. He found her with her family a short time later. Lennox circled them once and landed before the family of seven. They bowed their heads to him in respect, something he never took for granted.

"I'm sorry to disturb your day," Lennox began. *"I wondered if I could have a word with Noma."*

The father nudged one of the children with his wing. *"Certainly, sire."*

"Thank you," the mother hurriedly said. *"For coming. It means a lot to all of us that you would take the time to talk to*

us rather than make a hasty decision. Even if it is the same choice other Kings of Kings have made."

"It is no simple thing for a dragon to find their mate. It's my duty to take any issue seriously, and there's nothing more important than this." Lennox turned his attention to Noma.

The young dragon stepped forward hesitantly. She wouldn't meet Lennox's gaze for more than a heartbeat, but she didn't shrink away either. He remained silent until the rest of the family left, giving them privacy. Then he turned to look at the surroundings. Most of the territory for the Yellows was flat with mountains far to the north and oceans to the east.

"Your declaration has caused a bit of a ripple," he stated.

"If I had a choice, none of this would've happened."

Lennox turned his head to her and found her gray eyes locked on him. *"You're certain about your mate?"*

"I am, sire. I wouldn't risk my family and clan if I weren't. There's no mistaking what Ariston and I feel."

"There will be some who say otherwise."

She lifted her chin. *"That's because they can't think outside of what has always been. They're afraid of change and what might come after. We're dragons, sire. Every being on this realm fears us. We should blaze a trail of inclusion and revolution instead of being rooted in tenets that no longer serve."*

Lennox admired her courage to stand up for what she believed in when so many others—including her own clan— didn't. She would make a formidable Queen. *"You're verra outspoken. How is that going with Darald?"*

"As you could expect."

"*Aye,*" Lennox said with a nod of understanding. "*If I sanction this mating, where would the two of you live?*"

Noma shifted from foot to foot before wrapping her tail tightly around her middle as if fortifying herself. "*My parents have reluctantly offered us shelter here.*"

"*You doona seem keen on that idea.*"

"*Ariston will be an outsider.*"

"*The same will happen if you go to his clan.*"

She released a long sigh filled with resentment. "*We're all too aware of our predicament. There's nowhere we can go to be together, but…we can't be apart either.*"

"*What if there was a place for you to go?*"

Her head snapped to him, the faintest glimmer of hope in her gray eyes. It struck Lennox hard. He prayed he hadn't said too much. Hope was a tricky emotion. It could pull someone from the ashes…or obliterate them with a whisper when it was yanked away.

"*Where?*" she asked breathlessly.

"*It's simply a question, Noma. A what-if. Nothing more. Nothing less.*"

"*I understand.*" Her voice was calm, but her eyes danced with excitement. "*If there were such a location, we'd go.*"

Lennox wasn't shocked by her answer. "*You speak for Ariston?*"

"*We want to be together.*"

"*It doesna matter where the two of you are, nothing will be easy. You realize that, aye?*"

Her chin lifted once more, this time with defiance. "*Life is hard, my King. At least we would have each other. At least we would live.*"

Lennox's thoughts turned to Ailis, and he couldn't help but agree with Noma. *"And children? Have you thought about that?"*

"I have."

He remained silent, waiting while trying his best not to imagine what a child between him and Ailis would look like.

"Their life would be even harder," she finally answered, her voice so soft he barely heard it. Then she straightened to her full height. *"None of that changes the fact that Ariston is my mate."*

"Thank you for being so candid. I imagine things in your clan have been difficult."

"For my family, as well," she replied.

"Do any in your clan support you?"

"Oh, aye. Absolutely. They don't dare speak out, though."

And he knew why. Darald was against such a union, and none dared to speak out against their King publicly. *"I see. That's all I have for now. You can go unless you wish to ask me something."*

"I just want to repeat what Mum said. Thank you for coming." She bowed her head low.

Lennox returned the bow and watched her fly away. Then he started back to the seat of the Yellows, where every King of the clan lived. He spotted dragons flying near him and detoured to speak to them. Three of the five were adamantly against the union of Noma and Ariston, but two were in favor. Lennox asked seven other dragons with the same mixed results.

He was no closer to knowing what to do when he landed in front of Darald. The King of Yellows stood brazenly, annoyance in his gaze. Lennox ignored the look and strode past him into the cave entrance that took them belowground.

"*I hear you've asked my clan what they think of the union,*" Darald stated.

"*I have.*"

"*Why?*"

Lennox turned to face him. It would be easy to unleash his wrath, but that was exactly what Darald wanted. So, he did the opposite. "*It's what I expect you to do as a King, Darald. Our opinions doona matter. We're chosen to lead our clans, not propel our own agendas.*"

"*Past King of Kings have left things as they were for a reason.*"

"*Past being the operative word.*"

"*You're going to allow them to be mated,*" Darald stated with a sneer. "*I knew it.*"

Lennox fought against the explosion of rage that welled up. If Darald reacted this way to one of his clan finding her mate with another, Lennox couldn't imagine what he would think about Ailis. "*I've no' decided anything yet. I'm gathering facts. I'm talking to others. I'm getting a sense of how the dragons feel.*"

"*We both know you've already made your decision.*"

He and Darald had never been close, but there hadn't been outright animosity like there was now. "*What are you afraid of, Darald? This is Noma's and Ariston's life. No' yours.*"

"*It would set a precedent. Things are as they are for a reason, Lennox. Can you no' see that?*" Darald asked, exasperation dripping from his words.

"*You know Noma could leave at any time. Neither she nor*"

Ariston need your or Rolf's permission to mate. They need no one's approval, actually. She's remained out of respect for her family, her clan, and you."

Darald looked away, his face tight and closed off. *"We're no' meant to mix clans, Lennox. It is wrong. Verra wrong."*

"She found her mate. You would deny her that?"

"I doona wish to, but it must happen."

"You're so afraid of change that you would make her and Ariston suffer? Force both their families to watch their agony as they each die?"

Darald swung his head around and met Lennox's gaze. *"I'm no' the first King to do it, and I willna be the last."*

"What if it was you who found a mate outside your clan?"

"There would be no need to share the information and cause disruption throughout two clans."

"You say that despite having a mate. You can no' declare such things when you doona know what it's like for those who can no' be with their mate."

Darald said nothing in response.

Nothing Lennox said would get through to him. Not now. Possibly not ever. *"I'll call for the Kings after I've finished my investigation."*

Darald didn't follow him out. It was a much shorter flight from the Yellows to the Coppers across the border. The same border where Noma and Ariston had met. Rolf didn't come out to meet Lennox. Instead, the King of Coppers stood at the seat of their rulers and waited for him.

Rolf was somber as he greeted his King. *"I didna expect you so soon."*

"I thought it better for everyone to sort things out quickly."

"Quite right. Have you spoken to Noma?"

"I have."

"And?" Rolf asked, his curiosity clear.

Lennox noted that the Coppers kept their distance from him and Rolf, allowing them to speak privately. The differences between the two clans were clear with just a glance. *"She's smart and brave. She knows her mind."*

"Ariston, too," he said with a long sigh. *"I had hoped the two were mistaken."*

"It has happened, though it's rare."

"Their lives will be harsher than they understand." He sighed again. *"Would you like me to bring Ariston to you, or would you rather go to him? You can use my cave for privacy."*

Lennox glanced at the other dragons milling about. All of them looked as miserable and desolate as Rolf. *"Bring him here, if you doona mind."*

"It's done," Rolf said a heartbeat later.

"What are your thoughts about the matter?"

Rolf opened his wings slightly and then snapped them closed. *"My sister found her mate outside our clan. It was all my father could talk about for years. There's no forgetting the sight of what happened to her. It haunts my entire family. There will always be those who find their mates outside the clan, and they shouldna be punished for it."*

"You would change things if you were in my place?"

"In a heartbeat. Though I'm no' naïve enough to think there willna be massive repercussions."

Lennox nodded once. *"Aye."*

"You're doing more than past King of Kings, Lennox. You're speaking to others and giving them a voice. It's a step none have taken before."

Ariston's arrival cut their discussion short. The young dragon hovered in the air until Lennox called him down. Rolf exchanged a look with the youngster before walking away.

"I think it would be better to have this conversation somewhere private," Lennox said. He motioned Ariston to follow as he made his way through the wide entrance at the base of the snow-capped mountain.

"I willna change my mind. I can no'," Ariston said before they reached the cavern.

Lennox entered the cave and faced the dragon. *"I'm no' asking you to."*

"Noma's my mate, sire. Neither of us wanted this, but it happened."

"I've spoken with her."

"She told me. She also told me everything you said. If there is a place we could go, we'd accept that."

Lennox eyed the dragon. *"So Noma said. Did she also tell you that I asked about bairns?"*

"Aye." Ariston swallowed loudly, his worry evident. *"I didna think that far ahead, but it still doesna change things."*

"How does your family feel?"

"They're upset. Obviously."

"Would they support you?"

Ariston's navy eyes flashed. *"They're my family. They know this isna something I have control over. They're there for whatever we need. Noma and I belong together, sire. No one has the right to stand in our way."*

He was correct. No one had that right.

CHAPTER TWENTY-THREE

Ailis walked along the water's edge. She only kept the candles near the bed lit. Just in case. Lennox said that no one would dare enter his cave without permission, but she didn't want to give anyone reason to investigate.

Her thoughts drifted from her meeting with Osric to Lennox venturing off to speak to the dragons from different clans who wanted to be mated. Ailis tried not to think that her arrival had somehow caused the division between the clans, but it was difficult for her mind not to go there. Whether she was the trigger or not, Lennox and Osric had shifted in her presence.

That was worrisome for them. It certainly was for her. She had thought that shifting was perhaps something special that Lennox could do. Then Osric had transformed and forced her to rethink everything.

Knowing what should be done and actually doing it were two different things. She knew the best course of action would be to leave Earth. Lennox could go back to his life without keeping a secret or worrying the Kings would find out. Her heart would remain behind, but knowing Lennox was safe would keep her going. She would spend the rest of her days alone—however long that might be. Because she wouldn't return to her realm. She would seek out another. Perhaps she could find a place to live. Maybe she'd have to go to yet another realm. It was also entirely possible that she would fail and get caught between realms.

She had a bleak future ahead of her, no matter how she looked at it.

That was *if* she could leave. They had discussed it, and she had thought about it. Both of those were altogether different from actually doing the deed. Ailis wasn't sure she was that strong. What she found with Lennox was unexpected and astonishing. Even before they had ever touched, she had felt a pull toward him. Like an invisible connection linked them, becoming stronger and more intense the closer they got to each other.

He spoke of destiny. She had wanted to dismiss his words, but she couldn't. The way they were drawn together, the passion between them, it was too tangible to reject. They had been brought together. Fate, destiny, or some higher power had set this plan in motion. She could look back and see all the reasons she'd come to this realm. What she couldn't see was the future. She had no idea what she should do.

Ailis wanted to stay. With every fiber of her being, she wanted to remain. She wanted to spend her life loving Lennox and sharing the ups and downs. She wanted long discussions and even arguments so they could make up with kisses and mind-blowing sex. She wanted to explore every corner of the realm with him. She wanted to meet other dragons, to see them hatch, fly, and live their lives.

She wanted it all.

And a part of her feared that was asking too much.

She stopped when she came to the wall where the water narrowed and continued flowing to the next mountain. Ailis turned on her heel and retraced her steps. There was no one here she could talk to. No friends or family. Not that she would ask Bea what to do even if her aunt were here. Bea's response was always to follow her heart. Well, Ailis's heart belonged to Lennox.

The love she had for him was bigger, stronger, and more encompassing than she thought possible. And that love had her thinking about the dragons and any changes that might arise from her remaining on the realm.

Change was inevitable. It happened regardless of what anyone thought or if they tried to stop it. By Osric's account, it was long past time for someone in Lennox's position to allow dragons from different clans to mate. She saw in Lennox's eyes that he agreed with his friend, but that didn't mean he would amend the current decree. For one simple reason: the resulting consequences.

Even she could see that while the current directive was far from great, it was part of the dragon culture. Those who found their mates outside the clans suffered, but they got over it. Altering it would result in utter chaos. Not to mention the formation of a new clan.

All she had to do was look at her parents for confirmation. They had followed their hearts and ignored their family's wishes. Her father had left his ways behind to become Dark. Without support from his family and friends, all he had was her mother. As for her mum, she went back on her word about marrying someone from a very powerful Dark family that her father had chosen to strengthen their family alliance. The result had been a war between the two families that had lasted hundreds of years.

Neither of her parents had any kind of support system. They hadn't cared. They'd trusted that their love would give them everything they needed. If Bea was to be believed, it had. At least for a while. They leaned on each other, which had brought them closer. Neither had status in the community, though, which made it more challenging for them to achieve anything. Ailis barely remembered her parents. She didn't know if they'd fought or not. She remembered her mother humming to her at night and how she used to ride on her father's back as he crawled on his hands and knees pretending to be a horse.

After that, Bea was all there was. She was the one who'd protected Ailis from everything—including her own family, who wanted to exact revenge at first and then secure a marriage later.

Single, do-whatever-I-want Bea, who had lovers aplenty but never found anyone worthy to hand over her heart. That was who Ailis had as a role model for relationships. Bea and stories of her parents that may or may not be true.

Ailis never imagined that she would have to decide on her happiness or what was right for a realm. She changed direction and walked to the bed. Pausing beside it, she wondered if she would ever be able to look at a bed again and not think about Lennox's hard body, their tangled limbs, and her sighs of pleasure. Or the way he held her as she drifted off to sleep.

She removed her shoes and crawled under the covers. With a thought, she put out the candles. She cradled Lennox's pillow as she rolled onto her side and shut her eyes. It had been a long day, but the night would be even longer.

Ailis.

The sound of Lennox's voice as he called to her had her bolting upright, sleep forgotten. She knew exactly where he was, and she didn't hesitate to jump to him. She found him standing in moonlight beneath a frozen waterfall.

"I wasna sure it would work."

She threw herself at him. He caught her, holding her tightly as she buried her head in the crook of his neck. "I heard you. I'll always hear you."

"You're shivering, lass."

It was cold, but his warmth surrounded her.

"What is it?" he asked. "Did something happen?"

She shook her head and leaned back to look at him. "I'm just happy to see you."

"Perhaps I should go away more often," he teased.

"I'd rather you didn't." Ailis looked around then. The frozen waterfall was massive, the long shards of water coming to a lethal point about fifteen feet above them. "Where are we?"

"The northern territories. This is one of the areas Osric spoke about that belongs to a clan but isna used."

The icy desolation was probably why, but she kept that to herself. Ailis used her magic to cover herself with a jacket and thick boots, though she noticed that Lennox wore only his trousers. "Are you not chilled?"

"Nay," he said as he released her and moved to stand beside her. They faced the white world beyond them. "You wanted to see snow."

Ailis grinned as she looked out over the landscape blanketed by endless white against the backdrop of the midnight sky. "So I did."

The trees were so thickly covered with snow that their shapes were barely discernable. Some were bent over from the weight of the white powder. She spotted large footprints, which must have come from Lennox when he arrived. The depressions went at least waist-deep on her.

Movement caught her eye. She spotted a small creature with white fur, large, pointy ears, and a fluffy tail darting from behind a tree. It leaped into the air and dove into the snow. When it came up again, it had an animal in its mouth. It ran away to consume its meal.

"It's crazy how something that can look so bleak can also be so striking."

Lennox nudged her with his elbow before pointing up. "Take a look at the water."

She moved from beneath the waterfall. The outside of the frozen water was white and sparkled like crystals, but deep within was the brightest blue she had ever seen.

"Come," Lennox said as he took her hand and led her into the cave behind the waterfall. "There's more."

She hurried after him, a smile on her face. He led her through tunnel after tunnel. She halted to stare in amazement at the frozen world around her, each turn bringing something new and amazing. Bright white cave gave way to various blues, each more beautiful than the last. In some parts, the ice looked to be about thirty feet thick.

Despite the plummeting temperatures, she couldn't get enough. They walked for hours through the maze of passageways until they returned to the waterfall. Ailis could no longer feel her nose, and if it weren't for Lennox's hold, her hand would be completely numb. Yet it was quite possibly the best night of her life.

"Why don't any of the dragons use this?" she asked.

Lennox wrapped an arm around her, bringing her flush against him. "They did at one time, but it's been a few generations since. The Burnt Oranges tend to stick closer to the food source."

"Are you thinking of using this for the new clan? If you create one, that is."

"There is another option."

"Why not create two clans, then?"

He shrugged absently. "Neither of the locations will be easy for the dragons. Food is scarce out here. They'll have to travel far, which will likely mean running into other clans."

"Which would result in a fight, I gather."

"Aye."

He didn't say more, and she took that to mean he didn't wish to speak about it. She leaned her head back against him when he moved behind her and wrapped his arms around her. They looked out from the cave, and suddenly, waves of green, purple, and blue lights began moving in the sky like a child trailing a ribbon behind them as they ran.

"What is that?" she asked in awe.

He pressed the side of his face against hers. "We've always called them the northern lights."

"They're…"

"I know," he said with a soft chuckle. "They amaze me, no matter how many times I see them."

Ailis was absolutely mesmerized. The colors changed, growing darker, then lighter, then darker again as they undulated and swayed. "Does the magic create this?"

"Maybe. I can no' say for sure."

"They look like they go on forever."

"Up here, they almost do."

She wanted a closer look. She wanted to reach up and touch them, and she almost asked him to fly her up. "Is this the only place you can see them?"

"You'll find them all around the upper regions. This is a good night. Sometimes, they are no' so large or bright. We've seen them a few times at the capital, but no' like this. Never like this."

She turned in his arms and looked into his pale green eyes. "Thank you."

"I'm sorry we need to stay hidden."

She shook her head. "Don't say that. It feels like it's just you and me on this realm. And that makes it special."

CHAPTER TWENTY-FOUR

Lennox wished he could've returned to his cave with Ailis, but word had spread among the dragons. They knew he was talking to clans, and they would be looking for him. Lennox made Ailis return to his mountain when she couldn't stop shaking. As soon as she was gone, he shifted and took to the skies.

He altered his course several times, flying over areas he hadn't seen in a few years. The vast oceans where the Clarets dove from lofty heights, their wings tucked against them before plummeting into the water, only to rise with large fish in their jaws.

Then there was the great desert. The ever-changing hills were a sea of sand that stretched as far as one could see. The wind took the grains and created new works of art each day. The desert was one of Lennox's favorite places. Those who didn't live there believed it barren, when in fact, the dessert was plentiful. One just had to know where to look.

He dipped his right wing, turning ever so slightly southeast. He flew for another hour before coming upon the oasis. The palm trees were plentiful, the water clear and blue. The Browns reclined among the trees. The clan was large, and there was only a handful below him, but Lennox took the opportunity to stop and talk to them.

"Sire." One of the largest males rose and bowed his head.

Lennox greeted them all. *"I'm sorry to disturb you. It's been too long since I've come this way, and I couldna resist a look. I've always loved this place. From the first time I saw it."*

"We're honored to have you," the male replied.

Lennox shook his head. *"I only wanted a closer look at this tranquil spot and perhaps a few moments of your time."*

"About the couple from different clans?"

Lennox knew word traveled fast, and this proved it. He inclined his head to the male. *"Aye. I've spoken to each of them, their Kings, and some dragons among their clans. I've also stopped along the way to talk to other dragons to get their thoughts."*

"That's a first."

So many had said those exact words. Lennox wondered why none of the other Kings of Kings had talked to the dragons. Or had they been right, and he was the one in the wrong?

The male glanced around him. *"Are you really interested in what we think?"*

"I am."

"Then I will give you what you ask. I think mating outside

the clans should be allowed. I know it willna be easy for the couples, but it should be their choice."

"*I agree,*" replied a female.

Another older female nodded.

Behind her, an older male growled to show his displeasure. "*It isna so simple as you all think. We have our ways for a reason.*"

"*That doesna make it right,*" the big male replied.

Lennox held up a hand before an argument broke out. "*There are mixed reactions everywhere. As well as good arguments for and against. This is a weighty decision, one I willna make easily. I want to take everything into account.*"

"*You willna please everyone,*" the older male stated.

"*I'm aware. Thank you for sharing the oasis.*"

Lennox spread his wings and launched himself into the air. The dragons were firmly split on what they wanted. There was more for it than he had anticipated, however. That only proved that it might very well be time for a change. But no matter what he decided, there would be an uproar and protests.

He didn't stop again until he spotted his mountain. His gaze darted to the vast Dragonwood. The trees stood tall and sturdy. He had walked among them as a dragon, but only in a few places because he hadn't fit everywhere. However, he'd be able to explore all of it if he shifted. It was a temptation hard to resist.

Lennox greeted the Kings at the capital, but he didn't stop to talk. He landed and entered his mountain. He shifted and didn't bother with pants. Then he jogged to the water cavern, where he found Ailis sitting naked on the bed.

His gaze raked over her beautiful body. She held out her

hand and beckoned him with a finger. He stalked to the bed, desire coursing through him. Once there, he put his knee on the mattress and wound an arm around her.

"You smell like the wind," she told him.

He grinned and looked into her red eyes. "I was racing to get back to you."

"Took you long enough."

He pressed her back onto the bed and braced his hands on either side of her head. "Eager, are we?"

"For you? Always."

"Then perhaps I should make you beg."

"I could return the favor," she replied with a seductive look.

Lennox kneed her legs apart and ground his hard cock against her. "Or I could take you now."

"Stop talking. I need you inside me."

He entered her in one thrust, sighs of pleasure falling from both their lips.

"Do you want to talk about it?"

The question pulled Lennox from his thoughts. He kissed the top of Ailis's head and spread his hand on her back. She was draped over his chest with their legs intertwined, just as he liked her to be. "I doona know where to begin."

"Tell me about the female."

"Noma knows her mind. Neither she nor Ariston are hesitant about what they feel."

Ailis's head lifted, her face slackening with surprise. "You thought they were making it up?"

"No' making it up, but maybe mistaken. It's rare, but it happens."

"I see." She laid back down. "Now that you know what they feel is genuine, does it change your thoughts?"

He grunted. "I wouldna say it changes them exactly. Her family is prepared to welcome Ariston."

"But the clan won't?"

"Some will. Some willna. Darald is against the mating. Rolf, however, supports the couple. He would welcome Noma to his clan, as would Ariston's family."

"That's good, at least, but I have a feeling it still won't be enough."

"Sadly, it willna. I talked to various dragons, and everyone is split."

"Leaving you to shoulder the decision."

He put his free hand behind his head. "It was always going to fall to me."

"I know Osric told you to think about our situation, but I don't think that's wise."

Lennox's brows snapped together. "Why?"

"You must take us out of the equation. This is about more than you or me. This is about your people and their way of life. It's about allowing love to triumph or fear of change and grasping at old ways to win again."

"I know your opinion," he said with a soft chuckle.

She tilted her head to briefly meet his gaze. "I'm not from here. I don't really understand why the change is so difficult, but, aye, I think these couples should be allowed to do what they want. They should have a place to go and thrive. A community of their own, where their children are welcomed and loved. I think there will be more of them than you realize."

"I agree. I know for a fact that dragons have found their mates outside their clans and never disclosed the information."

"They live a lonely life, then. How sad."

Lennox didn't correct her. He didn't know why he didn't tell her what became of a dragon who found their mate and couldn't have them. Even when he knew he should, the words wouldn't come.

"You hesitate to make the decision. Why?"

"Those against it are verra loud. There will rise up to oppose it."

"You're King of Kings."

He wound a midnight lock around his finger. "That doesna mean they willna protest."

"But they must listen to you."

"Aye."

"After you're…gone…can the next King who takes your place undo your decision?"

He thought about that for a moment. It actually hadn't been something he'd considered until she brought it up. "Technically, he could. I'd like to believe he wouldna, but that's just wishful thinking."

"Let's say you do form a new clan, and this couple and others flock to it. They create a community and begin to have children. Would a new King really break that up? It would only create even more upset."

"Depends on who the magic chooses and his thoughts on the matter."

"Did you ever think that perhaps this is the very reason the magic chose you. To make this change?"

Lennox blew out a breath. "I stopped trying to guess why I was chosen. There will never be an answer, no matter how much I want one."

"You were selected. That's enough."

He closed his eyes and rested his chin against her. Despite the turmoil, having her beside him helped him relax. "You wanted me to set us aside, but I can no'," he told her. "You and I are mixed in this."

"I don't think it helps to make your decision. If you decide to leave things as they are, you'll have to keep me hidden."

"And if I create a new clan, I could show you the world." In whatever time he had left before he was replaced.

"You and I both know that couldn't happen immediately. You'd need to give the dragons time to adjust to the change. The last thing you'd want is for them to have two major adjustments back-to-back."

He twisted his lips, hating that she was right. He didn't want to keep her secreted away. Everyone should know how wonderful she was.

"Then again," she said, "if they had me to focus on, they might accept the new clan faster."

"I willna do that to you."

She shrugged. "It's a suggestion. By the way, is Osric mated?"

"Why?" He didn't like the jealousy that rose within him.

Ailis playfully slapped at his stomach. "I have you, and you're all I need. I'm just curious if he has chosen his mate."

"He hasna."

"Do you think it's because he's found someone in another clan."

"Nay."

She lifted her head long enough to look at him. "You said that definitively."

Now was the time to tell her what happened to dragons who couldn't be with their mates. And for the second time, he let it pass. "Osric would tell me."

"I'm sure he would. He's just very keen on helping us. I wondered if he had a reason of his own."

Lennox closed his eyes. "This kind of decision shouldna rest with one person."

"Let everyone vote."

"Vote?"

"Why not? I wish they would've done that on my realm. Instead, there was always someone on the throne making the decisions."

"How are your leaders chosen?"

She sighed, the sound filled with disgust. "By blood and cheating. Whoever takes the Dark throne is never on it for long. Many covet the position, but they're always betrayed and killed. Whoever slays them then gets the seat."

"That sounds horrific."

"It is. There is no trust among the Dark. The Light are ruled by the royals. I hear their court is as political as ours, but they don't murder their people. That would turn them Dark. Nay, they just lie, cheat, and steal. At least with the Dark, you know everyone is an enemy. I'm not sure I'd like the Light. You think someone is a friend, but they can be your biggest adversary. Whether Light or Dark, those on the throne make the decisions. They never consult the Fae."

He grunted, trying to imagine the two courts. "Allowing others to vote takes the power away from some."

"Exactly," she said, a smile curving her lips.

"What a radical you are."

She rolled onto his stomach. "You like it."

"I love it," he murmured, pulling her to him for a kiss.

"Don't start something you can't finish," she warned.

He grabbed her legs and pulled them up until she straddled him. He grinned when her eyes widened at the feel of his thickening arousal. "I'm waiting for you."

Her sexy smile sent a thrill through him.

CHAPTER TWENTY-FIVE

Ailis sighed and stretched beneath the weight of blankets, a sign that Lennox had left the bed. She heard a splash and rolled onto her side as she lifted her head from the pillow. She caught sight of his firm backside as he slid elegantly through the pool.

That was when she noticed there was a light under the water. She hugged the thick fur blanket around her and sat up. Lennox swam the length of the pool, flipped, and swam back without coming up for air. He broke the surface and smoothed his hair from his face before glancing her way.

"You're finally awake," he said with a grin.

She stifled a yawn. "Someone kept me up all night."

"I'll be sure to have a word with him so he doesna do that again."

"Don't you dare," she said with a smile. Her body still tingled from the hours they had spent loving each other. "I expect it every night."

His grin widened as he swam toward the side nearest her. "Every night? That's asking a lot."

"What's wrong? You don't think you can keep up?"

"I'm no' worried about me, lass."

She laughed at his knowing look. "What can I say? A girl can only take so many orgasms before she needs to rest. You seem to enjoy waking me from sleep."

"That I do." He pulled himself from the water. Droplets coursed rapidly down his hard body as he made his way toward her.

Suddenly, a loud boom reverberated through the mountain. She looked up before meeting his gaze. "Was that thunder?"

"Aye. There's a big storm headed toward us."

"Does that keep you out of the skies?"

He wrung out his hair. "No' all of us. Some enjoy the thrill of weaving through the clouds while trying to escape being struck by lightning."

"And if they do get struck?"

"A few dragons have the ability to create and harness lightning. It does nothing to them."

She looked pointedly at him. "And the others?"

"If they're unlucky, they die."

"Why would they do that?"

He quirked a brow at her. "Why would you chance going to another realm when you knew death was possible?"

"Point taken."

To her surprise, Lennox used his magic to dry himself. He rarely wore clothes now, preferring to walk around nude. Not that she minded. He had an amazing body that she couldn't stop looking at, touching, or wanting to feel. He climbed into the bed, but he didn't stretch out. Instead, he sat beside her, pulling the blanket across his legs.

Ailis slid her hand against his. He linked their fingers and glanced at her. In that one look, she saw the worry that still weighed on him. "You've still not made a decision."

"I'm evaluating all the options. I willna be able to see every outcome, but I'm trying to look at things from all sides. Whatever I decide will impact everyone. I doona take this lightly."

"I never thought you did." She glanced at the water. "A light beneath it. I never considered that. I like how it shines from the bottom."

He nodded, grinning. "Me, too."

"And you used magic."

"I knew you'd comment," he said, cutting her a side-eye.

She laughed, elbowing him. "Absolutely."

"You have a point about having magic and no' using it."

Ailis shrugged as she went back to gazing at the water. "You're right, too. The Fae use magic too much. There should be a better balance. Not that I'll ever convince any Fae to change their ways. I, however, can and will."

"I didna mean that you needed to alter anything."

She glanced at him. "You make me consider things, and another outlook is always good. I do fall back on magic easily and often. I don't know what I'd do if I ever lost it."

"You're made of magic. You wouldna lose it."

"You're made of magic, too, yet dragons consider the possibility they may not have it."

His fingers briefly tightened on hers. "Neither of us is wrong or right."

"I've learned a lot of things in the short time I've been here. I love that knowing you, talking with you, has expanded my views on things. You give me another avenue to consider that I wouldn't have."

"Aye, lass. Same for me."

Another boom of thunder that felt even closer than before sounded. A part of Ailis wanted to go outside and see it. She'd always been partial to thunderstorms. There was something wild and thrilling about the feral weather that could unleash such violence.

"I've called another meeting of the Kings."

Her head snapped to Lennox. "I thought you hadn't made a decision."

"I've no'. It'll take a few days for some of them to get here."

"I don't understand why you would call them without a decision."

His shoulders lifted as he took a deep breath and slowly released it. "I want to hear from all the Kings."

"You want them to state their opinion on such an important matter in front of others?"

His brow furrowed as he studied her. "They deserve a right to be heard."

"They may not wish for others to know their stance."

"Why no'?"

His genuine confusion forced her to try a different approach to help him understand. "You said yourself, this is an important matter. One that, no matter what you decide, will have consequences for everyone."

"Aye."

"There will always be some more than willing to announce their views on a subject. They're usually the ones who also like to debate topics. Mostly to try to change other's opinions to theirs, but sometimes they're mindful enough to also hear all sides."

Lennox's lips flattened. "I know dragons like that."

"Then there are those who will reluctantly give their thoughts. They might be the ones who sit back and hear everyone else, considering everything before they decide and announce it."

"There are fewer of those dragons."

She couldn't help but grin. "There are fewer of those anywhere. It takes someone not only intelligent but also openminded to be aware that others not only have opinions but that theirs could be better." Ailis licked her lips. "Which brings me to my last group. The ones who don't want anyone to know their feelings on serious subjects—the kind, like this one, that could impact everyone. They don't want to cause ripples in the water, so to speak. Nor do they want to take sides. It's easier for them to stay silent than anger anyone by having a different opinion, especially friends or family. It isn't that they can't decide. It's that they don't want others to know what that decision may be."

Lennox was silent for a few moments. "As Kings, we have certain things that need to be discussed among us. I know while I've been King of my clan and then King of Kings, nothing as significant as this has come up. There are always quarrels among the Kings whose land borders each other's, and there are Kings who aren't impacted and sit back to listen and watch. They would only speak up if I forced them. I never thought anything about it until now."

"Can you speak to each of them individually? A one-on-one discussion might be a way for them to give you an answer."

"That's a good idea. Is that what the Fae do?"

She wrinkled her nose. "Not at all. At least not the Dark. I read it in a book once and thought it was a good way to do things."

Lennox tilted his head slightly. "Osric wants to talk."

"Go see him," she urged.

"He probably has questions."

"Undoubtedly." Ailis pulled him toward her for a quick kiss. "Go to your friend."

Lennox winked at her and rose from the bed. He walked toward the cavern entrance and shifted without breaking stride. She smiled as she watched him leave. Ailis fell back onto the bed and closed her eyes. She could drift back to sleep, but she decided to rise and get moving. First, however, she wanted some breakfast.

She chose black pants and a long-sleeved shirt a shade darker than Lennox's scales. After she brushed her hair, she gathered the thick length behind her head and fastened it in place. Then she made the bed, propping the pillows against the rock wall. She walked to the edge of the water, still transfixed by the light at the bottom as she created her morning meal.

Ailis had eaten half of it when she heard Lennox call her name. She set aside her food and immediately jumped to him, only to be engulfed by darkness.

"Bloody hell," Osric said as he took a step back.

Ailis crafted a small light and tossed it into the air above her. Lennox was beside her, his eyes glittering with pride as he smiled. She wondered if there would ever come a time that her stomach didn't flip when he looked at her. She dragged her gaze from him and found Osric. Both men wore nothing but trousers. She raised her brows in question.

"You told me," Osric said as his eyes moved from Ailis to Lennox, "but I didna believe it."

"He has some questions that I'm no' answering very well," Lennox explained. "I thought you could do a better job."

Ailis shrugged. "Sure. What do you want to know?"

"I'm going to shift back and return to our mountain. Can you jump him there?"

Our mountain. Lennox had actually called it *theirs*. She would've done anything for him before, but now, she would move the very stars if he asked. "Aye."

He winked at her. "I'll see you back there."

Ailis turned to Osric as Lennox shifted and left. "So," she said to the Dragon King, "you can shift, but my ability to teleport is unsettling?"

"I doona understand how it's possible."

"Ditto, my friend."

He glanced down the tunnel at the exit. "Is it going to hurt?"

"I never feel anything."

"I understand that, but—"

Ailis grabbed his arm and jumped them to the water cavern before he could finish the sentence. In the next blink, they were there. She regretted her decision instantly as he looked a little green.

"You could've warned me," he said, breathing deeply in and out of his mouth.

She twisted her lips. "I thought it might be easier if we stopped talking about it."

Osric lowered himself to the ground and sat there for several long moments. Finally, he looked at her. "Can you do that with anything?"

"Pretty much. If I'm touching something, or if it's touching me, it'll come with me wherever I go."

"Fascinating. Do you think you could jump a dragon with you?"

Ailis shrugged. "Maybe. I'm lucky I can take someone my size. It's actually rare for a Fae to be able to jump with others."

"Well, I see you two made it," Lennox said as he walked in.

Osric pointed at her. "She jumped me without warning."

"Again?" Lennox asked.

"Again?" Osric repeated, his voice pitched louder.

She gave both men a sheepish look. "It always seems better to do it when you aren't aware."

"It isna," Lennox said. "Trust us on that."

Ailis gave them a thumbs-up. "Noted for the future."

"Now," Lennox said as he too sat on the ground, "Osric, ask your questions."

She eyed the hard ground before glancing at the bed. Then she created three chairs that she turned to face each other. She lowered herself into one and waited for the men to do the same. Lennox was the first to try it. He gingerly lowered himself, only to smile at the softness that met his backside. Osric was more hesitant, but he finally got there.

"These are chairs," she explained. "There are all different kinds. Some are simple and without padding. They can be big or small, sleek or oversized. I prefer these because the rock is just too hard after a while."

Osric nodded before pointing at the bed. "And that is?"

Lennox was the one to explain it to him. Ailis couldn't stop her smile as Lennox rose and tossed Osric a pillow so he could feel it. That wasn't enough, though. Osric was soon lying on the bed, his surprise evident. Some might say she was showing the dragons more than they could ever teach her, but those people would be wrong.

Dead wrong.

"Windows," Ailis explained. "They allow light and can be opened for fresh air."

She pointed out the roof, which she then took off and explained the inside. Lennox was especially interested in the kitchen. It seemed so foreign not to eat food raw but to have to cook it. Yet he enjoyed everything he had tried with Ailis. In fact, he wouldn't mind attempting to cook himself. The bathroom was another fascinating area. Again, not something dragons used, but captivating all the same.

Ailis didn't stop there. Next, she created the building where she lived in the city. She had already shown him this, but he liked getting a second look. She pointed out balconies and terraces and even expanded the model to show the roads and other buildings. Then she explained about eateries, as well as clothing and shoe shops.

Osric sat back, his face slack with overload. Lennox knew exactly how he felt because he had been there. In many ways, he still was. Ailis had told him much about her world, but he was seeing it anew, and it staggered him all over again.

"Why would you leave such a realm?" Osric asked.

Ailis moved her hands apart, and the model disappeared. She slid her gaze to Lennox. "Did you tell him about the Light and Dark?"

"Aye," Lennox replied.

Osric waved her words away. "Besides that. You had so much."

"As do you here," she answered.

Osric gave her a flat look. "No' like that."

"Advancements don't always equal peace and serenity."

"We doona have that here either," Lennox pointed out.

She shrugged. "More than I ever had on the Fae Realm."

"What about your magic?" Osric asked as he stretched out his legs and crossed his ankles.

Ailis gathered her hands in her lap. "What about it?"

"You can teleport, and you can create doorways to move about. What else can you do?" he asked.

Her throat bobbed as she swallowed. "Fae have the ability to use glamour."

"What's that?" It was the first Lennox had heard of it.

She shifted in her seat. "It allows a Fae to change their appearance. Like this." Her long hair was gone, replaced by a blond, shoulder-length style. Her red eyes were now a bright blue.

Yet, through it all, Lennox could see the real her beneath. "I see the changes, but I still see you."

"What?" she asked, eyes wide. "That's not possible."

Osric frowned. "I see a slight flickering, aye, but Ailis has blond hair and blue eyes."

"It's like the altered version of you is semi-transparent and overlaid atop you," Lennox explained. He looked at Osric. "You doona see that?"

His friend shook his head. "Nay, I see a changed Ailis, she's just a wee bit unfocused."

In the next instant, the glamour was gone. Ailis blinked a few times. "I've never heard anyone able to do that."

"You've also never run into dragons before," Osric said with a grin.

Ailis chuckled. "Good point."

"Do you use glamour often?" Lennox asked.

"I don't, but some Fae like to change their appearance."

Osric cleared his throat. "What other kinds of magic do you have?"

"Fae can also veil themselves. We can't do it for very long, but sometimes we don't need a lot."

Lennox frowned. "Veil? Do you mean disappear?"

"Sort of," she replied with a twist of her lips.

Osric grinned and jerked his chin to her. "Let's see."

Lennox watched her vanish. A second later, she was back. He frowned.

"Are you sure you didna jump away?" Osric asked.

Ailis laughed. "I didn't. A veil is great if we're teleporting somewhere and want a moment to look around before anyone knows we're there."

"Ah." That made sense to Lennox.

Osric leaned forward eagerly. "Anything else?"

"That's it."

Lennox leaned his forearms on his thighs. "When we first met, you held those balls in your hands."

"The orbs?" Ailis asked with a frown. Then she shrugged. "It's what we use when we're in battle."

"That's the kind of magic I want to know about," Osric stated.

Ailis's red eyes landed on Lennox. "I thought Osric had questions about being in this form."

"I thought he did, too." Lennox looked at his friend.

Osric shrugged. "I did. I mean, I do. But I'm also curious about the Fae."

"Let's move on from Ailis's magic," Lennox urged.

Osric sighed and bent his legs. "All right. Will we heal in this form as we do as dragons?"

"Why are you looking at me?" Ailis asked, affronted. "I'm not the one causing you to shift."

Lennox ran a hand over his jaw. "We're no' sure you are no' the cause either."

"I can tell you about being a Fae. I can't answer questions about healing or your magic while in mortal form," Ailis told them.

Osric lifted one shoulder. "My magic is the same in both forms."

"As is mine," Lennox confirmed.

"If you got here, Ailis, more Fae could come. We need to know what we're up against," Osric said.

Lennox's stomach clenched as he realized what his friend was getting at. "Osric, nay."

"We must know if the Fae's magic is stronger than ours. You know that as well as I, Lennox."

Ailis pushed to her feet. "If you're suggesting that I use my magic against either of you, you're out of your mind. I'm not doing it."

"That isna what he's proposing," Lennox said.

Osric rolled his eyes. "That's exactly what I'm suggesting."

"It's not going to happen." Ailis swung her head to Lennox, her jaw set. "I won't do it. Don't ask."

Osric stood. "Both of you know I'm right. You might no' want to admit it, but we need to know what we're up against."

"I'm not a warrior," Ailis added.

Lennox was pulled in two directions. Osric had a valid point, but at the same time, Lennox couldn't—and wouldn't—ask Ailis to use her magic on any dragon.

"You were prepared to fight Lennox," Osric continued. "You formed the orbs to protect yourself."

Ailis lifted her chin. "As anyone would if they felt threatened."

"Exactly. This is our home. We've welcomed you, but even you admitted to Lennox that other Fae might no' be so inclined to…how shall I put this? Realize this isna their world." Osric shrugged, as if the action said everything.

Lennox squeezed the bridge of his nose with his thumb and forefinger. "Osric, stop."

"What if Lennox came to your realm?" Osric asked, ignoring him. "What if you were worried about more dragons finding their way to your home? Would you no' want to know what you'd be up against?"

"Osric!" Lennox bellowed and lurched to his feet.

Ailis's voice was low as she said, "I would."

Lennox jerked his head to her. Ailis met his gaze, her smile sad. "You doona have to do this."

"But I do. I might not like what Osric says, but it's the truth."

"Use your magic on me," Osric said.

Lennox ignored him and closed the short distance between him and Ailis. He took her by the arms and fought against his need, the overwhelming demand to shield her from everyone. Including Osric. "There are other ways to compare our magic. You doona need to use it on anyone."

"If there's a—" Osric began.

Lennox silenced him with a look. He returned his attention to Ailis. "Tell me you understand."

"I do," she replied.

But he wasn't convinced. When she would no longer meet his gaze, he knew he had his answer. "If you're going to do this, then you'll use your magic on me."

"Absolutely not," she replied.

At the same time, Osric stated, "Nay, it'll be me."

Lennox dropped his hands and nodded at Ailis. "Whenever you're ready."

"It should be me," Osric said louder, looking between them. "Hello? Do either of you hear me?"

Lennox ignored him and held Ailis's gaze. "Go on."

For a moment, he thought she would refuse. Then she briefly pressed her lips together. "On one condition."

"What would that be?"

"You use your magic on me after."

Lennox fisted his hands. She asked the impossible. But he understood. She didn't want to do this either. If she did, then he would, as well. Lennox bowed his head in agreement, his instincts fighting him the entire time.

"What is wrong with both of you?" Osric demanded as he walked between them. He looked from one to the other. "Stop this madness."

Ailis twisted her lips in a rueful smile. "You started it."

"Because I expected to be the one getting hit with the magic. No' my friend." Osric's dark eyes were troubled, his brow furrowed deeply.

Lennox was tired of talking about this. He wanted it done. "Move away, brother. We're doing this. I'm the only one Ailis can do this to, and you know it. Because I willna retaliate if something goes wrong."

Osric parted his lips to reply but ended up closing his

mouth and stepping aside. Lennox found himself looking at his mate once more. There was so much reluctance in Ailis's eyes that he didn't think she would go through with it. Until the orb formed in her hand. It was small, barely bigger than her palm.

"Are you sure about this?" she asked.

"We need to know what your magic is like. I'm ready," he assured her. "It'll be fine."

"I'm sorry," she whispered before lobbing it at him.

The instant it struck his chest, Lennox had to grit his teeth to hold back the bellow. The pain was unlike anything he had ever endured. The orb sank through his flesh into muscle, ligament, and bone. He fought to stay standing. Dimly, Lennox was aware of Ailis frantically calling his name. He felt her soft hands on him, even as his knees gave way. The world tilted as he pitched backward, and then he hit the ground hard.

Osric was on his other side. Both he and Ailis were talking rapidly, but Lennox couldn't hear any of it. He was too busy trying to push past the agony that began to radiate through him with every breath, growing stronger and stronger until it was all he knew.

He didn't know how long he lay there, racked with agony. It could've been seconds or days. The pain began to lessen, and he felt his body healing.

"I'm sorry. I'm sorry," Ailis said over and over, tears streaming down her face as she rested her forehead on his shoulder.

Lennox cupped her cheek and lifted her head so she met his eyes. "I'm all right, lass."

She wiped at her eyes and saw for herself that he had

healed. Her face creased as she cried harder. Lennox pulled her atop him and held her, needing her as much as she needed him. He turned his eyes to Osric. His friend's face was ashen, his breathing harsh as Osric dropped back onto his arse.

"Bloody hell, Lennox."

"Aye," he croaked. The pain was fading, but he wouldn't soon forget what Fae magic felt like.

CHAPTER TWENTY-SEVEN

Ailis knew her hold on Lennox was tight, but she couldn't make her fingers loosen. The pain that had flashed over his face, the way his body had stiffened before he collapsed, it would all replay in her head for the rest of her days.

"Look at me," he pressed. "The wound has healed."

She shook her head, refusing to lift her cheek from his chest, from the very place the orb had pierced him. The way it had sizzled and sank into his flesh made it difficult for her to swallow. The sickening sound of it and the smell of burned skin was too much.

"Ailis."

His voice was tender but resolute. She slowly straightened and reluctantly looked into his pale green eyes. He sat up and took one of her hands, placing it on his chest. A fresh wave of tears filled her eyes, but she blinked them back.

"You did exactly what I asked. This isna your fault," Lennox said.

"The last thing I ever wanted to do was cause you harm."

His lips curved into a crooked smile. "I know, lass. It's done and over."

Was it, though? Ailis wasn't so sure. She glanced at Osric to find his brow furrowed, a worried look creasing his features. Then she took a closer at the two Kings. It didn't take a genius to realize they were talking.

"Nay," she said and pulled her hand from Lennox. "Whatever you two are discussing, you say it in front of me. I'm part of this."

Lennox visibly winced. "You're right. I apologize. I didna want to cause you more distress."

"Trust me, whether you say it or not, I feel horrible."

"Aye. I see that now." Lennox got to his feet and pulled her up with him. He released a breath. "Osric wanted to know what it felt like."

Ailis fought not to turn away. She wanted to pretend the question didn't hang between them, but there was no getting away from this. Besides, she had demanded to hear their conversation. It took everything she had to meet Lennox's gaze and ask, "It… sounded and looked ghastly. I imagine it felt worse."

Osric turned away and began to pace.

Ailis watched him for a moment before swinging her head back to Lennox. "Tell me."

"It burned all the way through me. Once it hit bone, it started to spread. The pain was blinding."

Osric spun toward her and pointed at Lennox. "Is that what happens to Fae? Is that what your kind do to each other?"

She parted her lips to reply, but he wasn't finished.

"You could've warned us!"

Lennox took a step toward his friend. "Osric, we asked for this."

"No' that!" he bellowed.

"Doona put this on her. We use our magic on each other," Lennox stated.

Osric scrubbed a hand down his face, looking sick.

Ailis understood because *she* felt sick. "We use the orbs in battle. We also use other weapons like swords, spears, and arrows. Both Light and Dark use orbs, but a Fae turns Dark for additional power. Which means our magic is different from a Light's."

"Deadlier, you mean," Osric bit out.

Lennox's eyes turned hard. "That's no' fair, Osric."

"It's fine," Ailis said and put a hand on Lennox to halt him from going to his friend. "Aye, the reaction is similar when an orb lands on a Fae. They're meant to cause pain and suffering, but nothing like I saw with Lennox."

Lennox flashed her a smile that didn't reach his eyes. "I healed. We know what your magic can do, but we've also learned that a King will heal. How long was I unconscious?"

"A matter of seconds," Osric replied.

Ailis scanned Lennox's upper body but couldn't even see a mark left from the orb. "It's time for you to use your magic on me."

"That's no' going to happen," Lennox stated calmly, firmly.

Surely, he wouldn't do that to her. "We had a deal."

"We did, but I can no' do it. I'm sorry."

Ailis gaped at him, part angry and part shocked. "Nay. Do it."

"Do you plan on returning to your realm and sharing any information on Earth and us?"

She blinked, taken aback by Lennox's words. "You know I'm not."

"Then there's no need for us to learn if dragon magic harms you."

Osric cleared his throat. "That's no' necessarily true."

"Stop," Lennox told him with a hard look.

Ailis closed her eyes for a heartbeat. "He's right. Just as it was important for you to know what a Dark's magic could do, you also need to learn if your magic can hurt a Fae."

"I thought I could do it," Lennox admitted after a long moment of silence. "That's why I agreed. But I can no'. I saw your face when I opened my eyes after you thought I'd…"

"Died," she said when he didn't finish, emotion clogging her throat.

Lennox's nod was barely perceptible. "I knew in that instant I couldna take the chance of me or…any dragon," he said, looking pointedly at Osric, "hurting you."

"You think I want to do that?" Osric asked with wide eyes. He shook his head, the shock rendering him speechless.

Ailis didn't point out that it was Osric who'd reminded them that knowledge of how a dragon's magic would affect a Fae was important.

"We have dragon fire," Lennox stated. "Nothing can withstand that."

Osric said nothing as he returned to the chairs and plopped

down. He rested an elbow on the arm of the chair and dropped his face into his hand. "You could've died, Lennox."

"I'm a Dragon King. Nothing can kill us but another King."

"Nothing on this realm." Osric lifted his head and looked directly at her. "We were reckless. It's no' a mistake I'll make again. Even if you were no' his mate, I'd still be against any of our magic being used on you."

Lennox tugged her after him as he walked to the chairs. They took their seats, the three of them sitting in a circle staring at each other.

"I should never have brought it up," Osric finally said.

Ailis shook her head. "I should've refused. At the very least, I should've explained what the orbs do to my kind."

"And I shouldna have put you in that position, Ailis. There's enough blame for all of us to share, but there's no point in it." Lennox looked between them. "It's done and over. I'm healed. We got important data. Let's leave it at that. Now, let's change the subject. Osric, do you have any more questions?"

The Dragon King shook his head of black hair. "I…I doona know."

"Take a swim. The water against skin versus scales is interesting," Lennox suggested.

Osric didn't reply, and Ailis couldn't find anything to talk about. The silence that descended in the cavern was deafening.

"If we doona move past this, it will haunt all of us," Lennox told them.

Osric swallowed, his throat bobbing. "I want both of you

to know how sorry I am. I got too caught up in the *what-ifs*, and didna think about the aftermath."

"None of us did," Lennox added.

Ailis leaned over and patted Osric's arm. "You made valid points. I hope the Fae never make it here. Earth is beautiful and unspoiled, and my people would change all of that. It's good to be prepared for the Fae or any other being who comes to your realm."

"Does the Fae Realm get visitors?" Lennox asked.

Ailis twisted her lips. "Not that I'm aware of, and with the way word spreads on the realm, we would've known."

"Even with the Light?"

"Even with the Light."

Osric perked up. "So, I was thinking of the worst-case scenario when it may never happen."

"Exactly," Lennox said with an easy smile.

Ailis forced her lips to curve into a grin. Her stomach churned, and she wasn't sure why. Was it because she had come to their realm? Did that mean she had somehow alerted the rest of the universe about Earth? There was no denying the growing pit of concern or the certainty that it was imperative the dragons be ready and primed for any visitors to their wonderful world.

"What is it?" Lennox asked.

She shook her head. "Nothing."

He simply quirked a brow and waited.

Was she so bad at hiding her thoughts? "I got here. It wasn't easy, but I did."

"You think others will come," Osric replied.

She shrugged. "I don't think it's a bad idea for everyone, from the Kings to the clans, to be ready for such an event."

"That would mean we let others know about you." Lennox snorted. "It's no' time for that."

Osric crossed his ankle over his knee. "I'm no' sure there will ever come a time for that."

"Then don't tell them about me. But you need to set the stage. Lennox, say you had a vision, or that another dragon somewhere did. Get the dragons trained. The one thing that will defeat any race, no matter how strong physically or magically, is division. The dragons *must* fight together," she stated.

Lennox shared a long look with Osric before resting his arms on the chair. "You make a good point."

"We could start hounding the clans about that. It might no' take with the current generation, but eventually, it will," Osric said.

"Agreed."

The relief that surged through Ailis was so great the room spun. She might be a stranger and know little about dragons, but she had fallen in love with one. And that tied her to the land and them more firmly than anything could. The dragons were commanding and powerful. She doubted anyone could bring them down for long.

Not as long as they had someone like Lennox ruling.

"Any other words of wisdom?" Osric asked with a smile.

She grinned. "I'm not sure where that came from. Just a strong feeling I couldn't ignore."

"I hope it isna a premonition." Osric laughed at his joke, but neither Ailis nor Lennox joined him.

Lennox held out his hand. Ailis immediately linked her fingers with his. His pale green eyes were clear and bright as they held hers. "You might no' have seen the future, but you felt something."

"Undeniably," she replied.

"Has it happened before?"

Ailis shook her head. "Never."

"Then there is only one explanation."

She waited for him to finish.

Instead, Osric gave up the answer. "The magic."

Ailis was so startled by their response that she started to refute it. Once again, something made her pause. She sat with the feeling for a moment. The apprehension was gone. It had left as soon as she told them about them working together. What swirled through her now was peace and calm.

It took her a moment to recognize it because she'd felt it from the instant of her arrival. She had believed it was because she had reached her goal. But she had to reevaluate things now. What if, all this time, the magic of the realm had been with her? If it was strong enough to decide who in the clans would be King, then there was no reason it couldn't also touch her. She was made of magic, after all.

Lennox smiled at her. "If there was ever any doubt that you were meant to be my mate, it's gone now. The magic rules this realm, lass. And it has welcomed you with open arms."

CHAPTER TWENTY-EIGHT

"You sure about this?"

Lennox stood atop his mountain and looked at the vast landscape of the Kings' capital. *"Aye, Osric. Whether the Kings want to come or no', I'll be listening to each of them individually."*

"You're going to have a long day. Maybe a long couple of days."

Wind blasted Lennox as Osric flew over him low enough that Lennox could have reached up and grabbed his friend's tail. It was a prank Osric had pulled from the first day they'd met. *"Perhaps you should remain with me."*

"No' on your life, brother. I've a female in mind to visit."

Lennox laughed. *"Try no' to have too much fun."*

There was no reply, but he didn't expect one. Osric was as loyal as they came. A true friend and brother in every sense of the word. He had already given Lennox his vote. Osric was ready to stand up and announce it to anyone who cared to listen, but Lennox bade him to wait.

So, with one check already in the *for* column, Lennox readied to hear from the other Kings. And he didn't have to wait long. A few whose clans were near the capital made the journey. A handful simply gave their vote and left, while others offered details for why they were on the side they were on.

By noon, more Kings were against allowing dragons from different clans to be together. Lennox tried not to feel defeated. After all, he had only heard from a third of the Kings. There were many more to go. Still, he was alarmed at just how many were unwilling for things to change—no matter how much it hurt other dragons.

Lennox didn't take a break. He remained seated atop the mountain, listening as each King connected to him telepathically. The sun was making its descent as he finished speaking to the King of Corals and saw familiar scales. He took a deep breath as Darald drew closer.

"I'm surprised to see you," Lennox said when Darald landed below him on his mountain.

Darald looked up at him, his orange eyes steady. *"I wanted to state that I'm against any changes."*

"I have it recorded. You didna have to make the journey here."

"I felt it was imperative."

Lennox lifted a brow at that, but he didn't respond to it. *"Thank you."*

"Why no' bring all of us together and ask?"

"Because I wanted to allow everyone to state their opinion without being singled out if it went against others."

"We're Kings," Darald replied. *"We're capable of speaking our minds."*

"True."

"Who are you protecting?"

Lennox held his gaze, not giving an inch. *"All of you."*

"What is your vote?"

"I'll announce that once I collect everyone else's."

"How do we know you're no' lying?"

The anger that welled within Lennox was nearly uncontrollable. Darald was attempting to rile him. He would not take the bait—despite how much he wanted to. *"I'm the King of Kings, Darald. The magic knows."*

"If you go ahead with this change, you'll ruin families and clans."

"Families and clans are already being ruined by those watching their loved ones die from no' being with their mates."

Darald's nostrils flared as he huffed. *"There's a reason other Kings didna amend our way of life. Think on that."*

Lennox held his tongue. A moment later, Darald flew away. Lennox sighed and gave himself a moment to regain his composure. Then he opened the link to the next King.

It was well into the wee hours of the morning before he had heard from all of them. He wasn't sure what he thought about being the only King at the capital. All of them were with their clans, which was odd. At any given time, there were at least a dozen Kings in residence.

He had too much on his mind to worry about that,

however. After he flew to the bottom of the mountain, he hurried inside and shifted. He found Ailis asleep with a book against her chest. Her fondness for reading was something he, too, had picked up. The moment he'd mentioned wanting to read, she'd produced a book and handed it to him. He had only gotten a few chapters in since he spent most of his time making love to her or dealing with the current issues.

Lennox removed the book from her limp grasp, careful to put the bookmark in place. He'd made the error of closing one of her books without that once, and he wouldn't make that mistake again.

She rolled over, her eyes blinking open as he climbed into bed. "Hello," she murmured sleepily. "What time is it?"

"Late. Or early. Depends on how you look at it." The bed felt good. She felt better.

"Is it done?"

"Aye."

She snuggled against him. "What's the verdict?"

"Firmly for the change."

"Really?" she asked, her voice rising slightly with her surprise.

He grinned. "Aye. It wasna at first, and I was disheartened. Talking to them separately helped. Many said they didna want their clans to know their thoughts yet."

"Meaning they wouldn't have shared it with the other Kings either."

"Aye."

She blew out a long breath. "Hmm. That's interesting. They don't mind telling you, and I gather they'll carry out whatever orders you give them, but they'll hide behind you when they do it."

"A handful, possibly. But I know many more willna hesitate to tell their clans their thoughts, be they the same as mine or no'."

"Was it the majority for the change that spoke to you privately?"

"Oddly enough, it was split. Many who were against it didna want to speak out."

"Why?"

Lennox rubbed his hand on her back. "They didna wish to incite anything either directly or indirectly."

"Oh."

"I applaud them for that. Everyone is entitled to their thoughts. Even Kings. But for us, things go much further. We must think of our clans, first and foremost. I didna speak with one King who had anything other than their clan in mind when they voiced their choice."

"Even Darald?"

Lennox thought about that for a moment. "Darald is loud and can be obnoxious. He came to me today."

"Really?"

"It's important for him to look others in the eye. I may no' always agree with him, but he's a good King. He trusts his instincts, and he knows that others' words and actions doona always coincide."

"Will he cause trouble if you create the new clan?"

"He may think about it. He may want to, but he willna." At least Lennox hoped he wouldn't.

Ailis paused before she asked, "I know I keep asking, but have you made a decision?"

"I have." He kissed her forehead. "I'm going to announce at noon that a new clan will be formed immediately for anyone wishing to leave their current one."

"That may ruffle some scales."

"No doubt."

"Is there a better way to s—"

Ailis was interrupted as hundreds of screams bombarded Lennox, resounding in his head. He clutched his temples and rolled to his side as dragons repeatedly shouted his name. The voices were so loud he couldn't differentiate between them. What he did know was that there was rage, fear, and hatred in the voices.

Finally, one stood out among the rest. Darald. But there were no words. Just a scream of fury. Over and over.

Lennox shut everyone out and rolled out of bed to his feet, attempting to clear his mind. But he couldn't stop hearing Darald.

"Lennox? Please. Talk to me. What happened?"

He turned to Ailis and saw her wide eyes and pale face. "Something has happened. I must go."

"What is it?" she asked, jumping from the bed after him.

He strode away, shaking his head. "I doona know. Hundreds, maybe thousands of voices. Grief, anger, sadness. Hate. All of it. I must find the cause."

"Be careful."

Lennox turned to find Ailis had stopped several steps behind him. He walked back to her and gave her a soft kiss before embracing her. "I'll return when I can."

"I'll be here."

He started to leave but hesitated. "I doona expect anything to happen but…" He trailed off, not able to say the words. "When I arrive, I'll let you know it's me by making a sound."

"That half grunt, half growl thing you do?" she asked with a grin.

He forced a softening of his lips. "Aye. If you hear anyone else—"

"I'll leave."

Lennox touched her face once more, then turned on his heel. He ran from the cavern, shifting in the tunnel to burst from the mountain and into the air. He flew faster than ever before, all the while trying to get Darald to answer him.

"Lennox!"

He was relieved to hear Osric's voice. *"Where are you?"*

"Coming to you."

"I've left the capital. I'm heading toward Darald."

"You heard him, too, then?"

That gave Lennox pause. *"You heard him?"*

"Aye."

"What about the others' cries?"

"Others?" Osric asked in confusion.

"Never mind."

"Want me to join you?"

Lennox had no idea what awaited him. It would be good to have a friend by his side. *"Aye."*

"I'm on my way."

Osric wasn't the only concerned King who contacted Lennox. It appeared others had heard the outcry, as well, but they only heard one voice—Darald. With his worry increasing,

Lennox did his best to calm everyone until he could sort out what had happened. Yet with each flap of his wings, the knot of unease grew larger.

He reached the Yellows' territory in record time. Lennox was breathing hard, his mind racing with thousands of possibilities. He shouted over and over for Darald but received no answer. It only doubled his concern.

Lennox spotted Yellows flying in the same direction and followed them. He heard the roars and howls long before he saw the crowd outside Noma's. His heart clutched, dread filling him. Lennox circled the growing crowd. When he saw Noma lying unmoving, he fought against letting loose his own roar of sorrow and rage.

But he held it in check. Now wasn't the time to join those grieving. They would look to him for answers—and retribution. He had to bury his distress for now. Forget the ire, the need to lash out. If he didn't want others to do the same, he had to be calm, rational. And it would be nearly impossible.

Lennox landed behind the group. They parted at his arrival and allowed him to get a closer look. It was the last place he wanted to be. Lennox didn't want to see the young female, but he made himself go to her anyway. He halted, startled by the claw marks scoring Noma's chest, deep enough to penetrate her heart. There was little consolation in knowing that she'd died quickly.

Noma's family was on the other side of her body. The fury on her father's face was understandable. Her siblings' utter sorrow distressing. But her mother's anguish was gut-wrenching.

"Why would anyone wish to kill my beautiful girl?" she asked Lennox.

He shook his head, unable to give her an answer. *"I'll find who did this. I willna stop until I uncover who took her life."*

Dragons occasionally stole, lied, and killed. But outright murder? There could be only one reason for such violence. Lennox had let the entire realm know that he was considering a change. Someone had taken it upon themselves to ensure that Noma and Ariston couldn't be together. While Lennox didn't want to believe there was a dragon more against it than any other, there was—Noma's King, Darald.

Lennox launched himself into the air. *"Darald! Answer me now. I summon you immediately."*

It was an order that no King could ignore.

"Lennox! You need to come to the Coppers as fast as you can," Osric told him.

Lennox didn't question his friend. He dipped a wing and swung toward the Coppers. To his utter horror, he heard more roars and howls. He braced himself, hoping and praying that he was wrong, right up until he found the Coppers gathered, much as the Yellows had been.

He finally let loose a roar of outrage when he saw who lay at the center of the group—Ariston, just as still as his mate had been. Sporting the same claw marks on his chest.

And mixed with the Coppers was none other than Darald.

CHAPTER TWENTY-NINE

Something was wrong. Dreadfully wrong. Ailis wrung her hands and wished she were with Lennox. Not that he needed her. It was more for her sanity because she hated not knowing what was happening. Was it because of her? Or worse, was it because of the couple and the questions Lennox had been asking?

Neither scenario was good, and both were volatile situations on the best days.

Ailis tried to sleep, but her mind raced with questions and possibilities, each ghastlier than the last. She finally gave up and paced. There was a chill in the air that had nothing to do with the light rain falling, and everything to do with the stricken expression Lennox had worn before he left in such a hurry.

He would tell her everything when he returned.

If he returns.

Ailis halted, squeezing her eyes shut. Why had the voice in

her head said that? She knew it was possible, but she didn't need the reminder. Lennox wasn't immortal. No one was. But he was the closest thing that she had ever come across. He gave the illusion of eternal life, allowing her to believe he was untouchable. He had even healed from her magic.

Somehow, in all her time with Lennox, she had forgotten one crucial part—any Dragon King could kill him. And eventually, one of them would be tapped by the magic to do just that.

The thought chilled her. What would she do once he was gone? Wander Earth, lost and utterly alone? That wasn't an option. She was welcome because of him. Once Lennox was gone, she would have no one. For the briefest of moments, she had held out hope there might be a day when the dragons accepted her as his mate. The realistic side of her knew it would never happen, and she couldn't blame anyone for that.

She wasn't just a stranger; she was different in every way that mattered.

Ailis didn't want to think about what she would do if she had to leave Earth, but it was a fact she couldn't ignore. She wrapped her arms around her middle and fought against the tide of worry and apprehension that threatened to drown her.

"Come back to me, Lennox," she whispered.

She closed her eyes and focused on him, on their love. Though she didn't know where he was or what he might be dealing with, she wanted him to know she was with him, offering whatever strength he might need.

Lennox dove from the sky, his hands outstretched. He closed his fingers around Darald's neck as he collided with the King, slamming the Yellows' leader into the ground. Lennox peeled back his lips to show his fury and growled long and low. Out of the corner of his eye, Lennox saw the crowd scattering to give them room.

"*What have you done?*" Lennox demanded.

Darald slowly shook his head. "*I didna do this.*"

"*You were firmly against their union. You made that abundantly clear to me as well as your clan. Bloody hell, Darald, you even let Noma know it!*"

Finally, he met Lennox's gaze. "*I was against it, but I wouldna...I couldna do that to a member of my clan. You must believe me, Lennox.*"

Lennox hesitated. The anguish in Darald's gaze was clear. As was the truth. Or was it simply what Lennox wanted to see? His anger was too great for him to think straight. He tightened his fingers around Darald's throat, his talons cutting through his scales, drawing blood.

"*Do it,*" Darald urged. "*I deserve it. She screamed my name. She called for my help, but I didna get there in time.*" He lowered his gaze dejectedly. "*I doona understand who would do that to her.*"

Lennox instantly loosened his fingers, his heart skipping a beat. "*Noma? You're telling me Noma called for you?*"

Darald's eyes jerked to him. "*Lennox, the fear in her voice shook me. I've never heard anything like it.*"

"*Why are you here? Did you no' go to her?*"

"*Of course, I went,*" Darald snapped, but the anger faded instantly. "*When I found her, the life was fading from her eyes.*"

Her family already surrounded her. I saw what had been so viciously done to her, and I feared she hadna been the only one targeted."

"So, you came here?"

Darald's head rolled to the side to see Ariston's slain body a short distance away. *"I did. Too late again."*

Lennox glanced at Ariston and tried to swallow past the thickness in his throat. He only knew for certain that someone had violently and needlessly taken a young couple's lives.

"I'm many things, Lennox, but I'm no' a liar," Darald said.

Lennox looked at him and saw the truth there. He released Darald and moved to the side so he could stand. *"I'm no' finished with you. Stay with me. I want details, so be ready to give them."*

Darald bowed his head in acknowledgment as he regained his feet.

Lennox then turned to look around at the crowd. His gaze lingered on each face, noting the horror, the misery, the fury. He recognized it because those emotions whirled through him in a savage, feverish storm. Whoever had done this would be shown no mercy, no compassion. His gaze finally landed on Rolf, who stood with Ariston's family. Two dragons, two families, two clans that had been hurtled into unimaginable loss—but this affected every dragon, now and far into the future.

"I will find out who did this," Lennox announced to those around him. *"I will bring justice to Ariston and Noma, their families, and their clans. There isna anywhere on this realm the murderer can hide. I will ferret them out, but I willna deliver swift justice. That isna our way. There will be a trial,*

and if found guilty, Ariston's and Noma's families will determine the punishment."

Lennox tightly leashed his rage and made his way to Ariston's family. They were too grief-stricken to pay him much attention. They didn't just mourn their son and brother, they grieved for Noma, as well.

"What can I do?" Rolf asked.

"Stay with your clan. If there's anyone you think could have done this, I want their name. As for the funeral, Ariston and Noma couldna be together in life, but they will be in death."

"That would be beautiful."

Lennox saw Osric flying in the distance, circling them. *"Someone saw something. We'll find the bastard, Rolf. I give you my word."*

"I know you will." Rolf glanced at Darald. *"Who do you think did it?"*

"We can no' rule anyone out yet." Lennox didn't want to clear or condemn anyone without calming himself and sorting through what he had learned. *"Did anyone move Ariston?"*

Rolf shook his head. *"He was found right there."*

"Who discovered his body?"

Rolf turned to look behind him at a dragon whose copper scales had begun to fade with age. *"Morten."*

Lennox made his way to the elderly dragon. *"I'd like to speak to you if I may."*

"Ask anything," Morten said, his voice shaking, partly from age and partly due to the events.

"What were you doing when you found Ariston?"

"Flying. I can no' go verra far these days, and I know my time is short."

Lennox understood. A dragon who couldn't fly lost a part of himself, and death soon followed. *"Do you normally fly at this time of night?"*

"I take to the skies whenever these old bones allow. I had trouble sleeping, and the night was beautiful. If I had known what I'd stumble across..."

Lennox studied the dragon. Morten was getting up there in age, but he was far from finding death. Muscle had yet to fade. It made Lennox wonder if Morten could have killed the couple. He would talk to Rolf about the elderly dragon later. For now, he returned to the business at hand. *"Did you see anyone or anything?"*

"I wasna looking until I found the lad. After that, I searched, but there was no one around."

"What did you do then?"

"I alerted Rolf. Once he saw the lad, he bade me to stand guard and went to his family. It wasna long after that they arrived, and then others. Word spreads quickly, sire."

"It certainly does. When did you learn about Noma?"

"When Darald came."

"And when was that? Before the family or after?"

"Before."

Lennox tried to remember if he had asked Darald that, but he didn't think he had. *"What happened when Darald arrived?"*

"Well, sire," Morten said, scratching his chin, *"he practically fell out of the sky. The shock on his face was there for all to see."*

"Did he get close to Ariston?"

Morten shook his head firmly. *"Nay, no' at all. He didna leave the spot you found him in. He only stared at the lad as if willing him to rise. I was the one who asked what had brought him to our clan. Darald mumbled something I couldna hear, so I repeated the question. His voice was no' much louder when he said the lass had been slain in the same manner. I doona know Darald, but to me, he didna look like a dragon who had harmed anyone."*

"He was outspoken about no' wanting the couple mated."

"A lot of dragons were."

Lennox eyed him, surprised that the dragon would admit such a thing. *"And you? What did you think of it?"*

"I never found a mate, sire. I always longed for one. No' being matched isna a death sentence like finding one and no' being together. But it isna a good existence. I've often wondered if my mate was in another clan or if our lives just missed each other this time."

"You didna answer my question."

Morten's purple eyes were sharp and clever. *"I did no'."*

"Care to give it now?"

"I feel—or rather felt*—for the couple. All they saw was each other and their love. They didna see the bigger picture and the effects their union would have. They were one drop in the water, the spreading ripples significant, aye, but no' enough to cause disorder. I can no' fault you for speaking to them or others. In fact, I applaud you for taking the time to ask what we think."*

"But?" Lennox pressed when he paused.

"If you allowed their mating, there would be others. That

ripple could turn into swells, then waves, and finally a tsunami."

"That's usually what change does."

"You think we need change?"

"I think any society, no matter who they are or where they are, can no' stay stagnant if they wish to evolve and grow. Otherwise, they wither and die."

Morten sighed. *"Maybe you're right. And perhaps the majority of dragons feel as you do. But one of us was so against it they took two lives to stop it."*

A new flare of rage shot through Lennox. If the murderer had intended that, then they would be disappointed. *"Thank you for your candor. If I have more questions, I'll let you know."*

Lennox looked at Darald to find the King watching as Copper warriors gathered around Ariston. Lennox caught Darald's attention. It was time they went to his clan and got more answers.

First, Lennox connected to all the Dragon Kings. He was succinct as he laid out what had happened. He bade each King to stay with their clans and ask around. Lennox intended to conduct his own line of questioning, but for now, it would ensure that the Kings would notice if a dragon crossed into his territory that shouldn't be there.

"Lennox?" Osric called.

"I've got this under control for the moment."

"Is it Darald?"

"I doona believe so, but I'm no' certain of anything just yet."

Osric made a sound in the back of his throat. *"I can no'
fathom who would do such a thing."*

"Me neither."

*"Go. Do what you need. I'm here if you need anything,
brother."*

The only thing keeping Lennox going was knowing that
both Ailis and Osric would be there when he needed to sort
through all the thoughts in his head. And he would need them.

CHAPTER THIRTY

It was the half growl, half roar that had Ailis bolting from the water cavern into the tunnel. She spotted Lennox as he shifted and threw herself into his arms. He caught her against him, his hold almost too tight.

She had so many questions, but she kept them to herself. He said nothing, just held her as if they had been apart for an eternity. The shudder that went through him brought tears to her eyes. Ailis smoothed her hands down his hair, giving him comfort and love.

Finally, he lifted his head. The shadows kept her from seeing his face, but she didn't need to. She could feel his despair, his sorrow. His palm slid down her arm to her hand. He took it and led her to the cavern. The light beneath the water remained, as well as the candles. He stopped beside the bed. His shoulders drooped, and his chin dropped to his chest.

She got onto the bed, leaning back on the pillows that rested against the wall, and tugged him toward her. Once he sat with his back to her, she curled herself over him, wrapping her legs around his waist and her arms around his chest. The silence stretched endlessly, but she didn't press him. It wasn't what he needed right now.

Finally, he took a deep breath. "Someone murdered Noma and Ariston."

"What?" Surely, she had misheard.

"Both killed on their clan's lands with slashes across their chests, penetrating to their hearts. They died instantly."

The emptiness in his voice told her so much. She pressed a kiss to his bare shoulder. "I'm so sorry."

"It's my fault."

"Why do you think that?"

"I asked for opinions. Everyone knew why I was going to the other clans."

Ailis shifted and turned him until they faced each other. She took his hands in hers and looked into his eyes. "This isn't on you, my love. You did the right thing."

"Did I?"

"All the Kings knew about the couple before you spoke to others. I don't know about your people, but with mine, rumors spread quicker than wildfire."

He nodded. "They do among dragons, too. If—"

"Nay," she stated firmly. "This isn't on you. Any of it. You were doing what any King in your position would—or should have. The sick individual who took those lives did it out of hate and narrowmindedness. They did it because they feared change."

"I should've seen that."

"You're not all-knowing," she said with a small smile. "You cannot shoulder the blame for this."

He ran a hand down his face. "It's so bloody fucked up. I keep alternating between uncontrollable fury and unmanageable grief."

"As many are, I'm sure." Ailis hesitated before asking, "Do you have anyone in mind who might have done it?"

"I thought it was Darald."

He had been in the forefront of her thoughts, as well. "But?"

"He was standing near Ariston's body. After I saw Noma's. I attacked him, but he didna fight back. He looked as lost as I felt." Lennox glanced at their joined hands. "Noma called out to him for help. He didna get to her in time."

"You believe him?"

Lennox nodded solemnly. "I do. I didna at first because I wanted it to be him. It would've made things quick and easy."

"Things rarely are."

"Aye." He swallowed. "I have the Kings questioning everyone in their clans while I try to sort through the facts, which are no' as many as I wish to have."

She ran her hands up and down his arms. "You'll find who did this. I know you will."

"I've already sworn as much. First, however, there will be a funeral. Normally, each clan takes care of their dead, but since someone sought to prevent Ariston and Noma from mating, they will be together in death. It will happen here, at the capital."

"I think that's an excellent idea."

Lennox sighed. "I can no' stay long. I must get to my clan. I pray the murderer isna among the Silvers."

"What do you need from me?"

"I just need to hold you."

She reached for him, and they fell together onto the bed, their bodies pressed tightly together. After another long stretch, Lennox told her about coming upon Noma and seeing the slain dragon. Tears pricked her eyes when he described her family's and clan's grief. She cried when he detailed going to the Coppers and locating Ariston.

Ailis felt his rage and panic when he laid out the conversation between him and Darald. She listened raptly to the exchanges he had with Rolf and Morten. Lennox had told Darald to stay near him, and the King did exactly that until Lennox sent him to his clan.

"What makes this so difficult is that no one saw anything," Lennox said.

She held him to her breast and slid her fingers through his hair. "Someone did. They need time to come forward."

"How much time do they need to do the right thing?"

"They may be frightened."

"Of me?"

"Of whoever did it."

He grunted at that. "It isna that dragons doona kill, but this is...different."

"Sadly, this would be normal for the Dark."

"How do you handle it?"

"I never have. Not really. You learn to block it out."

Lennox shook his head. "I doona think I ever want to get to a point where I'm no' affected."

"I don't think you should." She bit her lip, thinking. "You said the clans are tight. Yet they do mingle, obviously."

"They do, but it's not as if they're all friendly. Generally, it's those who live along the border. No' all do, but those who choose it know that they'll have to deal with other clans. Why?"

She rested her chin atop his head. "I'm trying to figure out if it's normal for dragons to cross clan borders."

"No' really. Some clans would outright refuse anyone outside their clan to even cross onto their territory, much less rest there."

"Are Darald's and Rolf's those types of clans?"

Lennox hesitated. "I wouldna say Darald's that extreme, but he's no' exactly welcoming. Rolf wouldna turn away anyone who needed rest or water, but he wouldna allow them to stay either. No King would."

"What about here? At the capital? Do dragons come?"

"All are welcome. It is where the magic is the strongest. They may make a pilgrimage to the Dragonwood, but they never stay past sunset."

Ailis consider that for a moment. "So, dragons do travel."

"Aye."

"Do you know when any are here?"

"No' unless I'm searching the Dragonwood." He lifted his head. "You think someone came to the capital before or after they committed the crimes?"

She shook her head. "I'm trying to figure out how easy it is for dragons to move about while also eliminating some."

"The Kings have the most freedom."

"As expected. Are they welcome in other clans' territory?"

His brow wrinkled. "They wouldna be turned away. No King would turn another away. Ever."

"In other words, dragons are used to seeing Kings move about frequently."

"They are."

"And how does a dragon determine who is a King and who isna?"

Lennox propped himself up on his elbow. "Their clan and the other Kings know."

"I was afraid you were going to say that."

"Do you have a theory?"

She smoothed his hair from his face. "Sadly, no. I was thinking if someone saw a dragon, they might be able to tell us if it was a King or not."

"This will take some time to sort through."

Ailis tugged him back down. "What happens when you discover who it was?"

"There will be a tribunal, where dragons are randomly chosen to be on the jury. One of the Kings, generally someone in my position, will serve as judge. Someone will list out the grievances against the accused. The defendant then chooses someone to represent them and can dispute everything. Witnesses are called to give testimony, and then the jury decides the fate of the accused."

She was impressed. "We have something similar, though few things ever reach court. I hear the Light have cases lined up for years. What happens if the defendant is found guilty?"

"In this case, the family of those murdered are allowed to decide what punishment they feel matches the crime. Ultimately, it's the judge's decision."

"How often do you have trials?"

"Maybe a handful a year."

Ailis kissed the top of his head.

"I think they killed the couple to stop me from making a decision," Lennox said.

She had been thinking that, too. "Will it?"

"I'll announce the creation of a new clan at the funeral. If their deaths were meant to change my mind, it has done the opposite."

"There's always a motive for killing. Jealousy, vengeance, wealth. Those are generally the main reasons to commit murder. I've been trying to figure out which category these deaths fit into. I think we can rule out robbery."

He pushed himself into a sitting position. "True. There might be an argument for jealousy, but I'm finding it difficult to make one."

"I agree, someone might be jealous that Noma and Ariston could be together, but you were considering changing a long-held decree. That would benefit anyone envious of them."

"Which leaves vengeance."

She crossed her legs and pulled the fur blanket over her lap, missing his warmth. "I could see someone wanting retaliation for Ariston and Noma being so vocal about wanting to be together."

"That's the thing. They didna. It was Darald who brought it to my attention. No' Rolf or the couple or their family. Other dragons have found their mates outside their clans, but they never shared the information with anyone."

"Because nothing can be done about it."

Lennox nodded glumly, his pale green eyes filled with remorse.

"Still, attention was given to the couple. What if someone was bitter about losing a family member because they hadn't been able to be with their mate? What if they took it out on Noma and Ariston."

"I hate to admit it, but you might be on to something. I think your theory and mine are viable options."

Ailis twisted her lips. "If they thought they could either stop you from deciding or change your mind, they took a huge chance."

"It could be that someone thought they were doing a kindness."

"Excuse me?" she repeated heatedly. "Killing them was a kindness?"

Lennox covered her hand with his. "If they thought change would happen. Once I create a new clan, the couple will have the choice to go there or remain with one of their clans. Regardless of where they decide to live, life will be incredibly hard. A new clan has no hierarchy. Even if I appoint someone, it will be messy. We have no idea how long the magic will take to choose a King—if it ever does."

"Why wouldn't it?"

"I can no' say either way. I'm laying out the problems. Eventually, one or all of the couples who find their way there would have bairns. Those children would then be locked in that clan."

Now, Ailis began to understand. "Starting the process all over again."

"Aye. It would work for some time, but a new clan isna the answer to everything."

"What is?"

Lennox shrugged. "I wish I knew. What I am sure of is that things will be in flux. Kings are already deescalating tension within groups who want revenge. Those dragons believe someone killed the couple to keep them from being together."

"You know, we may both be right. What if someone had two motives to kill?"

"Then I need to find them soon before they strike again."

CHAPTER THIRTY-ONE

A full day had passed since the murders, and Lennox was no closer to finding the culprit than he had been before. Talking to Ailis had helped. Being with her had done even more. He wanted to share his thoughts with Osric, but he couldn't. Until he narrowed things down, everyone was a suspect.

Everyone.

He left the warmth and comfort of Ailis's side before dawn. It had taken everything he had to rise from the bed. He hadn't left immediately, though. He stood beside it, his gaze locked on her face, at ease in sleep. They had talked long into the night. Then, she had reached for him, and he'd reacted as he always did—with a hunger that still shocked him. It hadn't been a quick coming together but a slow, sensual joining that caused his body to stir even now.

Lennox braced himself on the mattress as he leaned over and pressed his lips to her temple. Ailis stirred and blinked up at him. The moment her red eyes locked with his, she touched his face.

"You're leaving."

It wasn't a question. He nodded. "The funeral is today. Doona venture close to the entrance. I'm no' sure how many dragons will show, but I doona wish to chance anyone seeing you. No' now."

"I understand. Is there anything I can do?"

"Just be here when I come back."

"There's only one thing that could make me part from you. Death." She sat up and wrapped her arms around him.

He lowered himself to the bed as they embraced. They simply held each other for long moments. He wished she could be beside him today. He could use her strength, her quiet comfort. But that wasn't possible. It would have to be enough knowing that she was here, waiting.

Ailis leaned back to meet his eyes. "I may not be beside you physically, but I'm always with you."

"That may be the only thing that gets me through this day." Or the days to come. As tough as the funeral would be, the time after would be grueling until the murderer was brought to justice.

"You're the King of Dragon Kings. Everyone will look to you, but don't ever doubt yourself. Not for one second. You know exactly what your people need. Go be the King you were born to be."

Just one more example of what made her perfect for him. Her strength and love were everything he needed. "I love you."

Her mouth curved into a soft smile. "And I love you."

They shared a lingering kiss. Then Lennox forced himself to release her and rise. Otherwise, he would find another excuse to linger. He strode to the opening but paused to look back at her. The sight of Ailis sitting up in their bed, the covers dropped to her waist while her long, silky hair was still tangled from their loving made his heart swell. But it was her smile and her simple nod that propelled him. He took a deep breath and shifted.

All too soon, he was out of his mountain. The sky was a solemn gray, thick with clouds. There would be no magnificent sunrise to watch this morning. He soared above the capital, dipping a wing and spinning around to take in everything with one sweeping glance. Dragons already made their way, coming from all directions. Some in large packs, while others traveled in groups of two or three.

He passed through a valley, soaring as low as he could, his wings barely missing the sides of the mountains with only inches to spare. He spotted Rydel, King of Whites, Elstan, King of Pinks, and Cedric, King of Indigos exiting their mountains. They must have arrived last night. Lennox should've noticed, but he had needed time to himself. With Ailis.

Lennox remained in the sky for the next three hours. The clouds grew darker, denser. A few drops splattered against his scales. Before long, it started to drizzle. Then came a steady rainfall. It was as if the magic felt the weight of their losses, and this was its way of showing everyone that it mourned along with them.

The dragons bowed their heads to him in respect, but otherwise, they said nothing. Which was fine. He didn't want to talk either. His heart was too heavy with the deaths—and the fact that one of their own had been the cause.

Finally, he spotted Darald flying at the head of a group of Yellows, the strongest warriors carrying Noma, her family behind them. Lennox then searched for the Coppers. When he spotted them, it wasn't Rolf in the lead. The clan's warriors carried Ariston, and behind them was Ariston's family. Rolf brought up the rear.

Lennox remained airborne until Noma and Ariston had been lowered to the valley below. He scanned the area around him. There wasn't a single space on any of the mountains as far as he could see. Dragons sat at the top next to their Kings, others clung to the sides or lined up at the bottom. Still more remained in the air, watching the scene from above.

He felt every eye on him. Silvers waited on and around his mountain. He deftly landed atop it and folded his wings. Briefly, he wondered what the Kings before him—and even those who would come after—would do in his place. But none of them mattered. He was the one who had to shoulder all of this. He glanced to his left where Ailis should stand. Her body wasn't with him, but he still felt her presence. It was a balm he desperately needed.

Though he wasn't the only one. Everywhere he looked, he saw others' sorrow and indignation. They needed to be consoled, as well. And he would give it to them.

Lennox opened his mental link to connect with every dragon on the realm, a special ability that only the King of Kings had. *"I can no' remember a day of such monumental heartache. Two dragons found love and wanted to share their lives together. Love. The healer of everything. The greatest gift given to us. From our mothers and fathers, our siblings, our friends, our clans, but especially our mates. Noma and Ariston were prevented from sharing that love in life. Instead, they'll have it in death, until they're reborn and can find each other once more.*

"The honor of a ceremonial funeral is for Kings and the bravest of our warriors. Noma and Ariston were such warriors. They fought for love. Borders didna matter. Clan lines didna matter. The color of the other's scales didna matter. They only wanted each other. And a place where they could live out their lives together.

"Today, we celebrate their strength to stand for what they believed in. Their integrity no' to ignore the feelings within their hearts. And most of all, their love, no' just for each other but for everyone. Today, we celebrate them!"

Lennox jumped into the air and spread his wings. He saw a flurry of movement below as the warriors who'd brought the fallen lovers once again lifted them into the air. They followed Lennox to a clearing in the Dragonwood. He circled high above the forest as the warriors gently lowered the two into the clearing. They arranged Noma and Ariston so they faced each other, their tails and hands touching. It was a stirring moment.

As the warriors took flight, the other Kings fell in below Lennox, circling until they made a huge column with the warriors of the two clans at the bottom, flying over the top of the trees and brushing them with their tails and feet. Lennox tucked his wings and dove through the middle of the column until he reached the clearing. He spread his wings and released a mouthful of fire. The moment the flames struck the two lovers, there was a chorus of roars from every dragon. Lennox joined them as he soared upward. King after King followed him through the column, releasing their own fire. The roars didn't stop until the last of the warriors added their fire.

The Kings and warriors then flew back to the mountains. Lennox was the last to leave the Dragonwood and follow the others to soar through the valleys that coiled their way around the mountains.

Once he made his way in one direction, he circled back and did it again. He would continue his flight until the fire had taken the last of the dragons. Most of the Kings returned to sit atop their mountains. Only Osric, Darald, and Rolf remained with him.

Nothing burned hotter than dragon fire, but even then, it took over two hours for it to consume the lovers. Only then did Lennox land atop his mountain. And only then did the dragons begin their trek home. Not all left. Many remained behind, still struggling with what had happened. The smaller dragons walked through the Dragonwood while the larger ones flew over the vast forest to look at the burial site.

"Lennox," Osric called to him.

He opened his link to his friend. *"Aye."*

"That was a good speech. You did a fine job, brother."

"Thanks." But Lennox would've been happier if he'd never had to do any of this.

Osric blew out a breath. *"This isna the time, but I know how you want to find the killer."*

"Do you have something?" Lennox demanded, his head turning toward Osric. They were over a mile apart, but he could see his friend clearly.

"Possibly. I suspect two from my clan. They've been very vocal about their thoughts on mating outside a clan, but they have no' been the only ones."

"We've never censored anyone's opinions. However, I'm guessing you suspect this is more than just words."

Osric paused. *"Aye. I was hoping to come back to you and say no one in my clan could've done this. But these two have caused trouble before. Several times, in fact. It has escalated each time. The simple truth is that both were gone that night. And no less than eleven dragons saw them together, flying toward Rolf's territory."*

"Where are they?"

"Contained."

"I take it you've questioned them?"

Osric grunted. *"Of course. They willna tell me anything."*

"Then it's my turn."

"I thought you might want a go at them."

Lennox looked around. He should stay until every last dragon had departed, as was the custom, but he had to find the killer—or killers. This was the best lead he'd gotten so far, and the families deserved to know who was responsible.

"They're no' going anywhere. That, I promise," Osric said. *"We can wait."*

"I want to talk to them now."

Lennox didn't wait on his friend. He leaped into the air and headed south. Osric caught up with him, and they flew quickly. Others noticed, but no one asked any questions. Maybe it was the look on his face. Perhaps they could feel the urgency. Whatever the reason, Lennox was happy to be left alone. Because if the two dragons Osric had secured weren't the killers, he would be bombarded by questions.

They reached the edge of the southern territories where Osric's clan lived. The mountain range was vast, the green peaks like jagged teeth surrounded by stunning turquoise waters. Osric flew slightly ahead, leading Lennox toward the mountain with its uncomfortably small caverns used to hold those who had broken the law. Lennox landed at the base of the peak. To his left was a river that wound through the entire valley. Wildflowers blossomed along the shore as a soft wind bent them, the blooms swaying back and forth.

He waited as Osric called for his warriors to haul the two prisoners before them. Lennox was shocked to see that they were young. They weren't even fully grown yet, as was evident by the two towering guards on either side of them.

The one nearest Osric had defiance in his gaze, looking for a fight. Lennox had seen adolescents with that attitude before. Usually, it was because of a bad home or family life. Lennox might feel for the dragon, but nothing excused murder.

The other juvenile had his gaze on the ground, refusing to look up at anyone. Even the guards. Lennox took a step toward him. The youth actually tried to take a step back, but the guards held him. Lennox moved so close his nose nearly touching the teen.

"It's time we had a talk, lad."

CHAPTER THIRTY-TWO

The quiet brought Ailis to the water cavern's entrance. She heard nothing, but she knew dragons were there. She *felt* them. There wasn't flora or fauna within a hundred miles that didn't sense what was happening. The grief and despair seeped through the very rock around her.

Ailis thought about Lennox standing alone, the weight of the realm resting upon his considerable shoulders. No one was more capable of handling it. Yet she wished she was beside him. Not just to witness the funeral but also because she *belonged* beside him.

She conjured up all sorts of scenes in her head of what was happening outside, but they were probably far from the actual event. This might be her life for the foreseeable future. Always hiding, forever waiting. Never beside him when other mates would be beside their dragons. Yet she wouldn't trade her love for anything. If all she could get were stolen moments, then she would take them. Gladly.

The multitude of roars brought her to her knees, her hands over her ears. But it was the stark grief, the raw pain she heard in them that made her cry. Or perhaps she just imagined it because she knew what was going on. Still, it was there, and it was like a knife to her heart.

These weren't her people, but she belonged with one of theirs. She belonged on the realm. She wanted to share in their pain and lend comfort to whoever needed it. Isn't that what a dragon mate would do? She had no idea what another in her place would or would not do, but she wished with all her heart that she could offer comfort to every dragon on the realm, but especially the families who had lost loved ones. She knew the sting of losing family. It was a deep, keening ache that never truly went away. It might shrink to a dark corner, but it could rise up at the most unexpected moments and bring you to your knees.

Yet she cried now for a loss she wasn't part of. She cried for the families, for the lovers who would never know a life together. She cried for the division that cut through every clan, every family. She cried for Lennox and the worry and doubt that shrouded him.

She cried for all that could've been.

And all that would be.

She cried for her parents and Bea. She cried for being too afraid to be a Light and having to leave Bea. She cried for the love she had with Lennox, and their future—whatever Fate allowed them.

Ailis didn't know how long she sobbed. She didn't even remember hearing the roars stop. She had been too lost in her thoughts. She lifted her head, sniffing as she wiped her face.

Then she placed her palm on the stone wall and climbed to her feet. Lennox would no doubt be gone all day, but she couldn't allow him to see her like this. She would be strong for him.

Another kind of quiet settled over the area. Ailis heard dragons moving around in the valley, though the rock prevented her from knowing just how close they were. They were there, keeping her firmly tucked away in the water cavern. She tried to read, but her mind jumped from one thought to another. She finally gave up and sat in one of the chairs while watching the water.

She woke suddenly. She didn't remember drifting off to sleep, but something had stirred her from her slumber. Ailis was still, her ears straining to listen. That was when she heard something in the tunnel. With a thought, she doused the few candles around her and the light beneath the water. She was about to remove everything—including herself—when she heard a low rumbling growl that sent her heart racing.

Ailis froze. How close was the dragon? And what was it doing in Lennox's mountain? There was a scraping noise, like talons on rock, and then a sound she could only describe as chirping that began to grow dimmer. Another growl, this one shorter. This time, she could tell that it came from the entrance. The chirping grew farther and farther away until it stopped altogether.

She collapsed into her chair, her hand on her heart. It must have been a young dragon who had thought to investigate the mountain before one of their parents stopped it. Ailis was glad they had realized what was happening. It was a lesson to her, though. She couldn't freeze the next time. She had to be vigilant and ready to wipe away all evidence of herself at a moment's notice.

Lennox stared at the youth who stood dejected before him. It took all of five minutes of glaring before the adolescent broke. It took another fifteen to get the entire story since he was so frightened that he shook and stuttered over every other word.

"For fuck's sake," Osric muttered, relief and irritation mixing.

Both he and Lennox turned to the second dragon in custody. Lennox made his way to him. *"Do you have any idea what you two have done by no' giving the truth to your King? Do you know what crime we believed you had committed? If it had been leaked about what Osric suspected, dragons would've come for both of you. They would've killed you."*

For the first time since walking out, the young dragon looked uncertain. And a wee bit scared.

"Your friend told me the truth, which is why I'm no' going to dole out punishment. But you lied to your King. On top of that, you broke sacred laws by hunting across clan lines. Then there's the theft between two other clans to start a war. I'm no' sure if you're bored, stupid, or both. Only fools wish for blood and death. But you two are no' my concern. Your punishment is up to Osric," Lennox stated.

"I-I'm sorry, sire," the first youth stuttered.

The second still held onto his glower, along with his attitude, when he said, *"Aye. Sorry."*

"That's the worst apology I've ever heard," Osric snapped. *"And to the King of Kings. Lennox is right. You two are my problem, and you've caused enough trouble. I need to think about your punishment. Until I can sort through that and talk to your parents, you'll remain in custody. Take them back,"* Osric ordered his guards.

The two adolescents fought, each arguing for why they should be released, but neither Lennox nor Osric paid attention.

"Shite. I'm sorry, Lennox. I thought it was them."

He shook his head at his friend. *"They lied to you. They were too wrapped up in their own world and had no idea about the murders or what their lies might mean."*

"It was a waste of your time."

"I had to check it out." Now, however, he was back to square one. Lennox stared at the sky, wondering what to do. *"It would take me months to talk to every dragon. Many more months to check out their stories and verify facts."*

Osric snorted as he swished his tail in agitation. *"Unless they lie, and then it makes things twice as hard. And takes longer."*

"Aye."

"Fucking younglings," Osric grumbled.

Lennox cut him a knowing look. *"We both got into trouble as youths."*

"No' like this."

"Nay. No' like this."

"Fuck." Osric shook his head. *"What do you do now?"*

Lennox blew out a breath. *"I wish I knew."*

"I've been thinking about something. I can no' get it out of my head."

"What's that?"

Osric's eyes were troubled, his lips compressed tight. *"Kings cross borders all the time. Dragons doona heed them much. What if… Bloody hell. I doona even want to consider it, but…what if the killer is one of us?"*

"Ailis asked me something similar."

"And?"

"I doona want to think about it either, but…"

Osric's talons dug into the fertile ground. *"Are you sure it isna Darald?"*

"I am. The look I saw in his eyes, the slight tremor in his voice…he was as appalled and dismayed by the deaths as I."

"It wasna me. I was with my sister's family, meeting my new nephew. Several of my warriors saw me if you need to check my story."

Lennox nodded. *"I'm afraid I'm going to have to do just that."*

"Whatever you need, brother."

It didn't take long for Lennox to talk to Osric's sister and her mate. Osric had the warriors find Lennox. He spoke to each of the seven individually, and they all corroborated Osric's alibi. It was a relief to know that his closest friend was now cleared of the murder. That also meant Lennox could bounce ideas off him now.

"Come," Lennox bade Osric. *"We need to talk to each of the Kings before we do anything else."*

"Where do you want to start?"

He didn't want to start anywhere. He wanted to go home to Ailis. He wanted to hold her in his arms, test out another Fae meal, read more of her books, and laugh with her. But he couldn't do any of that until he found the murderer.

"We start with Jatix. He's the closest King to us," Lennox said.

It wasn't a quick or an easy process. Jatix was at first shocked and then outraged that Lennox suspected him. The King of Emeralds was quick to temper, but he was also quick to let it go. Once Lennox explained the situation, Jatix grudgingly understood.

Four hours later, after moving Jatix into the cleared column, Lennox and Osric were onto the next King. Lennox vowed everyone to secrecy. He wondered how many Kings would make that promise before one of them broke it. *Not many*, was the answer. One would tell a friend, who would then pass it on. Whatever surprise he had hoped to maintain while confronting the Kings was diminishing by the second. But he had no other choice.

It was well past midnight when they marked the sixth King off the suspect list. Lennox looked toward the capital where Ailis waited.

"Return to her," Osric urged him. *"We can pick this up again in the morn."*

"My comfort can wait. A killer is out there, brother, and I can no' take the chance he'll kill again."

"You doona have to do it all."

Lennox snorted and cut his eyes to Osric. *"Unfortunately, I do."*

"Where do you want to go next? Or should we split up?

We could cover more ground if we split up."

"We could."

"But you doona want to."

Lennox shook his head while also trying to shake off the weariness. *"You're my witness. And also the one who'll pull me off the bastard if we do find him."*

"I figured as much. Though you might have picked the wrong friend. I'm liable to lead the charge."

For the first time in over a day, Lennox grinned. It was brief, but Osric's knew just what to say to lighten the mood. *"He doesna stand a chance. Whoever he is."*

"You're sure it's a male?"

"As long as we're looking at Kings, aye."

Osric made an indistinct sound. *"Do you have any suspects? Someone who spoke out against the union, maybe?"*

"Other than Darald? No one."

"It would have to be someone against them, right? Because who would want to take their lives if they agreed."

Lennox squeezed his eyes closed as he realized there was a King he should've spoken to right after Darald.

"What is it?" Osric pushed.

"I know where we need to go next."

"Shite. You know who it is."

"I pray I'm wrong."

Osric swallowed. *"Who?"*

Lennox didn't answer. Instead, he jumped into the air and spread his wings. They didn't speak as they flew, and the closer Lennox got to the clan border, the more he hoped he was wrong. But he knew he wasn't.

They found Rolf alone, far from his mountain. Lennox

glanced at Osric to see his friend's face turning hard with anger and disbelief. Lennox landed first, with Osric behind Rolf.

"I wondered when you'd figure it out," the King of Coppers stated.

CHAPTER THIRTY-THREE

Lennox wanted to rage. He wanted to strike something.

Instead, he stood calmly before Rolf, looking into his green eyes. Without looking away, Lennox told Osric, *"Give us a moment."*

Osric flew away, but Lennox barely noticed. He couldn't wrap his head around what was happening. It had to be a dream. None of this could be real. Rolf was an honorable King, a male that others looked up to—even other Kings.

"You're wondering why." Rolf released a long sigh and slid his gaze to the side, looking out over his land. *"The simple truth is I knew what awaited Noma and Ariston. I knew that no matter what decision you came to, their lives would be filled with one setback after another. They would never have peace, and they would force that world onto their bairns."*

"That wasna your decision to make!" The words exploded from Lennox. He curled his talons, sinking them into the

ground so he didn't latch on to Rolf's neck. *"You overstepped. Gravely."*

Green eyes looked back at him. *"Perhaps, but then again, you've never had to witness someone you love wither away because they couldna be with their mate."*

"You didna give me a chance to make a decision."

"It wouldna have mattered if you approved the mating. How can you no' see they were doomed?" Rolf beseeched, pain in his eyes.

Lennox shook his head. *"You had to know you couldna get away with this. The magic will replace you."*

"I'm sure it's already found a new King for our clan. I expect a challenge anytime."

"Why did you no' come to me? Why no' tell me your fears?"

Rolf lay down and wrapped his tail around himself. *"Why? So you could carry those burdens atop the ones you already lug around? I think no', my friend."*

Lennox struggled to get his temper under control. He was furious. But he was also hurting. A King he respected and liked had taken two innocent lives. The reason didn't matter. There was only one outcome.

He drew in a deep breath and spotted Osric circling high above them. Lennox thought back over the last few days and went over every conversation he'd had with Rolf. The funeral that morning should've alerted him. It wasn't odd for a King to travel in front of a procession or behind. However, now that Lennox knew what Rolf had done, he was able to see the full picture.

Rolf hadn't just brought up the rear of his procession. He

had lagged behind. Lennox had believed it was because of grief. And that might have been part of it, but the truth was that Rolf knew he had no right to be there.

"*You had a good legacy for your family and your clan. Why would you do this?*" Lennox asked as he looked at him.

Rolf sighed loudly. "*My clan means everything to me. The day the magic chose me to lead was the best day of my life. Then I learned my sister had found her mate in another clan. I sat in a seat of power, yet I was utterly powerless. I welcomed him into the clan. I told them they would have a place with us, but he couldna do it. He doomed my sister and himself to the worst kind of death a dragon can endure.*"

"*Noma and Ariston would've gone through with it. Neither of them was backing out.*"

"*Maybe.*" He swung his head to Lennox. "*They would've been outcasts wherever they went. Dragons can no' endure that.*"

"*That was their decision, and theirs alone.*"

"*Tell me you didna worry about what would happen if you approved the mating. Tell me you were no' concerned that letting them be together would stir up more than if you left things as they are.*"

Lennox held his gaze. "*I can no'.*"

"*Exactly. I did what had to be done. What no King of Kings dared to do. I didna wish to do it, but no one else would have stepped up.*"

Lennox was now in a tight position. As King of Kings, he had every right to put Rolf on trial — or take his life himself. The trial would stir up the entire realm and divide the dragons more than they already were. Rolf would die. Be it by

Lennox's hand or the dragon the magic chose to be the next King of Coppers.

If, however, Lennox executed Rolf, it would serve a two-fold purpose. It would prove to all that Lennox had ferreted out the killer, and it would save the Coppers a battle. What he couldn't halt was the resentment and ire that would burn through not just the Coppers but also every clan around the globe.

"*Aye. Do it,*" Rolf said.

Lennox frowned. "*What are you talking about?*"

"*You're wondering if you should kill me or allow the challenge from the next King. You should do it. The dragons need to know where you stand.*"

Lennox turned away. He needed to think, but he couldn't take the time he really wanted. The magic wouldn't wait to replace a King. It never did. If only it would've acted before Rolf took two lives. No matter how much Lennox wanted to rail at the magic, he couldn't. Every dragon had the ability to make their own choices and deal with whatever consequences arose from those actions.

"*Lennox?*"

He looked up at his friend. He heard the worry in Osric's voice. "*Bring Darald and Heller. They're the two closest Kings. I need the three of you as witnesses.*"

"*Fuck me,*" Osric whispered. Then, in a stronger voice, he said, "*On it.*"

Lennox noticed the growing number of dragons who had noticed him. The anxious looks on their faces broke his heart. They wanted answers, as had he. And just like him, they would be staggered by the truth.

How had things gotten to this point? Had he taken too long? Should he have followed in his predecessors' footsteps and left things as they were? Where did he go wrong, and how could he ensure it didn't happen again?

He longed for Ailis. He needed her arms around him, to feel her softness against him. To bury his face in the crook of her neck and sink his fingers into the cool length of her hair. Whatever hope he had for them was slipping away like water through his fingers. If dragons couldn't accept two of their own from different clans being together, then they would never welcome her.

Lennox didn't have to demand that Rolf stay put. The King hadn't so much as twitched since he lay down. More Coppers gathered. It was as if they sensed something in the air. Maybe it was Rolf's acceptance of his fate. Perhaps it was Lennox's wrath and disbelief. The hope in their eyes would be replaced shortly, which was almost as ghastly as what he was about to do.

It wasn't until Lennox spotted a male headed toward them that he knew his time had run out. *"Osric? Where are they? I need all of you here now."*

Osric landed immediately on the other side of Rolf. *"They're almost here. Brother, you doona have to do this."*

Lennox didn't reply. What was there to say? No matter his response, Osric would attempt to talk him out of it. It didn't matter. Because Darald and Heller arrived. Lennox watched Darald's frown at Rolf's casual stance turn into rage. Osric kept Darald in check. Heller, on the other hand, stood like a stone statue, his disapproval of Rolf evident.

Osric hadn't told them. Lennox knew that for a fact. It

wasn't Osric's nature. The other two Kings had pieced it together once they took stock of the scene. For his part, Rolf kept his eyes on his clan. He paid no attention to anyone else. Lennox wasn't as fortunate.

The male hadn't slowed his approach, and by the narrowing of his eyes, Lennox knew what he had come to do. Did Lennox take control and get on with why he had brought the other three Kings to the clan? Or did he step aside? The easiest solution was rarely the right one. His current dilemma made it nearly impossible to know the correct choice.

Lennox looked at Osric to find his brother watching him. No matter what he decided, Osric would stand beside him. Because that's what brothers did.

"Sire."

Lennox briefly closed his eyes before looking at the male before him. *"I know why you're here."*

"And I know why you and the other Kings are here." The male lifted his chin. *"My clan doesna yet realize what's happening, but they will. They're going to need a strong King. One who shows them he will stand beside them, that he will stand for them against all enemies. Even those within the clan."*

Lennox liked him instantly. *"What's your name?"*

"Thad, sire."

"I agree with everything you've said. The magic chose you, which means you're what this clan needs. However, there's a reason I'm here."

"You did your duty. You found the murderer."

Lennox was impressed by Thad's tightly controlled anger. Lennox also knew Rolf wouldn't fight back. He had accepted his fate the moment he decided to take those lives. *"This is bigger than just your clan. This is about all dragons. And our future."*

"Rolf was a friend. He and I are close. Nothing will wash away the stain on our clan or the Yellows. I wish to punish Rolf. I looked up to him, and he betrayed us all." Thad paused, his breathing irregular as he struggled to contain his wrath. *"Yet I see the wisdom of your words and actions. I may no' like it, but I have no choice but to stand by it."*

"Right now, you want blood and vengeance. Trust me when I say there will come a time when you'll regret starting your reign with your hands covered in it."

Thad glanced behind him at the crowd. *"How are you no' incensed?"*

"Just because I doona show my emotions doesna mean they're no' there. As Kings, the clans look to us to know how to react. You wait until you're alone, with your mate, or other Kings before you let your emotions loose. Otherwise, you could start a war. I'm working hard to prevent that right now."

"I'm no' sure that's possible."

"Me either, lad. Me either."

"Thank you for the advice. I'm going to need all I can get."

Lennox nodded. Then he faced Rolf. The life of a King was what one made it, but the one thing a King never escaped was death. Either by doling it out—or receiving it. Lennox wished he was done spilling blood. With all his heart, he wanted to step aside and allow Thad to issue the challenge.

But then he wouldn't be the King he was.

He had no way of knowing if his actions would reduce the resentment or divide the dragons. Doing nothing ensured things would escalate. He started forward when Rolf gained his feet and faced Lennox.

"Let me do it," Darald said.

Lennox glanced at the King of Yellows but didn't reply. The crowd around them had grown beyond the Coppers to include Noma's family and others in her clan. All eyes were directed at the Kings. Confused faces were slowly turning to ones of shock and dismay—and fury.

He didn't know where the first roar came from. Honestly, Lennox was surprised it had taken so long to hear it. Once it was released, others joined in until the ground and the very air vibrated with it.

"I'm ready," Rolf said.

The King of Coppers didn't hang his head. He didn't advert his eyes. He stood proudly as a King would. If only he had been the King his clan needed.

Lennox took a deep breath and struck.

CHAPTER THIRTY-FOUR

Three weeks of hell. Twenty-one agonizing days of not knowing where Lennox was or if she would see him again. Ailis hadn't been outside the mountain at all during that time. She didn't dare when the realm was in such chaos.

She had gotten two hours with Lennox after he returned from passing judgment on Rolf. It had boggled her mind that a King would kill innocents. But what concerned her more was Lennox. He wasn't dealing with the betrayal—or his role as executioner—well. In those precious hours with him, she hadn't said but a handful of words, letting him talk instead. All the while, he had held her tenderly, lovingly.

She had foolishly believed they would have plenty of time with each other. But Lennox hadn't been surprised when conflicts broke out, and not just between clans—within them, as well. He'd issued his decree to form the new clan, but it did nothing to ease tensions.

He had then left her with a long, hungry kiss and a promise to return as soon as he could. She had been waiting ever since. Ailis would wait an eternity for him. But not knowing what was going on was hard for her to deal with. She had no idea if things had gotten worse or better. She worried constantly about him being injured. Because even she realized that Kings would eventually fight other Kings.

Ailis's apprehension occupied every waking hour. She wasn't saved in sleep, either. Her dreams—or rather her nightmares—were filled with violent images of losing Lennox. She hadn't slept through the night since he left.

On top of that was her concern that he would die, and she wouldn't know it until another dragon arrived in his cave. She set up a shield near the first cavern to alert her if anyone entered. That should've been enough to relieve her, but it wasn't. She couldn't relax or get comfortable anywhere.

Instead, she had taken to exploring to fill the endless hours. Crawling through narrow tunnels, climbing over boulders, and squeezing through tight shafts. Sometimes, she came to a dead end and would have to retrace her steps. Twice she got stuck. Thankfully, she was able to teleport back to the water cavern. Otherwise, she would've died.

In the early part of the third week, she found a place of her own. It took her three hours to crawl, climb, slide, and wiggle to reach it. She'd initially thought it was another dead end until she peered into the sliver of space between two boulders and saw it. Ailis then had to find a way around and over the rocks. In the end, she climbed up and over, which took all of her strength as well as some magic. Finally, she was in another tunnel that required her to crawl through. Then, she climbed inside.

It wasn't really a cavern. Not like Lennox's or the water one. Hers was more like a hollowed-out section within the rocks. She couldn't stand up straight because of the low, domed ceiling, but she didn't care. It was hers, and it allowed her to remain in Lennox's mountain without fear of being discovered by someone else.

After a little redecorating with some comfy pillows to ease the ache of her backside and candles in all the hollows and indentations of the cave, she sat back and sighed. The area was long enough to stretch out. She added a narrow mattress with plenty of blankets, and of course, her books. And with one thought, she erased every instance of herself from the water cavern. Just in case.

She wasn't leaving Earth as long as Lennox was alive. Maybe not even after. She hadn't just given him her heart, she had also given it to the dragons and their land. Regardless if they would have her or not. Lennox wanted her, and that was all that mattered.

No longer did she sleep for hours at a time because of the nightmares. Now, she took short naps. As soon as she woke from a dream, she would read or try to draw from her memories of the ice cave and other things with the love of her life. Her thoughts, however, remained constantly on one thing —Lennox.

Perhaps that was why it took her so long to realize that her monthly flow hadn't come. She had used her magic to prevent any pregnancy, so she knew that wasn't the issue. It had to be crossing realms. That must have messed up the timing. Earth's days were shorter than her realm's. Surely, that had done something. It would work itself out. She was sure of it.

Then the cramping started, just as she knew it would. Except they became far worse than anything she had ever experienced before. Not long after, the bleeding began. There was much blood. Too much. Racked with pain that had her curled into a ball, she realized this wasn't a monthly cycle. This was a miscarriage.

When it was finally over, she carefully folded the bloody blanket and clothes. She refused to just toss them away. A life was inside, one from Lennox and her. Ailis jumped to the water cavern. In the very back, against the columns of sharp rock, she lowered her baby and carefully placed rocks atop it, building a short mound with three rocks of decreasing size stacked on top of each other—one for Lennox, one for her, and one for their child.

Then she returned to her cave and cried.

Two more weeks went by before she heard her name. It wasn't Lennox, but Osric. Ailis teleported to him and found herself in his cavern. He looked haggard, his eyes vacant and drained. She waited for him to notice her. He blinked and tried to smile but couldn't quite manage it. That told her more than words ever could.

"Tell me he's alive," she begged.

Osric nodded. "Aye. He wanted to come, but he couldna. He's afraid…he's worried…"

"I'm not going anywhere."

"I told him that, but he's overwhelmed. Ailis…things are so verra bad."

She swallowed, her heart clenching at what she could well

imagine was happening. "Tell him I'm fine and he doesn't need to worry about me. I'll wait. I'll always wait."

"I will."

"Can you tell me what's happening?"

Osric ran a hand down his face and swayed, his exhaustion evident. Ailis rushed to him and called a chair. She eased him into it, her heart twisting at what the ravages of war could do to the strongest of males. If Osric looked like this, what about Lennox? Someone needed to be there for him since she couldn't.

"We gain ground, but it isna enough," Osric finally answered. "It's never enough."

"Everyone is still upset about the murders?"

He shrugged and leaned his head back, his eyes closing. "It's everything, Ailis. Lennox passed judgment on Rolf in hopes of avoiding this verra thing. He carries that, and few realize the implications. But it was all for naught, and that infuriates me. Our people are hopelessly divided."

"Mine have been like that for some time. Find a way to mend the rift. There has to be a way."

Osric opened his eyes as he rolled his head toward her. "If you know it, tell me. I've had little rest. Lennox has had none. He's pushing himself harder than any of us, and I doona know how much longer he can go on like that. He willna stop, though."

Ailis's eyes burned with tears. For Lennox, Osric, and every dragon. She knew what would come if something didn't change. If she couldn't tell Lennox, then she would send the message through his brother. She drew in a steadying breath and fixed Osric with a firm stare. "Make the dragons see what

Lennox is doing for them. They need to set aside their anger and fears and see him. See what all of the Kings are trying to stop."

"That will never happen."

She straightened and looked down at him. "Not with that attitude. My people are long past help. Yours aren't. Find a way. Talk to Lennox. Talk to the other Kings. Some out there want to stop this as much as you do. *Find them*. They're the key."

"I will."

"If you don't, this continuing war will break Lennox."

Osric lifted his head and sat up. "You should be out there with us."

"I would go in a heartbeat."

"Too bad you can no' shift into one of us."

If only. She forced her shoulders to relax. "Rest, and then return to Lennox."

"If my King doesna rest, I doona rest," Osric said as he pushed to his feet. He bowed his head to her. "Your words will bolster Lennox."

She turned as he walked past her. "Be safe, Osric."

"You are a queen. No' just his mate, but the perfect queen for all of us. One day, the others will see that. I'll make sure of it." He shot her a smile before shifting and leaving.

His words meant a lot, but they didn't lessen her worries. Ailis jumped back to her cave. She curled up on the pile of pillows and reached for her book, but she didn't bother opening it. Lennox always occupied her thoughts, but now her fear had ramped up a thousandfold. Osric looked ready to fall over. When Lennox returned, she would be ready to comfort him however he needed.

She refused to think that he might not come back. Though she knew little of war, other than what she'd read or had heard from others, the trauma could leave a lasting impression. Lennox was formidable, but everyone had their breaking point. She clung to the hope that he would make it through. Once they were together, she would help him sort it all out, one step at a time.

Eventually, she would tell him about the child she'd lost.

But not at first. He would need to heal mentally, physically, and emotionally. She would give him whatever he required, even if it was space and time alone.

"Come back to me, my love," she whispered.

The capital had been quiet for over a week. The rain had barely stopped in all that time, alternating from violent storms to soft rainfall. Ailis didn't think she would ever get warm again.

She marked off another day in her notebook. Lennox had been gone for just over eight weeks. There had been no other visits from Osric, which made the waiting even more difficult. Some days were harder than others. Occasionally, Ailis couldn't even get out of bed. She would simply lay there, lost in thought or sleeping fitfully.

On other days, she was a ball of energy. Wanting—craving—to do something. She explored more of the mountain. When that wasn't enough, she investigated Osric's. Then she felt horrible for intruding. She redecorated her cave, the cavern, and the water cavern dozens of times just for something to do to fill the time before promptly wiping it all away. She swam in the too-cold water. She drew anything and everything, from Lennox to the dragon on his body, to him as a dragon. None of it was ever quite right. She tried to sleep, but she could never do more than doze. There were no more nightmares, at least. Hard to get to those when she wasn't sleeping deeply enough.

She contemplated jumping to the doorway, but she wasn't sure why. Maybe just to see if it was still there. Possibly to get an idea of what was going on out there. Perhaps even to tear down the doorway to ensure that no one could ever come through. In the end, she did nothing.

Ailis sat on the pillows, her legs pulled up to her chest, and her head resting on her knees as she rocked back and forth. Suddenly, she stilled. Had she heard something?

"Ailis!"

Her heart jumped into her throat at the sound of Lennox's voice. She teleported behind him in the water cavern. She almost called out but paused just to take in the sight of him. He searched the empty space with a small bubble of light in his hand. He tossed it into the water and watched it sink to the bottom. Then he released a long sigh and turned around. The worry eased from his face as he smiled.

"Are you real? Or a figment of my imagination?" she asked.

"I'm verra real, darlin'. You're the only thing that's kept me going, and if I doona hold you soon, I'm no' sure I'll last."

Her face crumpled as they rushed to each other. She squeezed him tightly, reveling in the feel of him. All the days and weeks without him, the trepidation…his embrace washed it all away.

She squeezed her eyes shut. She was never letting him go. "I feared you wouldn't come home."

"Nothing would keep me from you. No' a damned war. No' even death."

CHAPTER THIRTY-FIVE

The weeks of blood and death, of horror and torment, melted away in Ailis's arms. Lennox never wanted to be apart from her again. He hadn't realized the depth of his loneliness until she came into his life.

She showed him new possibilities and opened his eyes to things he'd never dreamed were possible. Their passion was heady, wild, and commanding. And their love was the most powerful, prevailing phenomenon he had ever encountered.

Or ever would.

With her by his side, he had stepped into the role of King as never before. She didn't just make him a better male. She made him want to *be* a better male. He could search the universe for eternity and never find anyone as perfectly matched to him as Ailis.

Lennox gently held her face between his hands and looked into her crimson eyes. There was so much he wanted to tell her, but now wasn't the time for words. Desire sizzled between them. The torrid storm of need and hunger swept around them, consuming them in its blaze.

The moment his lips touched hers, all Lennox wanted was to be inside her. To have their bodies joined. He tasted her yearning, her fiery passion that excited him beyond measure. Their hands clawed at each other, trying to get closer, always closer. He grabbed at her clothes, uncaring when he heard fabric rip.

Finally, the clothes were gone. They were skin-to-skin, but that still wasn't enough. Lennox spun her around. He held her against him, her back flush to his chest as he kissed down the side of her neck and ran his hands over her body before cupping her breasts. A moan fell from her lips. It turned into a gasp when he pinched her nipples. Her hand reached up and back, tangling in his hair while she rocked her buttocks against his hard length.

He wanted to make her scream with pleasure, but he was past the point of waiting. Lennox turned her in his arms once more before lowering her to the ground. Just before her back touched, he used magic to spread a blanket. Her legs parted as her red gaze watched him. He knelt between her thighs. There, he paused, sending a prayer of thanks to the magic, Fate, and any other entity that had brought them together. Then he thrust inside her.

She arched her back, her eyes sliding closed as she moaned.

Pleasure burst through her. Ailis's breath locked in her throat as every nerve ending sparked to life once more. The male, the dragon who had stolen her heart and given her his in return, had found his way back to her. The fears that had plagued her, the worry that had consumed her were wiped away with one touch, one kiss.

Until it was only the two of them.

And their love.

She clutched at his shoulders as he began moving within her—hard, deep thrusts that pushed her beyond reckoning and thought. Beyond being. It wasn't just their bodies joined. It was their hearts. Their very souls. She felt his essence brush against hers and knew that no matter how many lives they shared, they would always find their way to each other.

Lennox's breath was harsh, his moans growing louder. Then he flipped them so he was on his back with her straddling him. Their gazes met. No words were needed. Their bodies said it all.

She rocked her hips and saw his eyes darken. His hands returned to her breasts, where he expertly teased her sensitive nipples until she shook with desire. She dropped her head back, lost in the beautiful, searing passion scorching hotter and hotter.

Ailis welcomed the fervent need. She embraced the searing desire.

She sought the flames that licked at her. The flames of a dragon.

Her dragon.

The sight of Ailis, head thrown back in wild abandon as she rode him hard was something he would never forget. Lennox sat up, needing to taste her lips. He tangled his fingers in her hair, wrapping the length around his fist even as she lifted her head to look at him.

Love and hunger sparkled in her eyes. His heart skipped a beat. Then she stiffened before pleasure washed across her face. He was already coming before her body tightened around his cock, milking him completely.

They didn't move for long minutes. Lennox felt tremors run through Ailis. Slowly, his breathing returned to normal, but he was loath to release her. Thinking of her, thoughts of finding her in his mountain had kept him functioning through the worst of things.

She was the first to stir. Her hands slid into his hair as her nails lightly scraped his scalp, causing prickles of sensation to run from his head down his body. She gave him a soft kiss before lifting herself to meet his gaze. The love he saw in her eyes was a balm to his battered heart and body.

"Where's the bed?" he asked.

Her nose wrinkled. "I became a tad paranoid about someone finding me, so I removed everything. It's back now."

"Good, because the floor is hard."

Her smile was blinding. How he had missed it. And her touch. He had missed everything about her.

Before he could move, Ailis jumped them to the bed. Lennox wasn't upset. He had no desire to pull out of her anytime soon. It was hard to miss the way her gaze searched his face, however. She had questions, and she deserved answers. Even if he didn't want to give them.

"You don't have to talk about it," she said as if reading his mind.

He shook his head. Then he gently unwound his hand from her hair. "I'm sorry I couldna return to you or call you to me."

"There's no need to apologize for that. I understood." Her hands gently touched his face, smoothing back his hair and caressing his frown lines. "Though I am glad you sent Osric. It was the not-knowing part that got to me the most."

"I'm glad I sent him, too. It wasna the same as seeing you myself, but it did the trick."

She frowned. "What do you mean?"

"I had been fighting against those who were revolting. Both the ones for and against cross-clan mating. Rolf being the killer was the spark that lit the mound of unrest. It would have happened regardless, though. I see that now, but I had hoped I could lessen some of it."

"You were fighting both sides?" Her eyes were wide with shock.

Lennox shrugged. "We attempted to control the situation. That worked for a wee bit before some of the Kings joined their clans."

"I suppose your decree of a new clan didn't help."

"Hardly. We would get one clan settled before we had to move to another, only to learn the previous clan had begun to riot again. The Kings were spread thin while also worried about their clans. No matter what we did, things kept escalating. I knew where we were headed."

She swallowed. "Civil war."

"I didna want that. I was prepared to do anything to stop it, but I couldna come up with anything. The other Kings were exhausted and weary of the fighting. We all knew we were losing. One suggested we let the two sides fight it out while we sat back and watched. But I couldna do that. So many had already died." He looked away when he thought about the children he had seen trampled by adults too angry to notice the bairns trying to run away. "It was too much."

Ailis pressed her forehead to his. "Oh, my love. I'm so sorry."

He met her gaze. "I needed you, but I could only ask Osric to look in on you. He brought back your words. They gave me exactly what I needed. Hope."

She smiled and lifted her head.

"I told the Kings to stop fighting. We were to break up any conflicts we came across, but we wouldna engage anymore. If we were attacked, we were to stop them without causing harm. And it worked. We were able to slowly end the strife and stabilize the situation. Emotions are still running hot, but I've dispatched the Kings to their clans to keep a careful eye on things. They know to contact me if something arises."

"And your clan?"

"I spent two days with them. I'll need to return, but I had to see you."

Her red eyes glittered from the soft light in the water. "I had no qualms you could solve things."

"I had a lot of doubt."

"You don't give yourself enough credit."

"It was your idea that resolved everything."

She smoothed her hands over his shoulders. "You would've thought of it eventually."

Lennox pulled her against him. "Maybe."

"I know you would have," she insisted before climbing off him and slipping beneath the covers.

He turned to face her. "I gather you didna have a good time either."

"I was worried about you and hated the uncertainty."

There was no mistaking the dark circles beneath her eyes. He had thought her safe in his mountain. Had he been wrong? "Did anything happen?"

"Nothing, I assure you. I let my imagination get away from me, which compounded my apprehension. I kept thinking that a dragon would come in and see me or our things."

"No' to mention you were bored. It was eight weeks without seeing the sky."

"Without you, you mean," she said with a wry grin. "I did create a sun and moon model so I knew if it was day or night. It was how I counted the days. It also allowed me to imagine the bright sky full of clouds or a starry night. You're right, though. I did get bored. I couldn't concentrate long enough to read, so I explored the mountain. I found a small cave where I could hide and attempt to sleep without worrying about someone finding me."

Lennox felt horrible. He smoothed his fingers down the side of her face. "I'm sorry, lass."

"That's where I was when you returned."

"I'd like to see it if you'll show me."

She grinned and laced her fingers with his. "I'd be happy to."

"Anything else happen?" He wasn't sure what prompted him to ask.

A dark shadow moved across her face, and she glanced away. "How long do I have before you leave again?"

There was something, but he wouldn't push. Not now. But soon. "The quicker I depart, the quicker I can return, but I'm no' leaving tonight."

"It's night out?"

"Aye. Do you want to see?"

Her eyes crinkled at the corners. "Please."

"Let me get up there, and I'll roar for you."

She nodded eagerly.

Lennox rose. He took a quick look around the cavern, missing the candles. That was when he saw the small pile of rocks with three stacked on top of each other above it. He paused and looked at Ailis. She was smoothing the covers on the bed and didn't see him. Something told him not to ask her about it now.

He hurried into the tunnel and shifted. Once outside, he flew to the top and let out a short roar. A moment later, his hand hid her. Her smile was luminous, her gaze locked on the stars.

If there was one thing Lennox had learned from the unrest that had rippled through his realm, it was that they would never accept Ailis. She would have to spend most of her life hidden if they were to be together.

Worse, he would never be able to officially have a mating ceremony. How could he bind them together when he knew another would come to take his place someday? He couldn't— and wouldn't—condemn her to that death.

CHAPTER THIRTY-SIX

Lennox was only gone for two days. They went by quickly for Ailis. The tension that had gripped her eased even more when she learned there had only been two small skirmishes that the Kings swiftly dealt with.

"Things are no' over completely," Lennox said. "It will take time, but we're on our way."

"Anything happening with the new clan?"

His lips flattened. "A couple and two single dragons chose the new one. Since they doona have a King, I'm keeping an eye on them."

"Do you think they'll stay?"

"Who can say? Rolf wasna wrong when he said that mating with someone outside the clan makes for a difficult life."

"Simply because your people are used to one thing. Change doesn't happen overnight."

He grunted. "I can attest to that. I will say, I like Thad. He has found his place quickly among the Coppers."

"So, all this discord and death, and nothing has really changed?"

"No' as much as I'd like, nay." He took her hand. "Show me your cave."

Ailis grinned. "Shall I jump us there?"

"I want to see how you found it."

"All right," she said and tugged her after him.

With his height and muscle, he scaled things faster and easier than she had. She led the way, but he never rushed her. In some of the tighter sections, it took him longer to turn his body to squeeze through, but he didn't complain once. It wasn't until they reached the last tunnel that they realized he wouldn't fit no matter what he did.

"How much farther?" he asked.

She glanced down the shaft. "About a hundred feet. Most all of it in the tunnel."

"If I'm going to see your cave, you'll have to jump me."

Ailis placed her hand on him and teleported them inside. "Mind your head," she urged.

Unfortunately, he banged his head on the ceiling at the same time. "Oof," he muttered, rubbing the spot that had connected with the rock.

She chuckled and motioned for him to sit. Ailis waited as his gaze moved around the small area that had been her sanctuary. He touched the pillows, his fingers playing with the fringe on one. He tilted his head and read the titles of books she had stacked together. He smiled at her pile of blankets folded neatly on the narrow mattress. He nodded at the candles.

Then, finally, his gaze returned to her. "It's verra nice. You made it yours."

"There's no need for it now that you've come home."

"I doona foresee a need for you to use this, but it's here if you ever need it. And as lovely as this is, can we return the water cavern to how it was before I left? Candles and all?"

She smiled and leaned across to kiss him. "I already planned on it." She sat back and laughed as he tried to find a way to move without bonking his head again. "There's not much room. It's really only suitable for one person. Ready to go back?"

"Aye," he said and glanced at the low ceiling.

Ailis jumped them to the cavern. He pulled her to him for a sultry kiss. Then he stripped out of his pants and dove into the pool. She smiled and watched his body glide effortlessly through the water. Her grin faded when her gaze landed on the pile of rocks where she had buried their child. She needed to tell him. It wasn't as if she'd kept it a secret, but the thought of revealing the truth and disclosing her pain seemed wrong.

He would be as hurt as she. They would share the loss together, but she didn't want to expose him to any more pain. Lennox had been through enough. Except he had a right to know.

Ailis put her hand on her stomach. She had added an extra layer of magic to prevent another pregnancy. It wasn't that she didn't want to have a child—his child. That would come later, once they figured out their situation. It wouldn't be fair to either of them to bring another life into the world at the moment. Things were too new to be so careless.

Yet she wondered how he might have reacted had she not lost the baby. Would he have been overjoyed at the prospect of their love creating life? Without a doubt, she knew he would have been jubilant.

The questionable future would've overshadowed that. She didn't miss the fact that he was worried about the new clan. It wasn't taking off as he had hoped. Or as it might have had Noma and Ariston lived to begin it. That meant it would be a longer, harder road for Lennox and her. If they were ever even able to travel such a path.

She pulled herself from her thoughts and dropped her hand to her side. When she looked at Lennox, he treaded water, his gaze locked on her. He didn't press her, but his expression told her that he knew something was amiss. So, he waited patiently for her to open up.

Ailis debated whether to postpone the inevitable, but the longer she put it off, the harder it would be to find the words. It was better to do it now. "There's something I need to tell you."

"No' if it causes you that much pain."

She didn't say more. The pain was there regardless. Lennox swam to the edge and pulled himself from the water. By the time he reached her, he was dry, his trousers in place. She took his hand and jumped him over the water before leading him to the grave.

Ailis felt his gaze on her. She fought the tears that threatened because she didn't want to break down as she spoke. "This is where…" she began and faced him.

She cleared her throat and looked into his pale green eyes. She wondered what color eyes their child would've had. What color hair? Would it have been a boy or a girl? What kind of magic would it have taken from each of them?

A dragon and a Fae.

Lennox's brow furrowed deeper. He took her hands as his gaze searched hers. "What is it? Tell me so I can help."

"I miscarried." The words tumbled out of her. They were frank and to the point, not the tender way she had hoped to share the news.

Lennox didn't move for a heartbeat. His face went slack, the color draining as he slowly lowered his eyes to the pile of rocks.

"It happened three weeks ago," she continued into the silence. "I should've told you as soon as you returned. It was just…it's just difficult."

His arms came around her, his body flush against hers. His hold was almost too tight, but she understood all too well the rush of emotions that slammed into him. She felt his pain, the unspoken words of loss he couldn't find to articulate his feelings.

The tears she had pushed away fell heedlessly now. She clung to him. They were each other's lifeline. With the release of the truth, it was like a floodgate had opened. Sobs racked her, and the harder she cried, the tighter he held her. His tears mixing with hers.

Ailis had never thought much about children. She had never seen herself as a mother, yet it felt like her heart had been ripped from her chest. The life that could've been was gone before she had even known it was there. If she had, she would've taken better care of it. Maybe then it would still be alive and inside her.

Being cradled in Lennox's arms and their shared grief helped to heal a tiny fraction of her heart, but nothing would ever truly mend the wound the loss of a child left behind. She might not have gotten to hold her baby or given it a name, but it had been theirs.

Lennox's hands moved up her shoulders to her neck and then her head as he gazed down at her. There were streaks of tears down his face, his pale green eyes watery. "Och, lass. I'm so sorry I wasna here for it. You should never have had to suffer that alone."

"You had other important matters to tend to."

"Nothing is more significant than my mate and our bairn."

She wiped at his tears.

He squeezed his eyes closed. His voice broke as he said, "Our bairn."

His raw anguish brought a fresh wave of anguish for her. They turned together, facing the grave. Lennox knelt before it and reverently touched the rocks.

"I wanted the baby close. I'm sorry if this isn't how you take care of your dead," she began.

He briefly met her gaze. "This is perfect." She took his hand when he reached for her. After a moment, he stood. "Did you know you were pregnant?"

"I didn't. I would've told you had I known."

Lennox ran a hand down his face, wiping the tears away. "You used magic."

"I did. It should've prevented any pregnancy, but it didn't."

He nodded slowly before he faced her. "Did you see the bairn?"

Ailis shook her head. "I saw nothing among the sheets and the blood. I couldn't bear to look. I wrapped everything and brought it here."

"What do you think a child of a dragon and a Fae would look like?"

"I've been trying to imagine it."

"And?" he asked eagerly.

She wound her arms around his neck and grinned. "I think such a baby would be beautiful and amazing."

"You're no' worried about half its form looking like a dragon?"

"I hadn't considered that. I thought…well, you can shift, so I assumed the child would look mortal."

Lennox linked his hands behind her. "How are your bairns born?"

The question surprised her. Didn't he know how something was born? "They grow inside us."

"Aye, I know that. I mean, are they in eggs?"

"They aren't hatched. Why do you ask?"

"Because dragons are hatched."

Ailis blinked. That wasn't something she had thought to ask. "I'm beginning to understand why you asked what our child might look like. You can shift, but you're still very much a dragon."

"Aye. I think…" He paused to clear his throat. "I think

that's why you miscarried. We might have produced a child, but it wouldna have survived."

The more she learned about dragons, the more she realized he was probably right. "That makes sense."

"It doesna diminish our pain," he whispered.

She saw a tear drop onto his cheek as he glanced toward the grave. "Nay, it doesna."

"We're parents."

"And our child will be with us always."

Lennox's throat bobbed as he swallowed. Ailis jumped them back over the water. She led him to the bed, where they climbed in and held each other. It was easy to get lost in the pain. She knew because she had done it herself for days. The only reason she'd pulled herself out was because of Lennox. The pain would always be with them. There was no getting around that, but she wouldn't let him suffer alone.

"I'm starving."

Lennox lifted his head and looked at her for a full minute. Then he nodded and sat up. "What will it be today? Something new or an old favorite I've already tried?"

"Up to you. What are you thinking?"

He took a second to consider it. "Something new. Something sweet."

"Aye," she said with a grin. "My thoughts exactly. Komove cake."

He pulled a face. "That sounds…interesting."

"You're going to love it. It's a little tart with some gooey goodness inside."

"If you say so," he stated dubiously.

Ailis crafted the cake with her magic and set it between them. Lennox leaned down to sniff the tall cake. She loved that he had to smell everything first. He looked at her and nodded. She laughed as she cut into the dessert. It wasn't until she put her fork through her piece that she glanced at the grave.

Their child would never be forgotten.

CHAPTER THIRTY-SEVEN

Peace. It had seemed so farfetched at one time, but it had
finally returned to the realm. Lennox flew over the capital as
snow flurries danced in the air. A heavy snowfall had coated
everything in layers of white overnight. There was a different
sound to the land during the winter. A soft hush the snow
seemed to bring. Every season had a sound, and winter was his
favorite. Many dreaded winters because of the cold and ice,
but not Lennox. It was the time for the land to rest. To sleep.
Just as dragons needed respite, so too did the realm.

He grinned as he thought about Ailis. She wasn't fond of
the change in seasons, though she never complained. She just
piled more blankets atop them. Instead of a fire where smoke
would alert others, a large area in the water cavern housed
sizzling coals to keep the space warm.

The first two months after he returned were rough. Not just
because they had lost a child but because he still had to leave
often to check on the Silvers. There were a few skirmishes, but

the Kings quickly got them under control. The last three months, things had returned to normal.

That meant he could spend more time with Ailis. The only thing he worried about was the new clan. There were five dragons living there now, and none of them were couples. Those dragons had left their clans for various reasons. What he had hoped would be a place for outsiders to fit in hadn't happened. Ailis kept telling him it would take time, but he feared the new clan would never take hold. Those that called it home couldn't find common ground. They kept themselves separate, even from each other. There could never be a new clan if they didn't come together.

Lennox soared over the Dragonwood, his gaze locking on the location where they had held the funeral for Ariston and Noma. Rolf hadn't gotten that honor. Not as a murderer. His body had been taken by Thad and the warriors to the edge of their territory and burned. Then left there.

A dip of his wing had Lennox swinging back around for another flyover of the forest. The pale gray sky hadn't allowed even a ray of sunshine for days, and that didn't look to be changing anytime soon. At the first sign it did, Lennox planned to bring Ailis outside. They had an arrangement now that had begun under the stars that long-ago night.

He would settle atop the mountain, holding his hand just right. After he roared, she would jump to him, settling within his palm so no one could see her. He made sure she got outside as often as she wished. Sometimes, twice a day. Once during the daytime and another at night. They had also jumped to the ice cave a few times for a trip away.

Lennox hadn't stopped there, of course. On his travels, he

found locations where he was alone and called to Ailis. He showed her the desert, a tropical island, and the grass plains. The joy on her face was always worth it. No matter how long they got to stay and enjoy each setting, she was ecstatic to visit. From the animals to the waterfalls to the plants. Everything interested her.

They spent time reading, talking, and loving. They shared hopes and dreams and wishes about their future. Occasionally, they spoke of their bairn. Of what the babe might have looked like and the life it might have led. Sometimes, they cried and held each other.

Not much could get Ailis down. But once every month, it would happen. Her cycle had yet to sort itself out. Sometimes, she was early, but mostly she was late. And the worry would set in. He would have to remind her that she had doubled her magic to prevent anything. She would nod, but her gaze would go distant. Then, a day or so later, her cycle would begin, and she would return to normal.

Today was the fifth day she was late for her cycle. She had always bled by now. Nothing he said soothed her. He asked if she could determine if she carried a bairn, and she flatly refused to try. The pain that flashed in her scarlet eyes was so great he had pulled her against him and swore never to ask her that again.

It was a punch to the gut every time he thought about her enduring the miscarriage alone. She'd had no one to hold her, wipe her tears, or help her when it was over. If he had known, he would've returned to her immediately. His role as King and the dragons be damned. She was his mate, the other half of his soul.

Lennox flapped his wings, knocking off the snow that had piled up. He turned slightly and headed back to his mountain. Osric was expected to return in a few days. Lennox thought his friend might have finally found a mate, though Osric was close-lipped about it. Still, Lennox held out hope. He wanted his friend to know the love he felt for Ailis.

He spotted Thad and Darald together. Darald had taken Thad under his wing, and the two Kings had become close friends. Darald was still loud, but he wasn't as quick to voice his opinions as before. The events had changed him. They had changed everyone, but Darald most of all. And Lennox didn't think that was a bad thing.

The two nodded in greeting as he passed them. He returned the motion and continued on to his mountain. He landed and shook the snow off himself before folding his wings and entering the tunnel, calling out to Ailis with a sound distinctly for her. Lennox didn't shift until he was past the main chamber.

He frowned when Ailis didn't come out to greet him as she usually did. He lengthened his strides and came to the entrance of the water cavern. There, he paused and searched for her. He knew she wouldn't be in the water. His first glance went to the grave, but she wasn't there. The second place he looked was the seating area near the coals and her favorite place to read. Again, no Ailis. Finally, he turned toward the bed.

He sighed when he found her sitting up with her back against the wall, her knees pulled to her chest. She stared off into the distance as if lost in a daydream. Lennox almost didn't disturb her, but something about the rigid way she sat alerted him that all was not well.

His feet didn't make a sound as he walked to her. She didn't look his way once. He sat on the bed, but she still didn't notice him. It wasn't until he touched her arm that she jerked and her gaze slid to him.

The shock he saw there made his heart catch. "What is it? Tell me."

When Ailis didn't reply, he moved closer and wrapped an arm around her. She rested her head on his shoulder and took in shuddering breaths. He fought against the need to demand she talk to him to ease the fear that had an unyielding grip.

But she said nothing. She took his other hand and brought it to her stomach. For several seconds, Lennox didn't move. He didn't dare believe. It couldn't be. Not with the precautions they had taken. Ailis lifted her head and looked at him.

He searched her gaze. "How?"

"I don't know," she whispered. Her gaze darted away briefly as she licked her lips.

The thought of having a child with Ailis sent a thrill through him. Then he remembered they were different species. She could lose this one, too. "How do you feel about it?"

"I'm not sure."

There was a hesitation in her voice that he understood all too well. "You're my mate, Ailis. I love you more than I thought myself capable of. I'll stand beside you whatever you want to do."

Her brow furrowed. "Are you asking if I want to be rid of the babe?"

"It isna what I want, but I'm saying I'd understand after what you endured the last time."

She looked at the water. "I lost our first baby before I even knew I was pregnant."

They had talked often about how she blamed herself, and it didn't matter how many times he told her that it wasn't her fault, she never believed him. But he would keep telling her that. Maybe she'd believe him one day.

"New world. New magic. New species," he reminded her.

"I know," she said, a ghost of a smile on her lips as she glanced his way. "I'd be lying if I said I didn't think about our future with children. I know it would be challenging. They wouldn't be dragons or Fae. They wouldn't belong in either world. Wouldn't fit in anywhere."

"Like Noma and Ariston."

Ailis nodded slowly. "Is it right to bring an innocent child into such a world? No matter how much love is shared between their parents. I embrace this life because of you." She turned her head to him. "I chose to be here. I don't care that I'll spend my life hiding with only Osric knowing I'm your mate. This child, and any more we might be blessed with, won't have that option. It would be forced on them."

"Finding a mate wouldna be easy for them," he added.

"If they even could. Do I want this child? Aye. With every fiber of my being, but we have to think about the baby and its future. I won't have our son or daughter hunted. No matter how we look at it, we won't always be around to protect them."

Lennox inhaled sharply and released it. "They would have Osric, but he wouldna always be here either. If we knew the child would look like a dragon or even shift into one, they might be able to blend in here."

"With your color scales, perhaps."

"Aye. Good point." He hadn't thought of that. Had just assumed.

"And that's supposing it looks like a dragon. What if they look like me? Or a combination?"

Lennox shook his head. "Nay. That wouldna happen. The magic wouldna allow it."

"You put a lot of faith in the magic of your realm."

"There's a reason for that."

"We can't ask it anything, and even if we could, I doubt it would answer."

He tightened his arm around her. "You raise valid points, but you forget there's another option. We leave."

"Nay, my love. That isn't an option. This is your world."

"You left your realm. I could leave mine. We could find somewhere else."

She smiled forlornly. "I can't ask that of you."

"You're no'. It would be my decision."

"You protect us here. I don't know where we would end up or if we would even find somewhere. All three of us would be out of place then. At least here, we have you and your rank."

Lennox scrubbed a hand down his face. Fuck. They should be celebrating, not debating the future. "I love you. I love this bairn, no matter its sex or what it looks like. It's our child, created by our love. I'll protect both of you until my dying breath. We belong together, and the magic wouldna have brought you here if none of this were supposed to happen."

Tears welled in her eyes. "Really?"

"Never doubt any of that, darlin'. We'll find a way. Always."

"I want to keep the baby," she said as a tear dropped onto her cheek.

Lennox tenderly wiped it away with his thumb. "I do, as well."

"I might lose it like the first one."

"I'll be by your side if that happens."

She wrapped her arms around his neck, smiling through her tears. Lennox looked over to the grave and sent up a prayer of hope.

CHAPTER THIRTY-EIGHT

Ailis smoothed her hands down the front of the gown. It was ridiculous to be nervous, but she couldn't stop shaking. She shook out her hands and took a deep breath. It was the first morning in a month that she hadn't been violently ill. Her body was still adjusting to the baby, and each morning she woke feeling the life within her, Ailis rejoiced.

She paced the cavern as she awaited Lennox's call. He and Osric had spent weeks searching for the right location. Apparently, they had found it, but now she waited for them to make sure no other dragons were around so they could exchange vows.

There would be no official mating ceremony. Ailis didn't need a ritual. She had Lennox, and that was enough. He, however, felt differently. It came down to the fact that they had no idea how long he would be King. While no one knew how long they had to live, it was different for dragons once they mated. The ceremony bound the two lives together. She and Lennox could have thousands of years. Or they could have one.

If they were officially mated and she carried the baby to term, but the magic chose a new King to replace Lennox, then Ailis would die with him. If they didn't have a ceremony, she could still raise their child. It broke her heart to see how he had worked so hard to lay it out to her while trying to hide his pain.

His anger at being unable to claim her as his mate to all rankled. Even Osric was upset by it. Ailis was the only one who didn't care so much. Perhaps it was because she had been on a realm where nuptials and separations happened all the time. A ceremony didn't bind people together. Love did.

Her thoughts skidded to the other fact that she had finally pulled out of Lennox. He hadn't been quite so eager to share the truth with her, and she realized why afterward. A dragon who couldn't be with their mate died—withered away in a slow, agonizing death. She never intended to leave him, but knowing what would happen if she did just solidified her vow to remain no matter what.

She sighed and looked at herself in the full-length mirror. The gown might be too much, but she was mating a King, after all. The *King* of Dragon Kings. That deserved a gown worthy of him and their love.

The color was a mixture of silver and white with some soft gray. The bodice molded to her like a second skin. White cords dotted with silver gems in the shape of dragon scales contoured to her breasts and created dozens of tiny Vs down the middle of her abdomen. There was more cording fanning out into an elaborate design around her hips and midway down the center of the dress. The ombre colors of the overskirt started with white, transitioning to silver at the hem. The underskirt was a stunning mix of soft gray hues.

But her absolute favorite part was the wings. They protruded from her back, extending out past her shoulders and falling to her calves. The same white cording outlined the silver wings, creating points that mimicked Lennox's. Additional cording strengthened the wings in the middle with long, sweeping lines and gentle curls. More dragon-scale gems were woven throughout the wings, with clusters along the outer edges.

She might not be able to shift into a dragon, but the love of her life was one. She lived among them, called their home hers. And she would represent them.

"*Ailis.*"

It was time. She closed her eyes and found Lennox. Her heart leaped as she teleported to him. She opened her eyes when she heard his gasp.

"By the stars, you're stunning," Lennox whispered.

A laugh bubbled inside her. "It isn't too much?"

"Never."

That's when she looked him over. Instead of just black trousers, he also donned a white shirt and black boots. The material of the top was soft and thin with threads of silver shot through it. "You look quite handsome yourself."

He beamed at her. "I'm glad you approve. And the rest?"

She had to pull her gaze away from him, but when she did, her mouth fell open. Mesmerizing turquoise water was to one side, while lush tropical trees spread around them. To her other side was a waterfall, cascading from a cliff high above them. "Oh, Lennox. This is perfect."

"It's part of Osric's territory. No one will bother us here."

She looked around. "Where is he?"

"Behind you."

Ailis turned to find Osric weaving through the trees. He, too, had clothed himself for the event in a shirt and trousers similar to Lennox's.

Osric came to stand before them. He grinned at Lennox before turning to her. "Ailis, Lennox is my King, but he's also my brother. Today, as the two of you share vows of love, you become our queen. The realm may never know you, but I do. Your impact on us and our world will be with us for eternity."

She didn't know what to say. It was wholly unexpected. All of it. She was still standing in shock when Osric kissed her on the cheek before embracing Lennox. And then he stepped away, shifted, and took his place atop the cliff near the waterfall.

"I…" she began but couldn't find the words.

Lennox took her hands in his. "I was as surprised as you. I had no idea he was going to do that, but I'm glad he did. If we were mated, you would be queen. It's your right."

Ailis swallowed and blew out a breath. "I would've been happy doing this in our mountain. You didn't need to go to all this trouble."

"I do this for myself, as well. We deserve this, darlin'."

"That we do," she said with a smile.

"Shall we begin?"

She nodded.

Lennox cleared his throat, his pale green eyes locking on

hers. "Ailis, I knew from the moment I saw you on the banks of the loch that you would change my life. You've opened my heart and my world. You've given me strength and resolve. But most of all, you've given me unconditional love. I'll stand beside you throughout this life and the thousands of lifetimes ahead of us. For we are bound in ways that supersede death. You are my mate, my soul. My verra heart."

Her eyes burned with unshed tears. The air around her felt different, and if she didn't know better, she would think it was the magic. She tightened her fingers around Lennox's and pressed her lips together before beginning. "I thought I left my world in search of adventure. It turned out I was searching for you. I was drawn here, doing magic no other Fae had done before. Because of you. Because our souls found a way to each other across time and space. I don't know how many lives we've had before this, but I know you. I knew you from the moment our eyes locked when you came out of the water. My heart and soul have always been yours. They will always be yours. You are my mate."

"I am yours," Lennox said and moved closer.

Ailis closed the last bit of distance between them. "And I am yours."

"For now."

"And always."

Their lips met, the kiss beginning slow but turning heated quickly. Above them, Osric let out a loud roar that shook the ground.

Lennox chuckled as he ended the kiss and met her gaze. "Did you feel it?"

"What?"

Instead of answering, he raised his brow.

Ailis shut out Osric, who continued to roar, and opened herself to her surroundings. There, a shift in the air, the same thing she had felt before. It was stronger now, wrapping around her and Lennox separately and then together.

Her eyes snapped open. "Is that...?"

"The magic."

When she could, she would walk the Dragonwood and find the magic's source. But for now, she held out a hand and smiled, silently thanking it for welcoming her. Ailis was sad when she could no longer feel it, but she knew it was there. Always. Just like her love for Lennox.

"Ready to go home?" he asked, holding out his hand.

"I'm ready to go anywhere with you, my love."

EPILOGUE

Eight months later…

Lennox was beside himself. Every day their child lived was a celebration, but the worry was still there. He knew little about bairns, even of his own kind. He knew less when it came to the Fae.

Ailis had told him it took nine months. Well, it had been nine months, and he didn't understand why their child hadn't made an entrance yet. Not that he was prepared for the bairn. He couldn't wait to hold their baby, but once it was born—if it ever came—an entire new set of uncertainties and concerns would need to be addressed.

He was so riled up that Ailis had sent him out of the mountain so she could rest. There was only one other he could go to in a time like this. Thankfully, Osric was at the capital.

"You're going to wear a hole in the stone with that

pacing," Osric stated in a flat tone as he lay on a boulder, his fingers pinching the bridge of his nose.

Lennox raked a hand through his hair but didn't stop. "I saw Ailis wince this morning."

"Brother, she has a life growing inside her. I doubt that's comfortable."

"I do have to help her up and down many times. She's no' been sleeping well either."

Osric sighed, his frustration evident. "Again, it can no' be comfortable."

"Yet there's nothing better than feeling the bairn kick my hand when I lay it on her stomach."

At this, Osric sat up, his eyes crinkling in the corners as he swung his legs over the side of the large rock. "I saw the wee thing press its foot against her stomach the other day."

"Aye." Lennox smiled, nodding. He finally came to a stop, loving nothing more than being able to talk about his mate and child. "My son or daughter seems to be constantly moving. I can no' tell you how many times I've been kicked in the back while we're lying in bed. Ailis can only sleep on her side, and she likes to throw her leg over mine, which means she's turned toward me."

"Your bairn is going to be a warrior."

Lennox heard the barest hint of envy. Osric still hadn't found a mate, and he was getting discouraged. Lennox held his friend's gaze. "If this is too much, I doona have to speak about Ailis or the bairn."

"We're brothers, Lennox. I'd been angry if you didna come to me. I'd just hoped to have my own mate by now."

"You'll find her. I know it."

Osric shot him a crooked smile that didn't quite reach his eyes. "And she'll never be able to know about our shifting, Ailis, or your child."

"Nay."

That was one thing the three of them had agreed on. No one could know about Ailis, but the one secret they would keep above all others was their child. He knew Ailis couldn't stop worrying about losing the bairn. He kept her spirits up, but he shared the concern. It had been hard enough losing their first so early. If something happened to this child now, it would devastate them both.

"Stop," Osric said as he vaulted to the ground. He walked to Lennox and clapped him on the shoulder. "Stay positive. Ailis has carried the bairn this long. All will be well."

"You and I both know that some eggs never hatch."

Osric's dark gaze never wavered. "True."

"We doona even know what the child will look like."

"It will be half dragon, from one of the greatest Kings to ever serve, and half Fae, from a great explorer. The child will know love unlike any other on this realm."

Lennox gave Osric a curt nod. They had been over this many times. "If something happens to me…" he began.

"I'll take care of them," Osric finished. "I've given you my word."

It wouldn't be safe for Ailis and the bairn on the realm once another King replaced him. He was asking a lot of Osric to step in. If she were left alone, Ailis still hadn't decided if she would take the baby and return to the Fae, remain on the realm, or go elsewhere. Lennox wanted his child to stay on Earth, but there were many reasons that wasn't feasible.

"It's been half a day, brother. Go check on your mate," Osric said and gently shoved him toward the entrance with a grin.

Lennox drew in a breath and shifted to his true form to return to his mountain. The moment he entered, he issued a low rumble to let Ailis know it was him. It had been many months since she'd greeted him. Her belly was so big that she could never get out of the chair before he reached her.

He cleared his mind of all worries and smiled as he entered the water cavern. It vanished as soon as he saw Ailis bent over, clutching the arm of the chair with one hand and her stomach with the other. Damp hair cascaded around her face, hiding it from him. Alarm surged through him as he raced to her.

"Ailis? Love, what is it?"

She looked up at him, her face a mask of pain and dotted with sweat. "The baby is coming. Nearly here," she ground out before doubling over again.

Lennox was helpless. He didn't know what to do. Or if he *could* do anything. "Tell me what you need?"

"Catch…them," she bit out between breaths.

He blinked. He was down on his knees behind her before his mind processed what she had said. Gently, he moved away the long, loose skirts she had taken to wearing. He glanced up to see she leaned both arms on the chair. She barely made a sound as she pressed down. Lennox saw the crown of the bairn's head.

"Bloody hell," he murmured in surprise. "I can see our child, love. You're doing great."

At least he hoped she was. He was flying blind here, and

that terrified him. It wouldn't do to let Ailis know that. She had her own fears about childbirth.

She grunted, her legs shaking as she bore down again. Lennox held out his hands as the baby slipped from Ailis's body. He gaped in wonder at the tiny bundle in his hands while Ailis crumpled against the chair.

Lennox glanced around for something to wrap the bairn in. There were many blankets, but none soft enough for his daughter. He created one with his magic and carefully folded her in it.

Ailis looked over her shoulder at him. "Is she breathing?"

Fear gripped him, but he refused to give in as he cleaned out his daughter's airway and lightly pressed on her chest. It would be too cruel for Ailis to have carried the babe to term only for it not to survive now.

"Lennox?" she asked with a sob.

He sent a silent plea to the magic as he continued helping his daughter breathe. Then, finally, he saw her tiny fist move. A moment later, she let out a loud wail. He lifted his gaze to Ailis. Tears ran down her cheeks as his clouded. He gently set aside the bairn and cut the cord connecting mother to baby.

Then he reached for his mate. Her hand shook as she grasped his. With her face red from exertion, she was the most beautiful thing he had ever seen. "You did it."

She swallowed and straightened, never releasing his hand. In a blink, her soiled clothes were replaced with clean ones. She gave his hand a squeeze before teleporting to the bed. Lennox gathered the bairn in his arms and brought her to Ailis.

The moment he laid his daughter in Ailis's arms, a serene

look came over his mate's face. She gently stroked a finger down the baby's cheek as their daughter flailed her arms and feet. Ailis moved aside the blanket to look at the baby. "She's beautiful. And perfect."

"Aye. Just like her mother."

Ailis met his gaze, and they shared a smile.

"Rest," he told her. "Let me clean our daughter."

Ailis allowed him to take the baby. He spent several minutes gently cleaning the bairn using warmed water. Then, he returned to the bed. Ailis patted the mattress, urging him to crawl in beside her. He cradled Ailis as she held their precious child.

"You should've called out to me," Lennox said.

She chuckled and twisted her lips. "I thought I had time."

"When did it begin?"

"This morning."

"You knew before you sent me away?" he asked, appalled that he had spent so long away from her.

Ailis shrugged. "I know some Fae spend hours in childbirth. If you had been here the entire time, you would've been wringing your hands with nothing to do."

"No doubt."

"I didn't know the babe would come so quickly. You got here just in time." She turned her head so their lips met.

"She's the most perfect thing I've ever seen," Lennox said as he softly cupped her wee head. She had fallen asleep as he cleaned her.

"She is that."

"What shall we call her?"

Ailis rocked slowly from side to side. "She's the daughter of a King."

"And a rather intrepid Fae explorer," Lennox added.

Ailis smiled. "She needs a strong name. One suited to her lineage."

"A name for the most special of children. One that will bring forth her true nature and the future meant only for her." Lennox felt the magic of the realm rise up and surround the three of them before enfolding his hand and daughter. He sucked in a breath at the words that filled his head and then spilled from his mouth—words that came from the magic, not him. "She has a pioneering spirit that will make her a natural-born leader. She will be highly focused and achieve great things. She is a keeper of secrets with a serene soul. A child that straddles two important worlds. Her name is Melisse."

Just as the magic slipped away, it gave Lennox one more revelation, one he refused to let pass his lips. He stared down at his daughter, the greatest joy of his life dimmed slightly. Ailis beamed with pride. He wouldn't tell her, he couldn't. Not now. Maybe later. Or perhaps never. The magic could have it wrong.

After all, how could one small child endure such torment, such hardship? The magic couldn't know everything. Could it?

"Melisse," Ailis whispered. "It's perfect." Her gaze met his. "That wasn't you speaking."

Lennox pressed his lips to her temple. "It was the magic."

"It has blessed us."

"It certainly has." Lennox shoved the niggle of worry to a far back corner of his mind for another day. This was too special a moment to concern himself with things that might not even happen. He had the family he'd never thought to have. And he would embrace every moment with them.

Melisse stirred, crying softly. Ailis shifted, showing the bairn where to latch on to feed. Lennox released a long sigh as he held his girls. Fate had given him so much. There had been strife and blood but love prevailed. It would always triumph.

"Do you want to tell Osric?" Ailis asked.

Lennox shook his head and held her tighter. "Later."

He couldn't take his eyes off his daughter. Their future would be different from any other, but they would be together. And that was all he could ask for.

"I love you," he whispered to them both.

Melisse waved her tiny fist.

Ailis leaned her head against him. "And we love you."

Thank you for reading **IGNITE THE MAGIC.** I hope you loved Lennox and Ailis's story as much as I loved writing it.

Have you read the Dark Kings or Dragon Kings series yet? Dive into the Dark Universe with the stories that started it all in DARK HEAT...

The Dragon Kings are sworn to defend an ancient legacy of magic. But their fiercest challenge lies in the modern world, where a woman's love conquers all.

To find out when new books release
SIGN UP FOR MY NEWSLETTER today at
http://www.tinyurl.com/DonnaGrantNews

Join my Facebook group, Donna Grant Groupies, for
exclusive giveaways and sneak peeks of future books.
http://bit.ly/DGGroupies

Keep reading for a peek at DARK HEAT…

The dark immortal warriors were never meant to experience human desire. But when Guy, a member of an ancient order of shape-shifting warriors, meets Elena—a mere mortal whose beauty and blind ambition shakes him to his core—all bets are off…

Dawn's Desire

For centuries, the Dragon Kings have hidden their shapeshifting powers from the world. But when a mortal enemy threatens to expose them, the warrior Banan must leave his secret lair in the Highlands to risk his life for the dragons within—and resist the temptations of human love.

Passion's Claim

Banan has been waiting for centuries for someone like Jane. Guy knew it was love at first sight with Elena. Can two Dragon Kings commit to two immortal women for eternity? Or does fate have something else in store?

A sneak peek at DARK HEAT…

Hal shut and locked the doors to the distillery for the day before he turned and looked out over the land. Snow blanketed everything and the light the crescent moon cast upon the ground made it look almost as if it were glowing.

The need to lose himself in the land in the forest sometimes was overwhelming, as it was this night. Other times he could ignore the call, but not tonight.

Hal didn't bother to tell the others where he was going. He simply walked down the steps and into the night. The weather didn't faze him.

His boots crunched in the thick snow, but he never noticed. His gaze was trained on the forest ahead. Every one of them answered to something, and for Hal it was the forest.

Always had been.

Always would be.

Once he was in the trees, he took a deep breath and lifted his face to the sky. Snow landed on his lashes and rain dripping from the limbs above pelted his face.

It was glorious.

Hal smiled and spread his arms wide. He touched his chest, through his jacket and sweater, to the tattoo beneath.

A person could get lost in the glens of the Highlands, and there were thousands of glens. Which made it a perfect place for Hal and the others like him to stay hidden.

It had been a long time since he'd allowed his other self to show, his dragon self. And for some reason, this night he desperately yearned to spread his wings and fly.

To feel the wind around him as he soared through the sky.

He still remembered flying low over the trees, the leaves brushing against his underside as the sun beat on him. He hadn't needed to hide then. For once upon a time, he had been able to call to his brethren and listened to their roars fill the forest.

So very long ago he had lived a completely different life. Back before the humans betrayed them, before a war that changed everything.

A sound off to Hal's right had him turning his head in that direction. He dropped his arms as his eyes fastened on a large, fast-moving animal loping through the trees.

Hal let his coat drop from his arms as he sprinted toward

the animal. As he neared, he realized it was a dog—a very large dog. And the only person near Dreagan land who had such a dog was Dan Hunter.

With more frustration than Hal wanted to concede, he came to a halt. He had been able to take flight, but now he had to chase a dog. For several moments he watched the Great Dane running, his tongue lolling out the side of his mouth.

There had been a few times in Hal's life where he'd felt that free, been that free. Those times were the barest of memories now.

When a person was as old as Hal, time blurred.

It was so easy to get lost in his memories, of what had once been, and what he had once been. But to allow himself to get absorbed in such recollections was not wise.

He pulled himself back from the brink and gave a loud, short whistle, which pulled Duke up short. The Great Dane turned his head to Hal and issued a deep, booming bark in greeting.

"Come here, lad," Hal called.

Immediately, the dog ran to him, his tail wagging.

Hal rubbed the dog's massive head. "It's no' like Dan to allow you to run like this. Nor is it like you to run off. What's the problem, lad?"

Duke jerked against the hold Hal had on his collar. Hal narrowed his eyes. He'd learned very early in life to listen carefully when animals tried to speak. They might not be speaking your language, but they were talking. It was obvious Duke was trying to tell him something.

"Show me," Hal said, and released the collar.